Kane opened fi...
Sin-Eater again...

"Lakesh, we've got trouble. I just hit Durga with an implosion grenade, and all it did was knock the wind out of him."

The Sin-Eater's heavy slugs tore into sections of bared flesh, but no blood trickled from the scale-shorn meat. Durga lifted his head, golden eyes filled with fury and disdain for the human who simply would not die.

"Keep fighting, mammal," Durga growled. "The longer you survive, the more time you give your friends to make peace with their gods."

"What makes you think you'll survive killing me?" Kane called back.

Durga laughed, rising to rest on the coiled trunk of his serpentine lower half. He hadn't recovered fully yet, but scales began to form over the flesh that had been scoured by the implosion grenade. "You amuse me, Kane. I'll name my first extermination camp after you."

Other titles in this series:

James Axler

Outlanders®

SERPENT'S TOOTH

A GOLD EAGLE BOOK FROM

WORLDWIDE®

TORONTO • NEW YORK • LONDON
AMSTERDAM • PARIS • SYDNEY • HAMBURG
STOCKHOLM • ATHENS • TOKYO • MILAN
MADRID • WARSAW • BUDAPEST • AUCKLAND

Recycling programs
for this product may
not exist in your area.

First edition February 2009

ISBN-13: 978-0-373-63861-1
ISBN-10:   0-373-63861-2

SERPENT'S TOOTH

A Countryman's son by accident trod upon a Serpent's tail, which turned and bit him so that he died. The father in a rage got his axe, and pursuing the Serpent, cut off part of its tail. So the Serpent in revenge began stinging several of the Farmer's cattle and caused him severe loss. Well, the Farmer thought it best to make it up with the Serpent, and brought food and honey to the mouth of its lair, and said to it: "Let's forget and forgive; perhaps you were right to punish my son, and take vengeance on my cattle, but surely I was right in trying to revenge him; now that we are both satisfied why should not we be friends again?"

"No, no," said the Serpent; "take away your gifts; you can never forget the death of your son, nor I the loss of my tail."

INJURIES MAY BE FORGIVEN, BUT NOT FORGOTTEN.
—Æsop's Fable

The Road to Outlands—
From Secret Government Files to the Future

Almost two hundred years after the global holocaust, Kane, a former Magistrate of Cobaltville, often thought the world had been lucky to survive at all after a nuclear device detonated in the Russian embassy in Washington, D.C. The aftermath—forever known as skydark—reshaped continents and turned civilization into ashes.

Nearly depopulated, America became the Deathlands—poisoned by radiation, home to chaos and mutated life forms. Feudal rule reappeared in the form of baronies, while remote outposts clung to a brutish existence.

What eventually helped shape this wasteland were the redoubts, the secret preholocaust military installations with stores of weapons, and the home of gateways, the locational matter-transfer facilities. Some of the redoubts hid clues that had once fed wild theories of government cover-ups and alien visitations.

Rearmed from redoubt stockpiles, the barons consolidated their power and reclaimed technology for the villes. Their power, supported by some invisible authority, extended beyond their fortified walls to what was now called the Outlands. It was here that the rootstock of humanity survived, living with hellzones and chemical storms, hounded by Magistrates.

In the villes, rigid laws were enforced—to atone for the sins of the past and prepare the way for a better future. That was the barons' public credo and their right-to-rule.

Kane, along with friend and fellow Magistrate Grant, had upheld that claim until a fateful Outlands expedition. A displaced piece of technology…a question to a keeper of the archives…a vague clue about alien masters—and their world shifted radically. Suddenly, Brigid Baptiste, the archivist, faced summary execution, and Grant a quick termination. For

Kane there was forgiveness if he pledged his unquestioning allegiance to Baron Cobalt and his unknown masters and abandoned his friends.

But that allegiance would make him support a mysterious and alien power and deny loyalty and friends. Then what else was there?

Kane had been brought up solely to serve the ville. Brigid's only link with her family was her mother's red-gold hair, green eyes and supple form. Grant's clues to his lineage were his ebony skin and powerful physique. But Domi, she of the white hair, was an Outlander pressed into sexual servitude in Cobaltville. She at least knew her roots and was a reminder to the exiles that the outcasts belonged in the human family.

Parents, friends, community—the very rootedness of humanity was denied. With no continuity, there was no forward momentum to the future. And that was the crux— when Kane began to wonder if there *was* a future.

For Kane, it wouldn't do. So the only way was out— way, way out.

After their escape, they found shelter at the forgotten Cerberus redoubt headed by Lakesh, a scientist, Cobaltville's head archivist, and secret opponent of the barons.

With their past turned into a lie, their future threatened, only one thing was left to give meaning to the outcasts. The hunger for freedom, the will to resist the hostile influences. And perhaps, by opposing, end them.

Chapter 1

A parrot squawked and its multicolored wings blurred as it exploded from its perch in the lowest branches of the tree. The bird's shriek was close enough to the cry of a woman being murdered that the expedition froze in startled anticipation of violence.

Austin Fargo's hand dropped to the massive revolver on his hip, his other tightened around the handle of the machete frozen in midstroke at a green branch barring his progress. It took several minutes before the explorers had recovered enough composure to breathe steadily.

Had this been sooner on their journey, Fargo would have relaxed his tightly wound nerves with a laugh, but the hard rubber checkering on his handgun dug into the pads of his fingers and his throat was so tight that he almost choked. Two days earlier, when the expedition set out, Fargo was looking for a gold mine of technology, the materials that the Millennial Consortium would need to wrest control from such adversaries as the rebels of Cerberus redoubt or the Tigers of Heaven. Stockpiles of weapons in the Kashmir region would give the consortium an edge in creating their new empire. Which was why Austin Fargo had twenty trained soldiers and twice that many technicians on hand. The hundred bearers packing their supplies were paralyzed with worry, and only

Fargo's display of stern discipline kept the lot of them from deserting the human train as it crawled through the uncharted forest.

It was one thing to be cut in two by the snarl of a Calico machine pistol, and even the slash of a machete brought a quick demise. The coiled loops of leather that hung on Fargo's hip, on the other hand, peeled flesh from the body in inch-wide strips, one lash at a time. The Indian deserter whom Fargo had singled out was a giant, six and a half feet with a barrel chest, and long arms and legs as solid as tree limbs. Fargo took his time, peeling the big Indian's skin off with the crack of tightly woven leather. After an hour and a half, Fargo's arm started to grow tired. The Indian hung by his wrists, bared ribs and shoulder blades gleaming where the whip had flayed skin and muscle away.

The deserter had been reduced to a gibbering mass, a once powerful man stripped of his strength by the cruelty of Fargo's whip. Eyeless sockets cried tears that flowed in crimson rivers down his cheeks. The bearer begged for death, for an end to the pain. Finally, well into the third hour of his exhibition, Fargo wound the whip back up, hanging it on the metal hook in his belt. Somewhere in those last few minutes of lashing leather, blood loss or shock had stilled the big man's heart.

Thoughts of rebellion were crushed. Fargo would make them pay, and the display of violence was foremost in the thoughts of the Indians laden with the expedition's supplies.

That should have been enough to keep everyone well behaved, but then the ghost sightings began. Humanoid shadows flitted in the darkness just beyond the path that the expedition carved in the forest. The soldiers fired on the ghostly forms, but no blood was spilled by the chattering weapons. Fargo hated to call the stalkers ghosts, but the only other whispered explanation came from the primitives who had borne the supplies on this arduous trek. They called the shadows Nagah, legendary snake creatures that lived beneath the surface of the world, interacting with men only when they chose to. Fargo was well acquainted with the idea of reptilian humans from his adventures in England to interactions with the Annunaki overlords and their scaled Nephilim slaves. The snake men, with their hinged and poisonous fangs, were feared by the natives of postskydark India.

The Kashmir region had for centuries been a contested territory, warred over by the nations of India and Pakistan for strategic purposes and for the vast agricultural benefits it had provided. While Fargo saw evidence of ancient combines, overgrown and now conquered by weeds and new tree growth, he couldn't imagine this land as farmland. It was too empty, too abandoned. On the other side of the forest, the remnants of Pakistan's survivors held their ground. Likewise the Indians stayed on their side of the edge of the forest. No one even went to the tree line to harvest logs to create more housing in the snarled shantytown. To leave such resources untouched nagged at Fargo.

A shadowy figure, manlike in size and shape, stepped onto the trail ahead of him. At first, the millennialist thought it was a figment of his overactive imagination. His fingers wrapped around the black rubber grips of his .45-caliber revolver as he realized it was more than just a phantom. Gleaming yellow eyes, partially obscured by a silhouetted hood, flashed as the figure's nod acknowledged Fargo's attention.

"Have you not listened to the men you have enslaved?" came a harsh, sibilant challenge.

"I come to you representing the Millennial Consortium. I am here to make contact with the keepers of a trove reported in this area. We are a peaceful group, seeking to negotiate a deal with you," Fargo answered. His thumb rested on the teardrop-shaped hammer of the big hogleg in its holster, ready for a fast draw. The challenger's golden-yellow eyes flicked down to his hand.

"You're well armed for a mission of peace," the hissing silhouette noted.

"I'd be a fool to come unarmed into a nation filled with tribal feuds and bandits," Fargo stated. "And in the south, there are violent cultists."

"They call themselves the Nagas," the shadowy sentinel added. "They believe themselves to be like unto us."

The jungle grew silent around them, as quiet as a tomb as birds and insects became too frightened to chirp. The shadowed, amber-eyed stranger was not alone. Odds were that the expedition was surrounded. Fargo glanced back to the Calico-toting millennialist enforcers and nodded.

Safety catches clicked off with the chatter of a sudden metallic rainstorm.

"This can either be peaceful or painful." Fargo's words punctuated the chatter of twenty machine pistols going from rest to wakeful readiness. "Your choice, stranger."

"Please, we seem to have gotten off on the wrong foot," the tall figure said. He stepped into a shaft of sunlight piercing down from the forest canopy. "My name is Durga, prince of the true-blooded Nagah."

Fargo watched Durga flip back the hood of his long, formless black cloak. Rising from his shoulders like a trapezoidal Central American pyramid, Durga's head and slender neck were blended into a flat, powerful sheet of muscle that instantly solidified the truth of the legendary cobra men of India. Save for the folds of the cloak that clung to broad, powerful shoulders, Durga was naked to the waist, his chest laden with large segmented plates in a paler hue than the scales that adorned his arms, face and ribs. The belly armor was the color of age-stained bone, while the smaller, finer scales glimmered metallic blue and green, shimmering almost like silk. The cobra man's yellow eyes remained locked on Fargo, and his thin, scaled lips were turned up at the corners in bemusement.

"Brothers, step out and introduce yourselves. Slowly and politely," Durga added as an afterthought.

Perhaps as many as thirty similarly cloaked figures strode from the shadows of the trees.

Like their self-proclaimed true-blooded prince, they were lean, slender figures. All were hairless, though not all of them had the perfect sheens of snakelike armor that their leader sported. On the Nagah men who weren't completely reptilian, bared patches of human flesh seemed like swollen, discolored rashes rather than normal sunburned flesh. Scales twinkled like dew-wet grass amid the untransformed flesh.

Fargo thought back to the semireptilian guardsmen in England, men genetically augmented to be more than human. The Englishmen so transformed looked pathetic in comparison to the powerful, graceful, cobra-hooded Nagah that Fargo looked upon now. The explorer wondered if the treatments of Lord Strongbow were clumsily copied from whatever procedure created the snake men he now encountered.

"Make your weapons friendly, lads," Fargo called out. "Muzzles down but triggers hot."

Fargo nodded to Durga. "Just a precaution."

Durga shrugged. His lean, powerful shoulders flexed, making his segmented chest plates ripple over tight pectoral and abdominal muscles. "Understandable. We are strangers. Indeed, we are obscenely alien to your mammal eyes."

Fargo shook his head. "Not completely. I have met others who have transformed themselves, but not as well as you have."

Durga nodded. "Ah, yes. The Englanders. Strongbow had sent scouts to seek a refinement of his crude process. We greeted them as brothers, but sadly, our lost relatives once more were lost. It is no wonder that our appearance does not panic you."

Fargo glanced back to his millennialist allies. He could hear the hushed whispers of Indians speaking among themselves in Hindi. "No. Not completely."

Durga's thin lips pursed in frustration. "Such a shame."

Fargo read the disappointment in the cobra man's words. Where the rest of his party displayed confusion, the millennial explorer's muscles tensed in anticipation of hell unleashed.

Durga took one step forward, but by then, Fargo had side-stepped, barely avoiding the slashing rake of unhinging fangs in the Nagah's mouth. A spray of fluid issued from Durga's venom sacks as they squeezed themselves out, disgorging their deadly payloads.

Fargo cracked his whip across Durga's flat face, a blow that would have lacerated any normal man down to the gleaming, bloody white bone beneath. It was a fast-draw slash that had split faces open from forehead to chin in the past. Instead, one yellow eye was clamped shut and Durga stumbled off balance.

The whip crack preceded the discharge of a half-dozen Calicos, but dozens of other men screamed in agony as venom seared into tear ducts and mucus membranes, burning like acid. Fargo whirled and bolted into the foliage, realizing that the poison-blinded guards and bearers had been neutralized.

The explorer trusted only two things to get him out of harm's way—his booted feet. They stomped through leaves, breaking saplings and low branches, putting distance between himself and the savage hisses behind him. Out of his peripheral vision, he could see the sinewy Nagah lunging at blinded, agonized humans, curved knives and distended jaws slashing into pink and brown flesh alike. Dagger and fang carved through human skin, cutting agonized wails short.

"Him!" Durga bellowed. "Get that miserable ape and drag him before me!"

Fargo noticed one millennialist unaffected by the gushing clouds of vision-destroying venom. His machine pistol hammered loudly, bullets chopping one snake man who staggered but still continued to advance. Mere handgun rounds deflected off the tough chest plate armor of the Nagah, though hits to the finer scales of the arms and thighs betrayed bloody swathes where copper-jacketed lead tore the weaker reptilian armor. Fargo left the fool to stand his ground, charging toward the frontier. The millennial gunman stopped firing, and the guard's fate was broadcast by a strangled death cry as hinged jaws and folding fangs stretched into a face-piercing lethal bite.

Other guns chattered sporadically, but were quickly overwhelmed by the coordinated assaults of the Nagah's ambush force.

Behind him, Fargo could hear the snap of branches and rustle of leaves. That could only mean that others were rushing

through the thickets after him. As no bullets speared through
the foliage, it had to be the knife- and fang-armed Nagah. The
cobra-hooded warriors were in hot pursuit of the fleeing archaeologist.

Move, he commanded himself, legs pumping. Vaulting
over roots, rocks and ruts with the ease of a man who'd run
for his life across six continents, Fargo avoided tripping and
stumbling. The Nagah hunters behind him snagged their feet
on vines or stepped into open space where they expected
solid ground. The snake men's yellow eyes had been focused
on Fargo, not the ground before them. For a moment, the archaeologist was elated that, despite their venom and tough
scales, they were as fallible and clumsy as any human. The
crack of a rifle, accompanied by the eruption of a tree trunk,
informed Fargo that the Nagah were perfectly willing to make
use of modern tools to slay their foes.

Fargo changed course and allowed gravity to drag him
down a muddy hillside. He rocketed to the bottom of the
slope and sprang into a dead run through a copse of trees.
Rifles chattered behind him, but Fargo kept up his frantic
pace. Soon the single shots changed to fully automatic fire as
machine guns were added to the mix.

Fargo plowed on, ricochets pinging and whining all around
him. Trunks thumped as they caught the storm of bullets
meant for him. He remembered his mental map, visualizing
a steep cliff bordering off into a turgid river. It had forced the
expedition to change its course by five miles, slowing the trek
to a tedious crawl. He remembered that the height of the
drop-off was around forty feet.

Boots filled with sloshing mud, wet pant legs clinging to
his calves and thighs, Fargo knew his pace would rapidly slow

off from constriction and lack of sure footing. One misstep would be the end of Fargo's explorations of the Kashmir region. While he would consider himself likely to catch an instantly fatal bullet, the ideal outcome was a splash in the river, its powerful current carrying him south and away from the serpentine assassins on his tail.

On foot, the Nagah warriors would not be able to keep up and shoot at Fargo at the same time, he suspected. The trees thinned out and the ground began to slope. Fargo's mud-caked boots turned into wet slicks, his footing dissolving into an arm-windmilling effort at balance as gravity whipped him into a wild slide. The rattle and crack of bullets around him faded as the slope pulled him below the arc of fire laid out by the cobra men. The skid downhill came to a sudden end as Forgo rocketed out into the air over the roiling waters beneath.

There was an odd, queasy moment of weightlessness as Fargo sailed to the waters. The surface of the river shimmered like ribbons of living, writhing glass. The world had gone silent around him, an envelope of calm providing him with a respite from the frantic race for his life. The snake men had stopped firing, it seemed, and in his peripheral vision, the millennialist trespasser knew why. Just before he knifed into the river, he had caught sight of a helicopter hanging over the tree line like a bloated, mechanical bee.

Fargo plunged under the surface of the roiling river, momentum pushing him nearly to the bottom as the water exerted its braking force on him. The current shoved hard, toppling him into a spin that he kicked out of, arms and legs dragging him toward the silty bottom.

With a twist, he looked up through the surface of the river, seeing the warped image of the sky and ledge hanging over him. Fargo knew that he had barely a minute before his lungs forced him to surface, but cold dread of that helicopter stilled his urge to swim upward.

Seconds ticked on as his lungs burned, wanting to return to their normal schedule of inhalation and exhalation. The helicopter's black shape poked out of the overhang of the ledge. Its fattened fish profile blotted out the sun while rotor wash created a flat dish in the water, creating a lens that the Nagah could see through.

Fargo had no trouble seeing the huge bulk as it hovered, and given the clarity of the river, he was easily visible to the airborne pursuers. A cobra man leaned out of the door and fired his automatic rifle, bullets knifing toward the millennialist. One plucked at his forearm, but Fargo bit his tongue to resist the urge to cry out, expelling needed air from his lungs in the process. The current dragged him along, a cloud of dark blood smearing behind him in a corkscrew.

Had it not been for the refraction of the crystal-clear water, the Nagah sniper would have riddled Fargo's chest. The explorer kept his cool, playing dead. His lungs burned as the enemy helicopter ascended and joined two more aircraft. Together they whirled in the sky for a moment before they broke north, back past the forbidden frontier that Fargo had dared to penetrate.

In three strong kicks, he broke the surface, sucking in sweet, life-giving oxygen. His arm ached badly. The bullet had glanced off his ulna, one of the strongest bones in the human body. Fortunately, the imprecise hit didn't have the power to cause more than a hairline fracture. Fargo knew it wasn't broken because he could still move his fingers, albeit stiffly.

He dragged himself to shore, crawling between two dense

bushes to shield himself from discovery in case the humanoid snake warriors saw fit to return.

With his good hand and his teeth, he tore a scarf from around his neck and fashioned a compress and bandage for his gunshot wound, sealing the puckered injury to control further blood loss and stave off infection. He had a strip left over from the bandages, but it wouldn't support his arm properly. He slipped his belt out of the loops in his pants and cinched the wounded limb to his torso, immobilizing it above the elbow. He wound the last strip of scarf around his forearm and the belt, multiple loops providing sufficient stability to the injured limb.

It would be dark soon, and he needed to get to a warm shelter. A fire was out of the question, not this close to the enemies who had killed more than a hundred trespassers with quick, ruthless efficiency.

No, Fargo needed something just a little better, perhaps the tall, intertwined roots of a tree or a nice cave, provided there were no native, actual serpents present within. The irony of dying from a real cobra bite after escaping a hybrid of man and snake would shame Fargo to no end.

·   The Millennial Consortium wouldn't be pleased at the loss of the expedition, especially now that it had been proved that there were operating aircraft in the stockpiles possessed by the Nagah. When the millennialists were disappointed, they tended to shoot the messenger. Already, though, the redoubt raider had a plan to minimize the blame and to appease the consortium.

For the plan to work, Fargo had to get to the Bitterroot Mountains.

The outlanders Kane, Grant and Brigid Baptiste could

succeed where a consortium expeditionary force had failed. If they didn't, they would still inflict horrendous losses upon the snake men, giving a new millennial strike team sufficient advantage to finish the job. Should Kane and company prevail, then a force meant to crush an army of serpent warriors would be more than enough to deal with the Cerberus interlopers.

It was the kind of win-win scenario that would allow the survivor Fargo a chance to retain his position and support within the consortium.

The journey of a thousand miles, however, needed to start with one step. Leaning on a branch for support, Fargo hauled himself achingly to his feet. With each stride, the explorer put distance between himself and the forbidden frontier. It was a temporary separation, though.

Austin Fargo would return, bringing vengeance to the snakes who had struck at him.

Chapter 2

The return to Cobaltville was meant to be a mission of mercy, but as Kane crouched in the shadows, watching the cold-hearts holding Brigid Baptiste and Grant at gunpoint, he was reminded that strength and mercy were two qualities that had to go hand in hand.

"Come on out!" the leader of the bandits snarled. "All we want are the meds, not trouble from you!"

Kane wrenched his fighting knife from the ribs of the raider who'd tried to ambush him. It had taken considerable effort to free the blade from where it was lodged in the breast-bone. Still, Kane was not a man to leave a perfectly good weapon behind, especially when he was outnumbered.

He would need information about the coldhearts, which meant that he would have to carefully get in touch with his companions over the built-in Commtact communicator implanted behind his ear and attached to the mastoid bone. "What happened?"

From his vantage point, Kane could see the massive Grant, clad in a tank top and cargo pants, clasping his hands behind his bald mahoghany-colored head as he was surrounded by raiders. Thick, powerful arms glistened like dark bronze in the sun. The big ex-Magistrate's lips didn't move, but Kane could see his jaw flexing as he subvocalized, loud enough for only the implanted transceiver to hear. "The fuckers popped out of the woodwork while I was moving crates. With my hands full, they swarmed us."

"I take the blame," Brigid's voice added. Kane's glance shot to the striking former archivist. Where he had a pang of concern for Grant, his fellow Magistrate for years and the closest thing to a brother that the lone warrior had, the sight of the flame-haired woman held at gunpoint was worth a full wince. "I should have waited until you returned from your errand, Kane."

"That's neither here nor there," Kane replied. He scanned the pair from his vantage point. Four bandits now surrounded Grant. It was always a risky proposition to bring medical supplies into the shantytown known as the Tartarus Pits, a sprawl that had grown in the shadow of the tower that housed the subjects of the hybrid barons. The medicine used by the healers at the Cobaltville clinic was almost as valuable as a cache of firearms in the lawless Outlands. Kane, Brigid and Grant were making the delivery, utilizing wheelbarrows to ferry the supplies to the healers who worked in the area.

Colin Phillips, the leader of the ragtag group of physicians and their assistants, had warned Kane and the others about the presence of the band of raiders. They were led by Lombard, a man familiar to Kane. The head bandit was a former Magistrate who operated almost exclusively in the Tartarus slums. The allure of easy money and quick satisfaction had corrupted Lombard, something the other Magistrates had done their best to ignore. Lombard disappeared after killing a fellow Mag, knowing his life was now worthless if he encountered any of the grim group that he'd betrayed.

With the barons now long gone from Cobaltville, most of

the Magistrates had also moved on, working as sec men for caravans or small settlements while the more corrupt went into business for themselves. Lombard saw Cobaltville as easy pickings.

Not that the ex-Mag was alone. Lombard had assembled easily a dozen men, according to Kane's observations, and he wasn't certain that there weren't more.

The bandit leader glared toward Grant and Brigid, alert enough to make out the low guttural subvocalizations as they communicated with Kane over their Commtacts. Lombard reached for the flame-haired archivist's chin, but Brigid jerked it away.

"Communicators?" Lombard asked as he gave her jaw a squeeze.

Brigid grabbed his wrist and pried the grubby, grasping paw away from her face. Around them, Phillips and his fellow healers remained still. They knew the drill, having endured previous raids, but Kane could see the frustration in their faces. The cold-blooded marauders had taken Brigid's and Grant's weapons at gunpoint, enticed by the new meat before them.

"So, where is your friend?" Lombard inquired. His thumb glided over the silvery plate of the Commtact implant behind Brigid's ear.

"It's a radio, not a radar unit, dimwit," Brigid retorted. "Besides, do you think that a Magistrate like Kane would give away his position to you?"

The predatory marauders were bold when it came to unarmed victims, but the presence of a Magistrate, especially the legendary Kane, would make the formerly cocky thugs pause. Kane flexed his forearm muscles, the sensitive actuators in his holster flicking his sleek, folding machine pistol into his hand. The full-auto Sin Eater would be necessary in the eventuality of a furious firefight, but Kane held his fire. The Cerberus warriors didn't want stray bullets to harm any of the healers whose only crime was endangering themselves for the sake of the huddled masses in the remnants of Cobaltville. Besides, Kane had learned long ago that mind games and intimidation could reduce the need for violence or control the reactions of his quarry.

The coldheart grimaced. "Fucking Mags? Kane nonetheless?"

Lombard glared at the massive Grant, a towering figure in his own right. The olive-green tank top left little doubt about the awesome power contained in his muscular arms and shoulders. It had been years since Lombard had last seen Grant. To assist with his disguise as just another guy the size of a colossal statue, Grant was wearing a pair of wire-rimmed glasses and had traded his forearm-holstered Sin Eater for a belt-holstered Heckler & Koch MP-5 K. In a nearby wheelbarrow Grant had hidden both a Sin Eater and a compact Copperhead assault rifle, ready to be reached through a precut opening.

"Then who the fuck are you?" Lombard asked.

"I'm just a delivery boy," Grant said. "Does she look like she hauls around crates full of this shit?"

Lombard glanced over to the slender but fit young woman. Brigid didn't look like a delicate flower thanks to years of adventuring across the globe. Though it was obvious that she was in very good shape, Kane knew that there was a mentality among his fellow Magistrates to dismiss women as incapable because of their softer bodies. At first even he had trouble adapting to Brigid's competence and capability as a fellow adventurer.

Kane also quietly admitted to himself the stomach-churning anger at Lombard's sneering familiarity with Brigid Baptiste. Though she could take care of herself, having proved her inner strength across several years and every continent on the planet, Kane still possessed an instinctual protectiveness for the archivist.

Brigid shrunk from the renegade Magistrate, and Lombard chuckled.

"Still, it's only one Mag bastard," Lombard said aloud, as if to calm his companions.

"Well, I guess if they measure those guys by you…" Grant said, shrugging.

"Ruben, if this overmuscled cock head talks again, shoot him with his own gun," Lombard snapped.

Grant looked down at the bandit Lombard had spoken to. Ruben, a young, tattooed punk wearing a leather vest, was a foot shorter than Grant. He gripped the machine pistol with whitened knuckles.

"Don't shoot yourself with that thing, kid," the big Cerberus warrior whispered to him.

Even without being close enough to see Grant's face, Kane could tell that his partner was smiling. The mind games against the coldhearts were now in full effect.

Ruben glared at Grant. "I'm not simple, you damned big freak."

"You could have fooled me," Grant replied. "You keep pointing that muzzle at your friends, too, and your finger's locked on that trigger. If it weren't for the fact that you haven't deactivated the safety on the gun, you'd have shot your partners twenty times over."

Kane could see Ruben's nearly comical double take as he

glanced down at the machine pistol. The Cerberus rebel fought to restrain a snort of amused derision at the reaction. His partner's mockery had struck another blow against the raider's confidence.

Kane dragged the corpse of his ambusher into a ditch and submerged the body beneath two feet of shantytown sewage. He had relieved the dead man of his walkie-talkie, as well as the twin single-action revolvers that he'd worn. The radio would give Kane even more intelligence against the bandits. The handguns were typical of what the robbers had, a blend of pump shotguns, bolt-action rifles and old revolvers, which explained Ruben's confusion over Grant's more complicated HK. In the two centuries since skydark, technology was no longer uniformly equal, and maintenance-intensive devices such as automatic weapons were nowhere near as common as manually cycled firearms and tough old solid-state circuitry, which could be reconstructed from simple wire. The bandit radio was one such cobbled piece of technology, presumably a simple circuit board, some magnets and wire wrapped in a hard little case. Kane figured that if he ran out of ammunition, he could use the boxy walkie-talkie to smash open an enemy gunman's skull and not even cause harm to the electronics within.

Kane thumbed back the hammer on one revolver, then cut loose with a terrified death cry. The revolver boomed, a cordite cloud filling the alley.

"Banyon! Banyon! Report!" the coldheart's voice cut over the walkie-talkie and the Commtact in stereo. "Second team! On Banyon's position now!"

Grant chuckled. "Good luck catching Kane."

Lombard whirled toward Ruben. "I thought that I told you to shoot that loudmouth!"

"I can't get the gun working," Ruben complained.

"You really think that shooting me is going to affect a hard bastard like him?" Grant asked.

"You're annoying me, shithead," Lombard grunted. "I've heard of Kane, and he's nothing special."

"No. He's only the most dangerous man ever to patrol the Tartarus Pits," Brigid countered. "Who else would I hire to protect us?"

Lombard grimaced. "Listen, bitch, Kane might have been hot shit in the old days, but I know all of his—"

"Lombard!" a bandit interrupted, shouting into his radio to the left of Kane's hiding place. "We found a puddle of blood."

"Banyon's body?" Lombard asked.

"Nothing," came the reply.

Sandwiched between two makeshift huts, Kane observed the search party that had stumbled upon the crimson slick that was the last evidence of Banyon's existence. Six marauders milled around, their eyes wide and fearful. Counting the five hanging around Lombard, watching Brigid, Grant and the doctors, that made a full dozen coldhearts, with a few more most likely still hanging back on perimeter security.

Sure enough, Kane's observation skills proved correct as a radio message crackled over his captured unit. "We found another wheelbarrow full of supplies. No sign of any Mags, though."

"Son of a bitch!" Lombard cursed. "Leave the meds for now. Find that fucking Mag before he turns everything to shit!"

"Where'd your bravado go?" Kane taunted softly into his radio, loud enough to transmit but not enough to betray his roost to the hunting bandits. From his vantage point, Kane could see the blood drain from Lombard's face.

"Show yourself, Kane! Or we start killing your people! And we'll make it slow!" Lombard snapped.

Kane decided to up the ante. "Go ahead. I already have the first half of my pay. I'm sure I could find a good buyer for the dread bandit Lombard's severed head, too."

Lombard dropped his radio as if it were a venomous snake, dancing back in fright. Nothing like striking a cruel, casual predator with the knowledge that he was nowhere near the top of the food chain. Where Lombard had set himself as a brutal ruler of the Tartarus Pits, the bandit now lived with the knowledge that an even bigger bastard was poised to snatch him and carve him apart for blood money.

"Pick up your damned comm, coward," Kane growled.

The rumble of Kane's threat attracted the attention of one of the brighter members of the marauders' hunting party. The shotgun-toting thug stalked cautiously along the alley between rows of huts, looking for a clear view of Lombard. Kane heard the man's approach. If it hadn't been for Kane's well-honed senses, the thief would have been stealthy. Instead, every footfall and kicked bit of debris locked Kane on to the approaching gunman like drumbeats.

Lombard tentatively reached for the radio. "Okay."

Kane reversed the revolver in his grasp and whipped the handle violently into the bridge of the curious bandit's nose. Steel and wood crushed bone, pounding splinters of skull into the marauder's brain for a sudden, decisive kill. Swiftly Kane snatched the still-standing corpse and hauled it between the two huts, jamming it down into the clutter on the walkway floor. He keyed the radio to Lombard. "You want the medicine, then you don't need to bully those sheep. Walk away and I won't have to waste any ammunition killing you fused-out pricks."

Lombard glanced at Grant, who let his powerful shoulders sag in a display of false helplessness. Brigid also put on the airs of cornered, helpless prey. It was a good act, and if Kane hadn't witnessed their efficacy against countless enemies, he would have been convinced. The two companions were figuring out the angles necessary to take down the bandits with maximum efficiency and the least harm to the Cobaltville healers.

"Where's Russ?" a searching bandit asked. "Fireblasted punk... Russ!"

Lombard turned his attention toward the source of the shout. In that quick glance, the marauder leader glimpsed the silhouette of the wolf-lean Kane. "There! There he is!"

The five raiders around Lombard spun in unison, ignoring their "harmless" hostages as they raised their guns to burn down Kane. The warrior in the shadows lunged out of his hiding spot, twin revolvers cocked in unison.

"That's right, idiots," Kane whispered to himself. "Follow the bouncing bogeyman."

GRANT EXPLODED INTO ACTION first, his long, brawny right arm circling Ruben's throat. With a hard yank, the bandit's feet were dragged into the air, whipping across the head of a second coldheart with stunning force. Ruben gurgled in surprise, watching his partner drop to the ground after the wrenching impact of booted feet on his skull. Grant's left hand clawed the MP-5 K loose from stunned fingers, thumb stabbing the safety down to full-auto. As a third gunman fired his bolt-action rifle at the spot where Kane's silhouette had been only moments earlier, Grant pumped a half-dozen bullets between the killer's shoulder blades.

Brigid was only a half heartbeat slower than Grant. She

pulled a box cutter from a nearby table and thumbed the razor edge out of its blunt-sheath nose. It was a quick, practiced movement. She whipped it in a savage backhand across the cheek and forehead of a fourth hostage-taker. The sharp blade carved skin and muscle down to the bone, the angled point raking through his eye socket. Milky fluid gushed from the gunman's ruined orb, and he shrieked in horror, dropping his weapons to free his hands for the task of holding his face together. She scooped up the half-blinded man's pistol in a lightning-fast movement.

Lombard and the remaining bandit were torn between the options of shooting Grant, Kane or Brigid. Grant rendered the dilemma moot with a withering hail of machine-pistol fire that stitched Lombard's shotgunner from sternum to forehead. Lombard took a fourth option and charged down an alley. Brigid hammered off a single round at the rogue Mag, but the bullet was just a second too slow to catch the fleeing coward.

KANE STEPPED INTO THE VIEW of his pursuers, both revolvers held at eye level, their triggers snapping down twin hammers in unison. One shot missed Kane's initial target, the buffoon who'd cried out for the clever but dead Russ. It was no matter, as Kane's other revolver shot punched through the loud-mouth's face. The slug gouged out his brain, and the back of his skull erupted in gore. The brutal death of their comrade stunned the remaining four gunmen. That bought Kane the time to cock and fire the revolvers in his hands twice more. One of the marauders folded over in agony, a bullet burning in his bowels. A second gunman whirled with a shattered shoulder joint, collapsing as he clutched his ruined limb.

Kane sidestepped, taking cover behind the corner of a hut,

but the remaining two bandits were in no mood to fight back. They were fleeing for their lives. Just to make certain, Kane put two more quick bullets into the dirt at their heels. The rebuffed predators only picked up speed, not even weaving to avoid being shot in the back. Terror, not tactics, ruled the minds of the pair. Any thoughts of returning fire had been abandoned with the elimination of their friends.

The man with the bullet in his belly lay in an ever growing pool of bright arterial blood. It had been only a few seconds since the initial hit, meaning that Kane had severed the bandit's aorta. Unable to be staunched by tourniquet or direct pressure compress, the marauder was doomed the moment the bullet tore through the central trunk of blood flow in his body. The other raider, his shoulder reduced to stringy, bloody pulp, fumbled with his rifle, flipping it across the alley toward Kane.

"I give up! Don't shoot!" the wounded man cried out. "I'm unarmed."

"You think I'm blind?" Kane growled, stalking closer to the surrendering bandit. "Pull the pistol from your belt."

The raider looked down at the handle poking from under the folds of his shirt. His left hand slapped at the gun, clumsily dislodging it while avoiding any semblance of grasping it firmly. The predatory instincts that had made the wounded robber into a thief had been quenched with his crippling injury. Kane stooped and helped the wounded gunman in his surrender.

"How large was Lombard's gang?" Kane inquired.

"There were twenty of us," the crippled prisoner answered.

Kane nodded, doing the math. "Baptiste, Grant, we've got about ten more raiders out there," he subvocalized over the Commtact.

"We've got two prisoners here that confirm those numbers," Grant responded.

"No medics were harmed, except for the initial rough-housing by the bandits," Brigid added. Over the Commtact, Kane could hear Brigid check the action of her 9 mm pistol. "Do you think Lombard will regroup and try to finish the job?"

"Lombard lost half of his crew trying to get these meds," Kane answered. "I don't know. Black market medicine is worth a hell of a lot, but money won't bring you back from the dead."

Kane escorted his prisoner to the intersection, seeing Brigid tend to Phillips. The medic had a cut on his forehead, and blood stained his white coat pink from the seeping wound. On closer examination, though, Kane was relieved to see that Phillips's eyes were focused.

"No concussion, just a mess," Brigid confirmed.

"Good luck for me at least," Phillips grunted.

"Us, too," Kane answered. "I wouldn't want to lose any allies here in Cobaltville. You're worth more than any five gunslingers we could recruit."

"Especially for rebuilding Cobaltville," Brigid added.

Phillips winced. "I appreciate the sentiment, guys. Just wish these bastards hadn't cracked my head open."

Phillips slowly got up and started dealing with the bleeding laceration of the man Brigid had carved with the box cutter. Kane had packed the shoulder of his prisoner with a kerchief and tied it down with a belt, so he wouldn't need immediate attention. Ruben was rubbing his throat, looking weak and sickly after being swung around as a human weapon.

An orderly looked at Phillips, then shook his head. "These guys attacked us. They hurt you."

"And they're not a threat anymore," Phillips snarled. "Damn it, even Kane, a Magistrate, tended to his prisoner's injury. Maybe you feel like you can pick and choose when to apply mercy, but that's not the oath I took."

Kane looked at the angered medic. "Besides, I don't think the danger's over yet."

In the distance, the rumble of diesel engines sounded.

Lombard had gotten back to his war wags, and from the sounds of things, they were returning to deal with Kane and his allies.

Chapter 3

At the sight of the stranger in the forest, Domi slipped her satchel full of scrounged books from her shoulder, hiding it in a corner between the raised roots of an ancient tree. The small but cord-muscled albino woman didn't want to lose her latest haul from the library in the event of a chase, or if the stranger had allies who would capture her. Armed with only her dagger and a pistol crossbow for catching game while in the wild, the youngest, most feral member of the Cerberus redoubt focused her ruby-red eyes intently on the newcomer, sizing him up.

The security of Cerberus had been breached many times in the scant years that Domi had called the redoubt her home. As commander of Cerberus Away Team Beta, however, she'd proved to be more than merely a wayward refugee in the ancient facility. She'd battled reptilian invaders with spacecraft and gods armed with technology that could have been mistaken for mythical weaponry, all in the name of protecting her lover, Lakesh, and the ever growing population of the predark bastion of technology, knowledge and security.

The man wending his way toward the Bitterroot Mountain stronghold had, no doubt, picked this arduous route to avoid Sky Dog and the Lakota Indians who were staunch allies of Cerberus. Domi had crossed this particular terrain with the nimbleness of a mountain goat, spring-steel leg muscles bounding her along the rocky, uneven path with preternatural ease. She noticed that the man was no stranger to hard journeying, but exhaustion weighed on his powerful limbs. Domi regretted leaving behind the Commtact implant at the redoubt as she observed the lone traveler. She had gotten into the habit of isolating herself on these solitary expeditions to achieve a measure of soiace, as Lakesh described it. Such trips were meant to escape the confines of the base, abandoning both people and modern technology. The act of shedding the Commtact was the ultimate statement of that mental journey. The machine-woven fibers in her tank top and shorts and the polymer materials of her crossbow were the only evidence of her connection to the Cerberus redoubt and the technology it represented.

Domi's thumb snicked off the safety on her crossbow. The bolt was now ready to be released with only the touch of her finger on the trigger. The broad-headed tip was an aggressive assembly of four vaned blades designed to inflict enormous trauma as it pierced the organs of animals as large and as fierce as bears. Domi avoided contact with the carnivores who hunted in this region, leaving them a wide berth. However, a shaft capable of killing a bear would be more than sufficient to take any human invader. She wondered at the stranger's affiliation and his motives for approaching the redoubt. From his focus and his direction, there was no way that he could miss the base. Nothing else was nearby for hundreds of miles.

The man was armed with a large revolver stuffed into a leather scabbard that rode on his thigh. A coiled bullwhip hung from a hook on his opposite hip. His machete sheath was empty, for now, as he was using it to hack through thick briars that halted his path. Hardly the arsenal of an invader, even with the two-foot blade in his grasp. Cerberus guards would easily overpower him in the event of a hostile confrontation, but Domi's curiosity had been piqued, and she strove to get in closer.

The man paused, wiping his brow with his brawny forearm. He laid his machete on a rock, then reached for his canteen. As soon as he was committed to pulling a swallow of water from the canister, Domi stepped out, crossbow leveled at his chest.

"Hold still," she challenged.

The man's eyes went wide with surprise. He managed a swallow, then tilted the canteen so he wouldn't waste his water by drenching himself. "Can I recap my canteen?"

"No sudden movements," Domi said. "Who are you?"

"My name is Austin Fargo. I am on my way to the Cerberus redoubt to meet with Lakesh and Kane, the men who rule there, to ask for their assistance."

"Anything you can say to them, you can say to me," Domi told him. "What do you need?"

"As I said, I am Austin Fargo," he began. "I am an explorer and scientist." He nodded to Domi in deference. "Can I move now?"

Domi flicked the crossbow's safety back on. "Any sudden movements and the crows will feast on your eyes."

Fargo chuckled nervously. "I don't doubt that. You must be Domi. Your name is almost as well-known as that of your companions."

"Flattery," Domi said, wrinkling her nose. "In my experience, that usually leads a lie."

"I'm just attempting diplomacy," Fargo returned.

"Yeah? Well, you're being diplomatic with the guard dog,"

Domi replied. "Follow me, and I'll confirm with the owner of my house that I was right for not chewing your face off."

"Don't denigrate yourself, Domi. You're far more than a mere guard animal," Fargo said as he followed the albino woman. They backtracked the two hundred yards necessary for Domi to retrieve her satchel of scrounged books. He paid special notice to the fact that her small but sinewy hand never strayed more than an inch from the handle of her fighting knife. From the stories that the Millennial Consortium had cataloged about her, the wiry little albino had the speed and skill to pull that blade and separate a man's head from his torso in the space of a heartbeat. It was an unspoken threat, a warning that Fargo had to keep on his best behavior.

"You're on the right path to meet up with my people," Domi said.

"Not the easiest, but for me, the safest," Fargo admitted. "Then again, my trek has been one of great effort."

"You can hold the sympathy dirge for someone who actually gives a shit. I caught you sneaking in my back door as a trespasser. Until you get approved by those who I actually do trust, keep your mouth closed," Domi growled.

Fargo took a deep breath. She could see that he was re-straining an insult. Domi didn't mind; she didn't care if strangers saw her as a snarling bitch just one flinch away from gnawing out someone's entrails. When it came to defending the redoubt and her loved ones, that image was exactly what she wanted to project. A harmless, cuddly defender rarely caused an intruder to shy away from hostile activity.

"I understand," Fargo spoke up. "You're only protecting your family."

"Damned straight," Domi replied curtly. Her tone was

meant to shut the stranger up so they could concentrate on scaling the back trail.

Cloaked in stern silence, they made their way to the redoubt.

THE SNARL OF DISTANT DIESEL engines reached Kane's ears as Grant scrounged the dead raiders' fallen rifles. The powerful Cerberus exile smiled as he picked up a gun that actually looked normal sized in his massive hands.

"What in the hell is that thing?" Kane asked.

Grant partially opened the lever action, finding a round seated under the hammer. "A Marlin .45-70. Just the thing for when you absolutely, positively have to kill a wag in three shots or less."

Kane sighed. "Should have figured these coldhearts would have wheels."

A gun in the distance thundered, corrugated tin roofs rattling as the walls beneath them shuddered under powerful impacts. The Tartarus residents screamed in terror as the distant heavy machine gun raked their shacks.

Kane grit his teeth. "They've got a Fifty…" He scooped up the walkie-talkie, transmitting his bellow. "Lombard! Cease fire!"

"Cease fire?" the bandit leader asked. "You kill my men in cold blood, and when I look for payback, suddenly it's off-limits? Fuck you, Kane."

"Damn it, Lombard! These people aren't involved in our fight!" Kane growled. "Stop shooting. You want me or the meds, we can make a deal."

"Deal?" Lombard broke out, his laughter rattling as if captured in a tin can. "Where's the cold bastard who executed ten simple businessmen?"

"There's no profit in killing these refugees. How much is that ammunition costing you?" Kane asked. "You want business? Fine. Even killing three people per bullet, there's no way your temper tantrum is worth the trigger pull!"

There was silence on the other end, and thankfully, the Fifty mounted on one of Lombard's war wags remained silent, as well. The only sound left was a chorus of frightened sobs. Thankfully, there were no cries of agony anywhere, but the Cerberus champions realized that the gunfight only moments earlier had sent the Tartarus inhabitants to cover. Kane glanced at Grant, then nodded. The two men knew that Kane was going to have to put himself in the line of fire to prevent an all-out slaughter. Of course, that meant Kane would have to rely on his partner's marksmanship. Grant took his borrowed monster rifle and a belt stuffed with spare ammunition, then disappeared into the maze of houses.

Phillips rose from where he put the finishing touches on securing a bandit prisoner's bandage, wrapping his slashed-open face. "We have to check for dead or wounded from that blast."

"No," Brigid said, placing a calming hand on the doctor's shoulder. "From the general tone, there are no cries of mourning indicating a death, nor calls for help. However, if you stray from this area, the next time Lombard's men do fire that cannon, there's a chance that some of you could be harmed."

Phillips grimaced, protest already flashing in his eyes. "But—"

"You and your people are too valuable," Kane added. "If Cobaltville is to have any hope of maintaining and improving on what little shred of civilization remains, then it needs smart healers. Stay put until I clear everything."

Phillips looked between Kane and Brigid. Given the penchant for bickering that they displayed, to see them in such solid agreement pounded the message through to the healer. "Be careful…"

Kane handed Grant's Copperhead to Brigid. "If things go rotten…"

"I'll escort the medical staff to safety," she replied, accepting the rifle. "Watch yourself, okay?"

Kane nodded, then jogged to the road. Over the Commtact implant, he heard Grant give a solemn whisper. "They're in my sights."

"What have they got?" Kane asked.

"Thankfully, just old military-style transport trucks. Nothing like the armored Sandcats," Grant said. "I wouldn't be able to punch a hole in one of those. These aren't quite as hard skinned."

"But they can still mount a heavy machine gun," Kane said.

"Only one," Grant replied. "The other truck has to make do with riflemen in the back."

"How many?" Kane asked.

"Five split between the two vehicles," Grant told him. "And there's literally someone riding shotgun with each driver."

Kane figured the odds. From the drone of the diesel engines of both trucks, he was getting close enough to eyeball the bandits and their transportation. "We're going to have to make these bandits very afraid."

"The old 'one Magistrate, one riot' strategy?" Grant asked. "I feed you intel and back you up with sniper shots, making you look like the baddest ass on the planet."

"That's the one," Kane answered. "Where's Lombard now?"

"Standing next to his machine gunner. He's got an automatic rifle of some form," Grant said. "He just reached for his radio."

"Kane! Come out and play!" Lombard shouted over the airwaves.

"I have been," Kane answered. "You're the one hiding behind the trucks. Now I'm thinking that it's time for me to quit being so kind and gentle."

"Kind and gentle?" Lombard asked. "What the fuck are you talking about?"

"I'm talking about it's time to stop playing with you and just put you down like the rotten little turd you are," Kane replied. "You're just some goon with some fancy guns. You don't even rank in the ten biggest gangs of bandits I've ever fought."

"He's telling his man to shoot," Grant warned.

Kane dived into a shoulder roll, zooming into the open just as a roar of autofire shredded the tin-and-wood hut he'd been hiding behind. Kane and Grant fired their weapons, both drowned out by the roar of the mighty Browning Fifty. Anyone watching, though, wouldn't have seen Grant's hidden muzzle-flash, while the Sin Eater's barrel blazed angrily.

The machine gunner jerked violently, his right forearm disintegrating under the impact of the monster hunting rifle in Grant's hands. The Fifty stopped its bellow, the gunner's screams piercing the air as blood sprayed in Lombard's face.

The men mounted in the trucks looked at the man who'd been at the controls of their crowd-killing device, then at the lone ex-Magistrate getting to his feet, out in the open. A tendril of smoke curled from the muzzle of the Sin Eater. Lombard scrubbed at his eyes, grimacing as the injured bandit wound a cord tightly around his arm to tourniquet the injury.

"You gentlemen think that because Lombard's with you, you know how to deal with a real Magistrate," Kane said, walking toward the trucks.

From the grumbles of discomfort among the marauders, he knew that his ploy had worked.

"That's bullshit!" Lombard shouted. "He's got to have a partner somewhere!"

Kane ignored Lombard, addressing the rest of the bandits. "Your partners are all dead. I killed them, because Lombard was just too stubborn to realize that he's second class. Now I'm going to appeal to you, because I hate wasting good ammunition."

"He didn't kill the others by himself," Lombard snarled.

"No, he didn't," a woman's voice called out. Brigid Baptiste strode into the open, Copperhead SMG held against her curvaceous hip. "He had the help of women and doctors. People with no combat training."

Kane repressed the urge to smile, remembering the steep learning curve of Brigid's early years at Cerberus, when the young woman had grown from an archivist to an adventurer who was a deadly shot and a tough fighter.

The bandits looked at Lombard.

"So you have a choice," Kane offered. "Ditch your boss and find somewhere else to hunt, or you can all die where you stand."

"How do you want him?" one of the bandits asked. "Dead or alive?"

"You fuckers!" Lombard spit. He lunged at the Browning, but Kane and Grant fired at the renegade Mag.

Kane's bullet plucked at Lombard's bicep, while Grant's cannon round smashed the belt of ammunition feeding into the machine gun. The mounted weapon and Lombard spun almost in unison under their respective impacts.

Marauders lunged at Lombard, seizing him tightly.

"Whatever is easier for you," Kane said, pushing his Sin Eater back into its holster on his forearm.

"God damn you!" Lombard shrieked as his men hurled him over the cab of the truck. He crashed into the dirt road, then clawed swiftly to his feet. Angry eyes glared at Kane, and he tensed. "This piece of shit isn't so hot!"

"Then prove it!" another bandit shouted. "You got a Sin Eater. Show us you're worth following."

Lombard looked around, confused. He eventually rested his eyes on Kane, who stood, arms folded, shaking his head.

"Not a good idea, man," Kane warned.

Lombard glanced toward Brigid.

"Don't look at her. She'd just as soon shoot you, but she's not paying for the bullets," Kane snapped.

Lombard's eyes flicked to the Sin Eater on his forearm. One flex, and the autoweapon would rocket into his hand. Kane knew, though, that a fast draw with the hydraulic holster was a perishable skill. The movement would be fast, but getting the first shot on target required regular practice. Lombard was a thief who attacked unarmed doctors, not a master gunslinger who constantly honed his skills.

In the meantime, Kane had just proved his lethality against younger, hardier men. Lombard reached slowly for the straps on his Sin Eater, unfastening them. The machine pistol landed in the dirt at his feet, and Lombard dropped to his knees, lacing his fingers behind his head.

Kane turned to glare at the truckloads of remaining bandits. "Go."

The new leader of the robber gang looked at the rest of his men. The diesels roared as the wags ground into Reverse, backing away from the edge of the town.

"They're not slowing down," Grant confirmed. "They've taken the hint."

Kane walked toward Lombard, pausing only to scoop up the renegade's fallen weapon. "What to do with you…"

"Grant…" Lombard snarled. "That big ape—"

Kane took a swift step forward and kicked him in the face. The impact split a seam of skin from eyebrow to the corner of Lombard's mouth. Blood flowed from the fresh gash.

"Talking about my partner like that is always a bad idea," Kane said.

"You're crazy!" Lombard snapped. His hands covered his battered, bloody face. "What are you going to do with me?"

"We'll see if Dr. Phillips needs someone to do grunt work," Grant said, rejoining his partners. "Though nothing too complicated."

"You lied when you said there weren't any other ex-Mags," Lombard complained.

"And you were dumb enough to not recognize me," Grant countered. "Your bandits were plain and simple outsmarted. We had the communication, we had the knowledge, and now you're just a footnote. Twenty marauders with big trucks and big guns, taken down by three people, two of them who you'd disarmed."

Lombard grimaced, then noted that Kane was disassembling the surrendered Sin Eater, handing magazines and the holster to Grant. They looked distracted by the menial task as they whispered softly to each other, probably discussing plans. Lombard reached down to his boot, coming up with a gleaming little pistol in his hand.

The deposed bandit leader pulled the trigger, but his gunshot jerked into the sky as Brigid pumped a single Copperhead round into Lombard's chest.

"Fool," Brigid muttered. "So busy concentrating on you two, he forgot all about me."

"Well, that solves the problem of what to do with the asshole," Grant said with a sigh.

Kane smirked. "A self-resolving problem, most likely. Thanks, Baptiste."

"What thanks?" Brigid asked. "I need one of you two to grab that last wheelbarrow full of meds. I'm not busting my back for it."

Kane chuckled, kicking the gun out of Lombard's dead fingers. "I love you, too, Baptiste."

Brigid returned the smile. There was an uncomfortable pause, but she regained her composure. "Let's go. We should get back to Cerberus to see if anything new has come up."

Kane nodded. "No rest for the wicked."

Chapter 4

Mohandas Lakesh Singh stood just outside the anteroom of the mat trans chamber as Kane, Brigid and Grant returned from their sojourn to Cobaltville. He waited alongside an impatient Domi, who paced like an anxious panther in a cage.

Kane looked the two people over and knew that whatever was going on, it couldn't be good. "Who showed up? Erica? Sindri?"

"Why would it be them?" Lakesh asked.

"Because Cerberus is still standing, but you're chomping at the bit to let us know some shit's up," Grant answered for Kane.

"Neither Erica or Sindri," Domi answered, her voice quick and clipped. "Ran into a millennial guy crawling around our back door."

Kane sneered. "Millennial Consortium? They found us here?"

"I know that they said they have extensive files on us, but I'm surprised that they know the location of Cerberus," Brigid stated.

"Why not? Erica knows. So do Sindri and the overlords. And the consortium has done business with each of them in the past," Kane said. "In fact, Erica's calling them allies now, after that blowout in China."

Brigid frowned. "And you let him in?"

"He wasn't in uniform," Domi replied. "No coverall. No button. No Calico. But he's consortium. I feel it."

Brigid glanced at Lakesh. "Any corroboration?"

Lakesh shrugged. "Nothing definitive. However, he's hale and healthy, with evidence of having received professional medical treatment. A recent scar on his arm confirms to DeFore that a real doctor stitched it up."

Reba DeFore was the redoubt's chief medical officer. With the influx of staff from the Manitius Moon Base, the position didn't weigh on her skills as much as it used to, but in the years preceding it, she'd gained a sharp eye toward medical treatment. The stranger's apparent access to such treatment left few options open as to his affiliation. The Millennial Consortium was a budding technocracy, seeking to rebuild America in its own image. Those in charge of the consortium paid lip service to the creation of a utopian society, but their ruthlessness in the pursuit of that goal had brought them into savage conflict with the Cerberus warriors on multiple occasions.

The consortium wanted a utopia, and its representatives were willing to kill every person who stood in the path to that objective. Unarmed foes were just as open to murder as the Cerberus personnel.

"I also inspected the stranger's gear," Lakesh told the others as he led them toward the briefing room. "His kit includes a leather bullwhip that appears to have bloodstains."

"He also couldn't stop buttering all of us up," Domi added as they entered a room where Sela Sinclair and Edwards, members of the Cerberus away teams, stood guard over a bored man.

"Worse than Lakesh in the beginning?" Kane asked, slipping into a faux Indian accent, trying to dispel his habitual unease with Balam's old stomping grounds. "'Friend Kane, beloved Brigid…'"

Lakesh rolled his eyes but chuckled at Kane's antics. "Not the same, but the man knows how to get his nose browned."

"What's his name?" Brigid asked. Looking him over, she seemed to be turning over a memory in her mind, not quite believing it.

"Austin Fargo," Lakesh answered. Fargo sat, dressed in a white shirt, brown pants and a battered old leather jacket. A wide-brimmed hat sat on the table in front of the man. "And yes…he's dressed almost note for note like the old movie archaeologist."

Kane tilted his head. "Has he gotten the earful from Sinclair about that?"

Grant rolled his eyes. "Yeah, she only made me sit through those movies three times."

Kane glanced toward his partner. "I thought you liked 'em."

"After the third time, with Sela saying all of Dr. Jones's dialogue line for line, it got tiring," Grant responded. He glanced nervously toward Brigid. "Not that memorizing things is annoying, mind you."

Brigid winked at Grant. "No offense taken."

Kane examined the heavy revolver, the machete and the curled bullwhip. He picked up the whip, examining its light tan leather bandings. "You think you found blood?"

DeFore knocked on the door, interrupting Kane's thoughts. The medic, a stocky, buxom woman with bronze skin and ash-blond hair, brightened from a dour mood, seeing that Kane and the others were back from their trip to Cobaltville. Despite this, she remained businesslike. "I brought some chemicals to run a test on the whip."

"It wouldn't mean much. He could have used it in self-defense, or the blood could have been from an animal," Brigid suggested. "Or the chemical could luminesce in the presence of copper, horseradish, even bleach."

Kane handed the whip to DeFore. "So, how many times have you seen someone flay a horseradish root with a bullwhip?"

"All other things being equal, the simplest solution is the best," Brigid returned.

Kane nodded. "And you say I never learn."

Brigid managed a smile. In the darkened observation deck, DeFore sprayed the whip, and iron traces left behind by blood illuminated the last four feet of the wicked lash, glowing brightly. She pulled some tweezers, digging into a seam between two strips of leather.

"What did you find?" Lakesh asked.

DeFore turned on a small lamp, and the two scientists inspected the scrap trapped between the tweezer's points. "Looks like skin. Dried out and desiccated, but skin. And this was just one clump of many that the chemicals exposed."

Kane glanced through the one-way mirror toward Fargo. "No fur?"

DeFore shook her head. "None on closer examination."

Kane looked at his friends. "And what does Fargo want with us?"

Lakesh looked at the whip as if it were a coiled cobra. "He said that he had discovered a cache of military technology in the Kashmir province of the subcontinent. A place between what used to be Pakistan and India. Both nations claimed the land before skydark, but it was always hotly contested, with terrorists and minor border skirmishes constantly erupting."

"So he came to us? We've got all the gear we could ever need here at Cerberus," Grant interjected. "And if not just here, there's also stuff at Cobaltville. Even the most dedicated army of looters couldn't take all of the equipment stored in a ville."

"There's got to be something more. Especially if he came to us, instead of returning to the Millennial Consortium," Brigid said.

"You think he's consortium now?" Kane asked.

Brigid nodded. "Your instincts are rarely wrong."

"What do you think?" Kane asked her.

Brigid regarded Fargo through the glass. "We've had troubles in India before."

"Scorpia Prime and her doomsday cultists," Kane noted. "Nagas, right?"

Brigid confirmed Kane's guess. "We might have solved the problem of Scorpia Prime, but the cult we dealt with may only have been a splinter of a much larger group."

"He claims to have encountered a much more dangerous group than just a few snake worshipers," Lakesh stated.

"They were savage enough," Grant said, remembering his horrific stay and the suffering he endured at the hands of torturers.

"No doubt, Grant," Lakesh returned. "My apologies."

"It wasn't you," Grant said, ending that branch of the conversation.

"He claims to have encountered a new party?" Kane asked.

"Different from the overlords. He even referenced the genetically augmented soldiers of England. I wanted you to get a look at him, figure out what he actually was before we all talked with him," Lakesh explained. "And if necessary…"

"Loosen his tongue," Kane concluded.

"Shall we?" Lakesh asked.

Kane picked up Fargo's gear, hefting the bullwhip thoughtfully. "We shall."

SELA SINCLAIR HEARD Kane's voice over her Commtact as she sat in the interrogation room with self-proclaimed archaeologist Austin Fargo.

"Talk to him," Kane said. "Make it seem like you give a shit what he's all about."

Sela grunted an affirmative. "So, are you a freezie, or did someone show you the movies?"

"Excuse me?" Fargo asked.

"The hat. The jacket. The bullwhip we relieved you of," Sela said. "Fairly iconic figure you copied your style from."

"Only her favorite vid hero," Edwards added. Obviously he'd received the same message from Kane on the Commtact. "If she wasn't going to ask, I would've."

Fargo sighed. "A traveling show passed through my town when I was little. It was a wag with its own generator and a widescreen monitor. When I saw him, I knew what I wanted to be."

Sela nodded. "This doesn't mean we'll be holding hands in the shower and taking midnight walks on the beach, so don't get too friendly."

"I'm not," Fargo answered. "I'm just an archaeologist, looking for what's still useful from the past."

"With skydark's destruction and the Program of Unification, I wouldn't think there would be much left to archaeolog," Edwards noted.

Fargo and Sela both raised an eyebrow at Edwards's newly invented verb. Fargo finally chuckled. "There is still preskydark tech not assembled by the unification program or various other parties. Besides, when the barons abandoned their villes, they didn't leave behind many of the keys to their kingdoms."

"And you get paid well for finding stockpiles of weapons, vehicles and electronics," Sela added.

Fargo nodded. "That's right. But my main goal is to discover what we have lost as a race."

Sela noticed that Fargo had allowed his voice to drop an octave, taking on a seductive tone. It hadn't been lost on the archaeologist that Sela was a survivor from another time, preserved in suspended animation for centuries, safe from apocalyptic turmoil. The past that Fargo longed to discover lived in the woman. His attention to her lithe, athletic figure also showed that more than a little lust had influenced his sudden focus on her. Fargo was a tall, handsome man in his own right. If Lakesh's and Domi's instincts hadn't been tripped by him, Sela wouldn't have minded the attention. The suspicions about Fargo's affiliations prevented any reciprocal appreciation.

The door quickly opened, jarring Fargo from his observation of Sela. Domi and Lakesh entered, moving with swiftness of purpose.

"My colleagues will be by shortly," Lakesh informed Fargo, taking a seat across from him.

"Kane, Grant and Baptiste?" Fargo inquired.

"The same," Lakesh answered brusquely. "The map you submitted is of interest. You claim to have encountered a hidden society in what used to be India. One in possession of twentieth-century military technology."

"My expedition was wiped out, and when I made my escape,

they pursued me with a helicopter," Fargo explained. "I also have a feeling that they possess genetic reengineering technology."

Lakesh frowned. "What did you say they called themselves again?"

"They called themselves Nagah, individually," Fargo stated. "No relation to the Naga cultists both your people and mine had encountered farther to the south."

Lakesh glared at Fargo. From a prior encounter, Lakesh knew that the millennialists had a penchant for trying to unsettle the Cerberus warriors by appearing astonishingly well-informed. "Interesting."

The door opened again, pausing the conversation as three more people entered the room. As large as Edwards was, Grant was even taller, his shoulders even broader. By contrast, Kane was a lean, tightly muscled figure, his body as sleek and efficient as if he were a wolf recast in human form. Kane's eyes held a predatory intensity as he glared at Fargo. The most interesting addition to the population of the interrogation room was Brigid Baptiste. Had her beauty been any less striking, she'd have been swallowed by the imposing ferocity of the two men she accompanied. However, even with her flame-tinted curls pulled back in a severe ponytail, and her voluptuous body wrapped in a plain redoubt bodysuit, Brigid was an explosion of beauty.

As the trio stared Fargo down, he could sense the flavors of their intellects. Grant emanated cynical distrust. Kane's hard glare tore deep, formulating the most efficient means to kill the archaeologist if necessary. Brigid's observations were cold and clinical, dissecting his every aspect like fibers underneath a microscope.

Without saying a word, the three companions had dispelled the chance that tales of their exploits were hyperbole. The trio had an energy to it that was unmistakable, a lethal mix of power and intellect. No wonder Fargo's fellow millennialists had considered the three adventurers the greatest threat to their goals of world superiority.

"Do I meet with your approval?" Fargo asked, trying not to appear cowed by the force of personality standing before him.

The bullwhip clattered on the table in front of Fargo, thrown there by Kane. "That's seen some hard use," the ex-Magistrate said. "Found bits of human skin in there."

"And despite the effort to disguise your allegiance, you possess considerable backing. Where else would you have received such competent medical treatment?" Brigid said, noting the line of the scar on his forearm. "Not to mention the quality of your clothing and other equipment."

Fargo glanced at Grant. The big man merely shrugged. "I got nothin' other than I do not trust strangers caught creeping around my back door."

Lakesh cleared his throat. "We were just discussing his claims of a hidden society operating in northwestern India."

"So the Millennial Consortium wants us to take a look where their own expedition failed?" Grant asked bluntly. Fargo raised an eyebrow at the sudden accusation, but Grant waved off the man's reaction. "Sure, think of me as the dumb muscle, but Brigid's implications only give me one real option. You're not some mind-controlled toady, so you can't be Erica von Sloan's errand boy. The snake-face survivors are too disorganized, looking for their old toys to bother with hairless apes. All that's left is the consortium."

Fargo nodded. "I've worked for them, but this is not their

call. They sent me to get a big, fat prize, and the force they supplied me with died. I left empty-handed and alone."

"So, the millennialists don't love you anymore," Kane mentioned. "Even if I believed that, why not try to ask the dragon queen for help? She loves ancient artifacts, and she'd provide a good word to get you back into the graces of the consortium."

Fargo chuckled, a rueful look on his face. "I'd taken a few of her things during a weekend at the Xian Pyramid. Since Erica joined up with the consortium, she's been looking for an excuse to expel me out into the cold, cruel world."

Brigid echoed Fargo's laugh, drawing Kane's attention.

"What?" Kane asked.

Brigid smiled. "Never thought that I'd sympathize with the wicked bitch of the east. You call yourself an archaeologist, but you're nothing more than a common thief."

Fargo shrugged. "Knowledge is power, but it doesn't keep a belly full."

"It pays the bills, right?" Brigid asked. "A lot of excuses for mercenary activity. After all, aren't you just seeking what we have lost as a race?"

Fargo's eyes narrowed. "I knew it. The waiting game was just to shake my tongue loose. You wanted the truth about me? Fine. I know you're not paranoid when you actually do have someone out to get you."

Kane smirked. "Spoken like someone who has plenty of enemies of his own."

"So what about the Nagah?" Grant asked. "They like the other cultists in the south? Snake worshipers?"

"Worship, nothing," Fargo said. "Scaled skin, hinged fangs, complete with venom sacs capable of spraying blinding poison. They also have hoodlike structures, webbing along the sides of their heads that leads down to their shoulders, capable of flexing like a true cobra's. Crazy is strong enough for a lot of things, but not enough to change a madman's species. That's why I said they possessed the facilities to reengineer genetics."

"It's possible to make enormous changes with the proper technology," Lakesh spoke up. "I'm living proof of that. Enlil-as-Sam utilized a swarm of nanites to rebuild my internal organs and store my youth."

"That was utilizing Annunaki technology," Brigid said.

"Nanites?" Fargo asked.

"Molecule-scale machines capable of deconstructing and reorganizing matter," Brigid explained.

When the look on Fargo's face betrayed his level of comprehension, Grant laughed. "Really tiny robots that can change an old man into a young guy, or a normal person into one of your cobra freaks."

"Thanks," Fargo muttered.

"I know how tough it is, listening to Brigid explain things for the first time," Grant added.

"Grant and I jockeyed to get first crack at science books when we arrived," Kane said. "Understanding the basics really helps."

"Do you two mind?" Brigid asked. "Besides, I thought you didn't trust him."

"We don't," Grant said. "We don't like or trust the murderous little prick."

Kane nodded. "But, like you sympathized with Erica, we can sympathize with him."

Lakesh sighed loudly, wishing to return to Fargo's story

about his serpentine adversaries. "The snake men seem to correlate with mythologies that extend back at least three millennia. Though the name 'Nagah' is localized to the Indian subcontinent."

"If you read between the lines, however, there are beings like mer-people, Lamia, even gods such as the feathered serpent god Quetzalcoatl. Snakelike humans are not a unique mythology," Brigid interjected. "As well, Lord Strongbow had modified his troops with reptilian aspects, obviously inspired by ancient creatures such as the Formorians."

"Durga mentioned Strongbow's people," Fargo said. "How they utilized an inefficient form of transformation."

Brigid tilted her head. "The Tuatha de Danaan and the Annunaki entered a truce and combined their technologies. However, one of the regions where they engaged in fiercest conflict was the British Isles. Perhaps the Formorians were these serpentine humans."

"I thought that was a leftover memory of when the snake faces and the Tuatha were at war," Kane said.

"Perhaps," Brigid said. "There is also a disturbing similarity between the reptilians that Fargo describes and the Nephilim that the Quad V hybrids evolved into."

Domi raised her hand and both Brigid and Lakesh looked at her. "Brigid, you were helping me do some research on reptilian humanoids, after we'd encountered the Hydrae mutants in Greece. There was someone... Yuck..."

"Icke. David Icke," Brigid replied. "It popped into my mind, as well."

Lakesh rolled his eyes. "I was around when he posited some of his ideas."

Brigid nodded. "Icke's theories were odd, but they may

have had actual scientific basis. He theorized that there were shape-shifting but basically reptilian creatures who secretly ruled the world in the twentieth century. They were purported to have had limited shape-shifting abilities, but his position that many world leaders were actually nonhumans strained credulity. This, of course, diverges from the traditional mythological texts where these creatures were not shape changers. As well, the Nagah were not an antagonistic race. They lived in a subterannean realm beneath India. There were also hints that the Nagah originated on another continent."

"Like Lemuria or Atlantis," Kane suggested.

"You've been taking notes," Brigid complimented him. "Which brings our friend's comparison to Lord Strongbow's troops full circle."

"So, the Nagah were not shape-shifters?" Fargo asked.

"Unlikely," Brigid answered. "Even Icke's contemporary John Rhodes stated that such accusations of saurian humanoids were unfounded paranoia. The 'reptoids' of Rhodes's description were, like the Indian Nagah, subterranean, but with origins in the era of the dinosaurs."

Fargo squeezed his brow. "That's a lot to bite off in one session, and I saw the fucking things."

The archaeologist glanced at Kane. "So, are you going to go to India?"

"Yes," Lakesh spoke up. "I want to come, as well. I proved I can handle myself in the field, with our last journey to India, and the sortie into China."

"You're not making me sit it out like you did in China," Domi said curtly.

"Darlingest one, it's too dangerous," Lakesh countered. The slap across his cheek wasn't entirely unexpected.

Lakesh, having seen Domi in conflict, knew that she pulled her punch, because his head wasn't swimming and he was still on his feet. Her ruby-red eyes glowed angrily in the interrogation room.

"I'm perfectly fine with danger. It's my job. Besides, you're too important to risk without having someone specifically looking out for you. Kane and the others will be too busy to babysit you, keep their eyes on Fargo and deal with high-tech snakes at the same time," Domi told him.

Lakesh nodded. "I forget. You're not some fragile flower."

"And it's not like I can tell you not to go, because you speak the language," Domi added. "So, I'm coming along. No bullying this time."

"Fine," Lakesh said.

He turned to Sela. "You and the other away team members can handle things here?"

"Absolutely, boss," Sela replied. "Just don't forget to bring me something back as a souvenir."

"What were you thinking about?" Fargo asked, slipping back into the role of seducer.

"How about your balls if you betray my people?" Sela asked.

Fargo glanced at Kane.

"Sympathy or no, if the consortium shows up to this party, you'll be the first one to catch a bullet," Kane told him.

Fargo didn't doubt the Cerberus warrior.

Chapter 5

The crystal-clear water of the underground pool slid off the shimmering blue-green scales of the naked serpent woman as she walked up the slope of the beach. She climbed past the water's edge on long, sinewy legs. The serpentess ran slender, deceptively delicate fingers down her body, wiping away droplets that clung to her curvaceous form. A sarong of flowered blue silk lay in a puddle on a flat rock that she used as a table, and she picked it up once she had assured herself that her scaled flesh had been brushed clean, no dewy droplets remaining to mar the simple wrap. The cloth snugged around her sleek, full hips, covering her from her vestigial navel down to just above her knees. With a deft fold, she looped a ribbon-like strap around her neck, covering her breasts, a throwback to her mammalian hybrid heritage. The wrap obscured her nearly invisible nipples in the center of each glimmering orb. The women of the Nagah, entitled Nagani, betrayed their half-human heritage, possessing the curves reminiscent of human female anatomy, and as such, had developed a need for concealing those differences from their male counterparts.

"Hannah, my queen, my apologies," the voice of her body-guard echoed to her. The echo of his words bounced from the cavernous tunnel to the subterranean lagoon. "May this unworthy servant enter thy glorious presence?"

Naji Hannah finished tucking her sarong down. "Come in, Manticor. There is nothing unworthy about you. And I am not queen yet."

The bodyguard strode into view. He was six and a half feet tall, lithe limbs resembling thick cords of steel cable, having a silvery burnish as they ran down from copper-brown shoulders. Manticor, like all Nagah men, was naked from the waist up, clad only in pants from his hips to his knees. The tough chest plates that rolled down his torso were the same hard, sandy shells that protected the soles of his feet, surer protection and traction than any hand-cobbled footwear. Like many of the Nagah, his toes had fused together, giving him the illusion of shoes. Those who had been gifted with the "change" and whose lower bodies had become truly serpentine were considered the children of their creator. Such instances were rare, resulting in beings who had to drag themselves along by their arms, resting on a long, undulating monolimb that was not designed for supporting the weight of a human torso.

"Naja Durga has returned from his recent expedition," Manticor stated. "He requests the company of his promised bride."

Hannah's eyes narrowed. "In other words, 'I'm home. Where's my fuck?'"

Manticor winced at the harshness of his charge's language. Hannah knew that Manticor was also pained by the thought of Hannah being pressed into a loveless marriage. "I am sorry, Excellence."

Hannah ran her delicate fingertips across the tough chest plates on the snake man's pectoral muscles. Her hazel eyes sought his, penetrating deep into their brown, smoldering depths. "I am sorry, as well, my loyal protector. I meant no crudeness for your ears. Tell my cousin that if he wishes to see me, he can find me in my chambers."

Manticor's scaled lips tightened into a bloodless line. "He won't be pleased."

"If Durga deems it necessary to punish you, he will never know my touch again," Hannah promised, rage giving edge to her voice. "No. He'll know the touch of my feet once I've finished kicking him to death."

Manticor stepped away from her touch. Shame had smothered whatever joy had been awakened by Hannah's caress. Manticor's duty was to the Nagah Protectorate, the elite who defended the royal family. That duty meant that he would give his life for the precious Princess Hannah. In the larger scheme of things, it meant that he had to ensure that the crown prince's bride would bear him the means to carry on his family dynasty. His life, influenced by an affection and attraction to Hannah, was commanded by an oath to see the thing he loved most in the world hauled off to an embittered being who saw her only as a means to extend his genetic viability.

Hannah regretted being so familiar with Manticor, speaking the thoughts that flashed behind dark eyes. She regretted that his devotion to her had sparked a kindred love. Manticor was the shining knight every girl wanted, be they human or Nagah. Tall, strong and selflessly committed to her, Manticor was Hannah's body and soul. All she had to do was ask, and he'd be hers forever. Were there a place for the two Nagah to flee in the human world, she would abandon her crown and leave with him. Instead, she was trapped. Serpents were not welcome aboveground, and the humans who interacted with the Nagah were rare outside of the underground realm. Hannah and Manticor would be hunted by snake and shunned by man.

"I will tell Naja Durga of your intentions," Manticor said. After a pause, he chuckled nervously. "Intention to wait for him in your chambers, not the kicking thing."

Hannah gave him a weak smile, then the official gesture of dismissal. Released, the bodyguard left the lagoon chamber, and his discomfort. She watched him bow as he left the private swimming area. Hannah made her way slowly to her chambers.

The dread-filled wait for Durga's arrival began.

DURGA ROLLED OVER, spent in his carnal energies. His member retreated back into its protective sheath of armored scales, smearing his and Hannah's mixed love juices on the flat plates of his groin. He licked at Hannah's hood, tongue trailing to the crook of her neck before kissing her. "Be a dear and clean our mess off me."

Hannah, panting and sore, glared at him. Her eyes flicked down to the glistening cocktail in his lap. "I am a princess of the blood, not some bathing maid. Get a washcloth."

She rolled on the mattress, pulling away from his grasp, staring at the tapestry on her chamber wall. Hannah hunched her shoulders, trying to create a wall between Durga and herself. Powerful fingers dug into her shoulder, and Hannah grimaced as he whipped her around so that they were face-to-face. She looked at the damaged scales over his right eye. The scar was a livid, jagged slash carved into his armored skin. His once golden iris was muted as it swam in a bloodshot orb. It was a memento of his encounter with the humans of the Millennial Consortium. The eye that peered at her looked harsh, unhealthy.

"Your king demands your service," Durga snarled threateningly.

Hannah's upper lip curled back, her fangs flexing int position. "You'll regret it."

Durga pushed her away, sitting up. "We are of the sam royal blood. Your venom would not harm me."

"No, but my teeth are still sharp enough to tear your dic to shreds," Hannah returned, exiting the bed to get away fron him.

Durga watched her move. Even angry, she had the grac of a dancer. "You would end the trueblood? For what Dignity? Even sucking me off, you're still a queen."

Hannah tugged her wrap around her naked form, steppin closer to the chamber entrance. "Then why act as if I'm jus a whore?"

"Take one more step, and it will be you who will harbo regrets," Durga promised. His hood flexed, flaring as th muscle stretched his neck in anger.

"If your touch leaves a mark, the Nagah will forget abou your pure blood and let you know how they feel about you bigotry," Hannah warned. "When the bulk of your people ar newbloods, you don't have much room to alienate them."

Durga smirked, his orange eye flashing like a fire in a pi "Manticor."

"You wouldn't," Hannah stated.

"He would follow my orders. He'd assault the gates of he armed with a toothpick if I told him to," Durga replied, sneerin at her. "He will do his duty, and his duty, ultimately, is my will.

"I would damn you to hell," Hannah said, sighing, "bi you'd be in charge inside of ten minutes."

Durga smiled. "Come here, lover. On your knees."

Hannah clenched her golden eyes shut, tear ducts burnin like acid.

"Your dignity or my majesty," Durga taunted. "Make your choice."

Hannah's eyes snapped open in a glare, but in her heart she knew the true choice didn't involve either of the royal Nagahs' pride. The life of a good, upstanding, selfless being was at stake. Even if Hannah hadn't harbored affection for the loyal Manticor, she couldn't allow harm to come to one of her people, especially when she had a say in the matter. It was her duty as ruler to sacrifice for her people, she told herself.

Not completely, she corrected. Self-service did play a role in her decision. As long as Manticor lived, there was a chance that they would have an opportunity to become lovers, to grow old together.

She stepped to Durga, knelt, closed her eyes and thought of Manticor.

WHENEVER HANNAH WAS CALLED to bed with the trueblood prince, Manticor always found it easier to be elsewhere in the ancient caverns of the Nagah. He wasn't blind to the affection that she showed him, but also knew that such love was a leash that Durga wielded to control his chosen bride. Hannah only alluded to her dealings with Durga, but the hints formed an ugly picture, that made Manticor regret the strength of his fealty to the royal family.

Durga's father, Garuda, had died defending their underworld realm, fallen as he battled against armored invaders from across the Pacific Ocean. The humans had called themselves Magistrates, and they sought the technology of the Nagah, most especially the ancient genetic-manipulation devices left behind by their creator, one of the dragon gods of the stars. The capacity for cloning and human alteration was too important to the hybrid barons who ruled America. Though they had their own genetics program and production facility, the thought of others possessing such advancements was anathema to them. Garuda, the fallen king, had offered to share with the barons, but greed had proved too much to allow such compromise.

The shooting war was brief and savage. Garuda led the Nagah warriors in a conflict against the baronial expeditionary force. The Magistrates had been exterminated, but at enormous cost, with Garuda dying as he destroyed the last of the Deathbird helicopters. Mortally wounded by the gunship's machine gun, Garuda struck the craft from the sky with a shoulder-fired rocket. The destruction of the human marauders became known as the Battle of Sky Spear, one of the greatest victories, and tragedies, in the history of the cobra people.

That was where Durga's spite for the mammals had been born. Durga was only in his teen years, a young warrior who fought alongside his father as a gunner on a jeep. He watched as the humans' bullets tore into his father's flesh, and his vengeful thirst had not been slaked in thirty years of bloodshed.

That was decades ago, and since then, Durga had spread the influence of the Nagah dynasty throughout the region. Raids against human settlements produced results that impressed the queen, Matron Yun. Converts among the imprisoned slaves were passed through the cobra baths, solutions of nanomachines in saline that stripped the majority of their mammalian nature, all save a warm-blooded metabolism, and replaced it with the serpentine perfection that had been a gift from the dragon god Enki. Human cultists were readily accepted into the ranks, provided they survived the harrowing trek to the Kashmir across the radioactive wastelands, bandit-controlled territories and the ferocious predators of the wilderness. Unfortunately, few of these believers, now called pilgrims, even knew of the hidden Nagah empire. Even fewer had the endurance to survive such a murderous journey.

Manticor's father had been one such man. His mother was a convert from the enslaved humans captured by the grim Prince Durga, in the time before the prince's rage consumed every waking moment. Technically, Manticor's birth by two newbloods, or converts to Nagah form, and the fact that he was born a serpent, not needing the cobra baths, made him a trueblood. Unfortunately, Durga had long ago decreed that only the royal family could call themselves truebloods, as they could trace their lineage back to the age of the dragon kings. Manticor didn't have the right to that title. The best that he could hope for was the mantle of pilgrim's son.

A cordon of guards entered the cavernous hall that Manticor had wandered into. A dozen pistol-equipped cobra men moved in unison, like a single entity. Manticor immediately recognized them as the ring of living armor that surrounded the queen matron as she moved among her citizens. The snake man dropped to one knee, lowering his head in deference to the grand matriarch. The phalanx of bodyguards halted in front of Manticor.

"Manny, child, rise and gaze upon your queen," Yun said.

Had she been human, her age might have proved more readily apparent. Still, six decades had done little to dull the copper-and-black leopard pattern of her scales, and her golden eyes were as bright and fiery as freshly lit bonfires. The only sign of her advanced years was a looseness of her skin and a softening of the firmness of her once tight, perfect musculature. Her lips turned up in a smile matched by the warmth in her gaze as she extended a delicate hand to Manticor.

"Matron," Manticor announced, nodding as he bent and kissed the scaled wrist offered.

"Manny, it's good to see you in health. How does my daughter-to-be fare?" Yun asked.

"She fares well," Manticor replied, kicking himself for not being looser, more genial with the Nagah queen. The response stuck uncomfortably in his throat.

"Ah, I take it my son is sampling the wine before he pays for the vinyard," Matron Yun suggested. Sarcasm dripped from her lips.

Manticor couldn't suppress a flash of a grin at the queen's crack. While Prince Durga's decades of warfare had expanded the safe zone around the Nagah's subterranean homelands, and had been responsible for tripling the population of the cobra folk, Yun had little patience for her son's recent, violent activities. She was troubled by the wanton murder of travelers, as well as the growth of Durga's increasingly militaristic personal guard. The rumors of his disrespectful relations with Hannah were particularly distressing. Hannah had survived far longer than her preceding suitors, young women who had died in accidents or quietly withdrew themselves from public life after a few meetings with the prince.

It had become an increasing concern that the matron would never have a grandchild to carry on her bloodline.

"I apologize, Matron Yun," Manticor said, catching himself. He knew the queen's feelings in the matter of her sole surviving child, but he didn't want word passing through the ranks that he had been amused at Yun's sharp criticism of Durga's behavior.

"My fault entirely," Matron Yun replied, releasing Manticor from his guilt. She winked at him, indicating that her cadre of defenders would not betray any indiscretion between the two of them. "My son has just returned from an expedition along the old Pakistani border and he claimed that he has found several items of interest. Since you seem weighted by your thoughts, I wonder if you would enjoy a distraction with an old, wrinkled serpent hag."

"If there were a wrinkled hag present, I'd do so," Manticor answered. "But for now, I am overjoyed to accompany a resplendent goddess of the blood."

Matron Yun laughed, resting her hand on Manticor's shoulder. "If I were a few decades younger, Manticor, I'd believe you."

She offered her hand and the cobra warrior crooked his arm for her. Yun smiled appreciatively. "It might even be that you carry some of the spark of Garuda in you. You resemble my husband, and his genetic code runs through every pilgrim."

"I'm flattered, my queen," Manticor replied. "But your son has likened the process to adding two drops of wine to sewage. It still remains vile waste, while adding two drops of sewage to a gallon of wine turns the whole to sewage."

"The Nagah, however, are neither waste runoff nor beverage," Matron Yun responded. "My son, in his advancing years, seeks to overturn the teachings of both great Nagah and humans, including the lessons of those who despised the institutional bigotry of caste systems."

"And yet, we are still a monarchy," Manticor countered.

"With safeguards and the ability to impeach those of royal blood. A human said once that the tree of liberty, at times, must be watered with the blood of tyrants and free men alike."

"Thomas Jefferson," Manticor said. "Words from nearly five hundred years ago."

"Truth does not cease to become truth because of age, my boy," Yun chided him.

The pair and the silent cordon of cobra escorts entered the alcove where Durga had deposited his discoveries. Off to one side of the underground hangar, the Nagah fleet of twentieth-century Black Hawk and Deathbird helicopters rested, a hundred aircraft only minutes from life should the children of Enki need them.

The airfleet had been recovered thanks to raids on Indian government installations. The Battle of Sky Spear taught the Nagah the need for air power as they had suffered terrible losses, aside from Garuda himself, to the Magistrates' assault helicopters. The Deathbirds and their utility transport counterparts were the backbone of a secure homeland, now.

Quarantined and protected by Durga's expeditionary troopers sat a strange and impressive object. It was sleek and silver, the size of the Black Hawk, and covered in burns and scars, as if it had been engulfed in lava.

Matron Yun gasped in horrified recognition.

"What is it?" Manticor asked.

The queen's lips drew into a tight line of concern. "The dragon kings. That is one of their craft, and if they have returned…"

"Returned?" Manticor asked. "But *Tiamat* was struck from the skies."

Yun's golden eyes flashed as she looked at the skimmer. "Death is no impediment to a god."

Chapter 6

Austin Fargo was glad to be in a set of clean clothes, and after the luxury of a hot shower, he felt like a new man. He cast a cursory glance toward the doorway of the locker room, noticing Lakesh brooding there. The Indian scientist looked far younger than the consortium's initial intelligence had described him. Fargo didn't think that nanotechnology existed at such a level to create that drastic a change of physiology, but the scientist was living proof. With such a display, it wasn't hard for the consortium explorer to agree with the theory of nanorobotic augmentation creating a posthuman species such as the Nagah.

"You had something to ask me?" Fargo spoke up.

"No, I came here to thank you," Lakesh grumbled in a tone belying his words. "It's not every day that the woman I love volunteers for such a dangerous journey just to babysit me."

"This is my fault?" Fargo asked, strapping on his gun belt.

"Absolutely," Lakesh challenged with a grimace. "You are the one who literally stirred up a nest of snakes. And don't think that we're not aware that you just might be setting us up."

"I've been threatened and bullied ever since your pale little bitch pointed her crossbow at me, Lakesh," Fargo snarled. "This shit has positively grown ancient fast. Do you honestly think I'm so smug that I don't realize your crew can kill me like a mouse in a trap?"

Lakesh's cheek twitched at Fargo's insult of Domi. His words came out in a controlled tone. "No one from the consortium has ever proved to be anything close to reliable or trustworthy, unless you specifically want a knife in the back. You cost them a lot in terms of your murdered expedition, so even if you're not offering us to the consortium on a silver platter, they'll be watching you."

"And I'm not going to lie that I don't expect them to make another go at the Nagah and their stockpiles," Fargo told Lakesh. "But you checked me over. No transmitters, no hidden comms, no locator devices."

"If Domi gets hurt, I will hold you personally responsible," Lakesh warned.

"Understood," Fargo answered.

Lakesh stepped forward and handed Fargo his confiscated revolver. "You'll need something more if you expect to pull your weight."

"I escaped the last time only because I carried a minimum of gear," Fargo answered. "I don't know about guys like Grant, but I don't carry the kitchen sink with me."

"I'm not a pack mule, either," Lakesh noted. He looked conscientiously toward the Detonics .45 on his hip. Domi insisted that Lakesh carry the pistol, and she had spent hours familiarizing him with the powerful sidearm. As neither Domi nor Lakesh had large hands, the .45 was ideal, being slim despite its power.

"I just can't see slogging all the way back to the Kashmir with bags of guns and grenades." Fargo sighed.

"Who said that we were walking?" Lakesh inquired.

"Yes. The mat-trans system," Fargo noted. "But would the facilities in the subcontinent be sufficient to get us close to the Nagah?"

"We have the means to travel…" Lakesh paused, debating whether to continue. He realized that he would not be able to disguise the interphaser's improvements on mat-trans technology.

"Your new invention? The one that lets you pop in on ancient temples?" Fargo asked.

Lakesh winced. The millennialists had representatives present at the tomb of Huan Di, intermediaries between the ancient Chinese warlord and the Annunaki to recover his rejuvenating armor. Obviously, they had reported back about the interphaser. Fargo cut into Lakesh's recollections with a new question. "How does it work? Magnetic fields?"

Lakesh maintained his silence.

"Come on, Lakesh. Who am I going to tell? And how could I even decipher the necessary mathematical formulae?" Fargo asked. "I'm a tomb digger, not a theoretical physicist."

"No, but that won't keep gun-toting thugs from trying to abscond with it," Lakesh stated. "It's been sought after before, and lives have been lost in the process."

"Do I look like I can let them in on your secrets? Do I have some magic, invisible phone to call them with?" Fargo pressed. He pointed to the Commtact behind Lakesh's ear. "Or a bionic transceiver, like you guys have?"

"No," Lakesh returned. "We searched you carefully. Nothing popped up."

"But you're still worried about me," Fargo said. "What kind of a trap could I put you all in?"

"I can think of twenty or thirty," Lakesh noted. "And with

all of those, I doubt any redundancy with the suspicions of my cohorts. Even without your friends in the consortium…"

"They are not my friends anymore," Fargo interrupted through gritted teeth. "Not after I blew it in India."

"Well, without them, you have the Nagah and whatever they have. Not to mention other interested parties who have access to technology that we can't detect," Lakesh said. "The Annunaki and other parties have demonstrated access to extrasensory means of communication."

"Others?" Fargo inquired.

"There are records of dozens of species of hybrid beings represented in mythology. The Nagah are only one such breed," Lakesh stated. "My compatriots and I have encountered others in our travels."

"The creations of the Annunaki?" Fargo pressed.

"Precisely," Lakesh answered.

"But what about *Tiamat?* That fireworks display must have taken care of them and whatever freak armies they had," Fargo said.

"Marduk is alive," Lakesh countered. "And he's looking for the means to regain his old status as a god. We stopped him once, but we may not be lucky the next time. There are also his surviving brethren, time travelers, colonies of malcontents in suspended animation…"

"So why are you rushing off to India?" Fargo asked. "If you're so certain that there are all these deadly threats out there…"

"I'd rather die trying than let those monsters go unopposed," Lakesh answered.

"Oh, so you lot are suicidal. Then why worry about me?" Fargo asked.

"Shut your fool mouth," Lakesh growled. "Suicide is the furthest thing from my mind. I hate risking the lives of my friends."

"But you are definitely damned if you sit on your hands," Fargo mused. "At least this way, you've got a snowball's chance in a lava flow."

Lakesh glared at the archaeologist for a long silent moment. Fargo squirmed under the harsh gaze, realizing that he'd pushed too hard.

"You say another word about failure, and I will personally strangle you to death."

Lakesh left Fargo alone in the locker room.

THERE WAS A GRIM SILENCE when Fargo finally joined Kane, Lakesh and the others in the mat-trans chamber. Obviously, Lakesh had spoken of their conversation. Domi's eyes had a particularly demonic aspect to them, the blood-colored jewels glaring at Fargo as if lit from behind by the fires of hell. The archaeologist winced, looking to the others, whose quiet demeanors held more than just impatience. He looked down to the floor of the chamber, spotting a small pyramid-shaped device.

"That's the interphaser?" he asked, hoping to change the subject.

"Yeah," Grant spoke up. "Go ahead and pick it up."

Fargo heard the unstated threat in the giant Magistrate's words, and wisely kept his distance from the pyramid.

"Dumb enough to talk shit about me," Domi spoke up. "Smart enough not to commit suicide…more or less."

"Enough," Kane interrupted. "We've got work to do. Brigid, fire her up."

Brigid input the coordinates, and the mistlike appearance of plasma waves surrounded the six travelers and the interphaser.

Fargo winced as the mat-trans chamber blurred from view. As reality opened around them, Fargo felt a momentary jarring, as if he were unplugged from the Earth. The reality of the situation wasn't much different from his initial perception. His body, and those of the others, were shunted through a wormhole and hurled across the planet at the speed of thought. The transit felt as if it lasted minutes for the millennialist, and when his senses returned to normal, he was in a darkened, cavernous temple.

He recognized the markings on the floor, despite the cracks and wear of antiquity. They were in northern India, and he didn't doubt that they were near the countryside where he'd encountered the murderous Nagah squadron. He remained still and glanced at the others, who were obviously accustomed to the disorientation of matter transfer.

"A temple?" Fargo asked.

"Many of the ancient peoples knew that there were places of power favorable to communicating with their gods," Brigid said. "Those areas were actually parallax points, convergences of magnetic lines of force that allowed access to other dimensions."

"Like Ley lines?" Fargo asked. "So where they cross, the fabric of reality is thin enough to open a wormhole?"

"Right," Lakesh confirmed. "The interphaser is programmed with remote access points."

"The little pyramid is useless otherwise?" Fargo asked.

Lakesh shrugged. "A good magician never gives away his secrets. You'll have to pry the secrets out of my skull."

"Don't tempt him, Moe," Domi cut him off. "Who knows who this bastard's shacked up with."

Lakesh nodded at Domi's warning, causing Fargo to exhale an exhausted sigh. "What do I have to do to get you assholes to trust me?"

"Die taking a bullet for one of us," Grant suggested.

"Or how about you quit calling us assholes?" Brigid added.

Kane returned from a perimeter sweep of the temple, and Fargo glanced at him for support. "They never let anything go, do they?"

"Not even if you *are* their friend," Kane answered, winking to Brigid in deference to their constant needling each other. "All right, the temple is secure. No sign of Fargo's buddies or walking snake men."

"I didn't think anyone else would be present. The Nagah keep a tight perimeter on their frontier," Fargo said. "Plus, to get here, they'd have to know the existence of parallax points, wouldn't they?"

The Cerberus explorers regarded Fargo as he stood, exasperated. Lakesh and Brigid loosened up, relaxing as Fargo's logic seemed to get through to them.

"He has a point," Brigid said. "Even if Fargo's alleged allies had some sort of psychic connection, the Nagah's defenses are between them and us."

"There's other threats to deal with here anyway," Grant noted, slinging his Copperhead on one powerful shoulder. "Bandits and local predators are just as much of a problem."

"I don't think that the Nagah would tolerate human bandits in their area of control," Fargo said.

Kane nodded in agreement. "And the bandits would not want to deal with a force stronger than they are. That doesn't mean that the snakes won't have humans on their side."

"So what's the plan?" Fargo inquired. "Stumble around looking for a snake hole?"

"Actually, we're going to avoid making the same mistakes you did," Brigid explained as Grant helped Lakesh set up a mobile field radio. Grant had hauled the unit along with him in a duffel bag.

"You're going to call them?" Fargo asked.

"Despite our success in turning societies upside down, we actually do try to be diplomatic," Kane noted.

"It's easier to make friends than enemies," Grant added. "Saves wear and tear on our guns, too."

"Would you please?" Lakesh admonished. "It's hard enough to seek out active communications bands without your chatter drowning out weak signals."

"Go chat outside," Domi said, waving the others away.

"I don't like the sound of this," Fargo continued to complain. "Just broadcasting…"

"Do we look like fused-out idiots to you?" Grant asked. "Lakesh is listening for short-range broadcasts that our satellites couldn't pick up due to atmospheric interference. He's listening for chatter first, boosting the signal through the field radio for further analysis at Cerberus."

"Are all of you so smarter-than-thou, or is it just you three?" Fargo grunted.

"First you want us to trust you, then you antagonize us," Brigid complained. "Make up your mind."

To lessen her frustration, she busied herself using a digital camera to record scroll markings on the temple wall.

"Can you make something out of this?" Kane asked her.

"Subcontinental pictograms aren't my forte. Plus, these

examples are considerably deteriorated," Brigid replied. "Still, look at these figures."

Kane squinted, leaning in closer to the markings. He could make out the images, worn by time, of normal-looking men interacting with cobra-hooded humanoids. "I was hoping there would be something more readable. It would be nice to know exactly who we are dealing with."

"Well, traditionally, the Nagah and humankind, in Indian mythology, interacted peacefully," Brigid explained. "The cobra, while a dangerous animal, is also respected and revered."

"The same goes for the Japanese and serpents," Grant interjected, drawing upon his knowledge of New Edo's culture. "Fear and respect."

"But the Japanese do not have an analog for the Nagah, as far as we can tell," Brigid said. "You'd have to go to the mainland, places like Thailand, for snakelike humanoids."

"That's not too far away, relatively speaking," Kane said. "Just sail along the coast, and you can reach Thailand easily. Not like crossing the South China Sea."

"There are also snake-human hybrid beings in Middle Eastern lore, such as the Lamia," Brigid added. "Though their examples display more serpentine bodies, which don't match the descriptions Fargo gave us."

"I saw Nagah at various stages of transformation, however," Fargo interjected. "Perhaps we will encounter serpent-like centaurs."

"Their atropian nature may be fluid if they were acted upon by an outside source," Brigid agreed. "Some genetic structures would be more resistant to alteration than others, while some might have mutated to become completely limbless."

Brigid snapped another picture, then leaned in closer. "Look at this. What does this resemble?"

"A snake face," Grant grumbled his slur for the Annunaki overlords.

"If the Nagah are on good terms with them, maybe diplomacy isn't the best tack," Kane mused.

"Not necessarily," Brigid countered. "Enki had sway over India, according to Balam's accounting of the rift between Annunaki factions. Enki was a beneficent being who was opposed to the enslavement of humanity."

"Enlil didn't like his brother too much," Kane said. "So he would work against Enki's pattern. The Nephilim are mindless drones, perfect for subjugation and as cannon fodder."

"So it might stand to reason that the Nephilim, in their reptilian nature, are Enlil's answer to Enki's creation," Brigid said. "This figure is definitely a respected and revered being, and his cobra subjects are bearing gifts of some form."

"These were not cannon fodder," Fargo said, looking over the pictograms. "The Nagah are bearing gifts of language, knowledge and invention. These beings are also noted as being his children, not his slaves. They were also his ambassadors to humanity. So what changed?"

"The Archon megacull and subsequent age of barbarism would have lowered the Nagah's trust of the human race," Brigid suggested.

Grant frowned. "It would have made things a lot easier if they were all good or all evil."

"Life rarely is that simple," Lakesh interrupted. Fargo looked at the Indian scientist, noting his dour mood.

"What's wrong?" Fargo asked.

"I picked up scrambled signals while monitoring Nagah transmissions," Lakesh said. "While I couldn't hear anything on the signals because of their encryption, I was able to have Bry analyze a sample."

"Let me guess. The overlords?" Kane asked.

"None other," Lakesh answered. "Actually, the signal resembles Enlil's work as Colonel Thrush, but with some modifications."

"That would make sense," Brigid said. "Enlil is currently without resources after the fall of *Tiamat*. He'd look for alternative means to bolster his power."

"And what better way than to steal his baby brother's children?" Grant asked, disgust coloring his words. "He gets revenge on Enki, and he grabs an army with access to the best military technology the human race has developed."

"Any clue who was talking?" Brigid inquired.

"No," Lakesh lamented. "The encryption also hampered signal triangulation. We do have one bit of news, though."

"What's that?" Kane asked.

Domi spoke up. "Fargo's sparring partner, the good Prince Durga, returned to their lair with a badly damaged spacecraft, according to a new report."

"The Nagah have found a drop ship," Lakesh added. "But did Durga take it or was it handed over to him?"

"Does it matter?" Fargo asked.

"It does," Kane answered. "Because if Durga was given the ship as a gift, it means that there's going to be a faction of the Nagah who won't have an interest in peace with humans."

"Durga without Annunaki technology fucked the consortium hard enough," Fargo mused.

"Crudely put, but to the point," Lakesh agreed. "We'll have to step carefully."

"But Enlil wouldn't have the resources to be a threat, would he?" Fargo asked.

"Maybe not," Lakesh answered.

Kane finished the thought that Lakesh couldn't bring himself to voice. "Just because the devil doesn't have his hellfire does not mean that he's without his other tricks."

The Cerberus warriors looked out into the forest engulfing the temple, dread smothering the air around them.

Chapter 7

Hannah reached out to a patch of undamaged hull, seeing the reflection of her hand before touching the smooth skin. She expected it to feel cold, but there was a warmth in the unblemished section, as if it were living flesh. She glanced at Queen Yun and Durga quizzically. "What is it?"

"It is the chariot of the gods," Yun whispered before Durga could answer.

"It's a ship that didn't quite escape the destruction of a larger craft in orbit. It had crash-landed on the border of Pakistan," Durga explained. "We encountered impostor creatures within."

"The Nephilim," Yun corrected. "The children of Enlil."

Hannah couldn't help but feel the frustration radiating off Durga as Yun spoke.

"Whatever," Durga grumbled. "There had been a few survivors in the craft, but we dealt with them."

"And brought their carcasses back for…what, display as trophies?" Hannah looked at the bodies laid out on tables next to the charred saucer. Save for their lack of hoods and their duller scale coloration, they could have easily been mistaken for Nagah. "And Enlil is just a creation myth, isn't he?"

"Enlil was the brother of our creator, Enki," Yun explained.

"Where Enki was wise and nurturing, Enlil was a schemer, seeking his own personal profit. The gods clashed often, and the Nagah were the greatest weapon of our father. Enlil's Nephilim had great strength and possessed powerful weapons, but they were no match for a free people who could think for themselves."

"That is ancient mythology, Mother," Durga retorted. "Who knows how the victors edited the history books?"

Yun's eyes softened into sadness as she regarded the Nagah prince. Hannah watched Manticor's hood flex in unspoken tension over Durga's disrespect for kin and queen. Durga's presence made every conversation a minefield. His barely contained rage seethed below the surface, seeking violent release over the slightest disagreement. It now seemed as if the raids against their human neighbors above the ground were no longer a sufficient distraction.

"Did you cause some of this damage?" Hannah asked, brushing her fingertips across the blackened, bubbled mass of scarring on the sleek, ovoid craft. She had seen fire-damaged metal, and this material had reacted more akin to skin. The latticework of distorted metal resembled the scabs of grill-seared meat. Nothing in the Nagah's weaponry, short of their stockpile of nuclear weaponry, could conceivably affect an alloy in this violent a manner.

"No," Durga answered, pausing to convey his reluctance to admit the answer. "We didn't do this. When we first saw the craft, it had already suffered this damage."

Yun wandered over to a table where one of the dead Nephilim lay. Hannah moved over to join the matron beside the corpse. The creature's chest sported five gunshot wounds, starred craters in the flexible alloy that wrapped his torso.

Smears where bullets had glanced off crisscrossed its muscular body.

"What is that?" Hannah asked, touching the metallic armor.

"The false god's children wear a sheath of smart alloy," Yun explained. "The false one so envied the love between Enki and the Nagah that he crafted these imperfect progeny. They are like us in many ways. Strong, armored, beautiful, but they are without the nobility inherent in us, for their master only had bitterness in his dark heart. Without the power to love, he had to make up for his mindless children's weakness with the tools of the Annunaki. As such, they are naught more than automatons."

"And yet, Enlil returned to the Earth, while our father has abandoned us," Durga interrupted.

Yun glared at her son for a long, silent moment. Hannah could feel the tension like an electrical charge that wafted in the air. "You know the legends, Durga. And yet you deny that the false one and his clan were cast down, exiled to this world. Our calling, handed down from Enki himself, is to watch and guard the Earth, lest the dark brotherhood make their play."

"Oh. Is that what we were doing when *Tiamat* loomed in orbit?" Durga asked, sarcasm dripping.

"Do not speak to your mother like that!" Hannah snapped.

"Mind your place, egg layer," Durga countered.

Yun's anger sliced through the hangar like a guillotine blade. Her eyes were hard as she expressed disapproval as harsh as the friction that had scoured the wrecked skimmer. Durga and Hannah both lowered their heads to the matron, admonished without a word.

"The star-born dragon was laid low by those we have been

charged to watch over," Yun said. "The three heads rose to the challenge and in the end succeeded, aided by the false god's own greed and pettiness. Our assistance was not needed. Not that you made any effort to contact them, Durga."

"The three heads," Durga grumbled, sneering. "The rebels from Cerberus. There were more than three of them, don't forget."

Yun glared at Durga's interruption. "The heart of that group are the three. Three whose true souls stretch back to the time when the dragon kings and the Tuatha de Danaan first strode the Earth as masters."

Durga frowned. "Regardless of the myths we're discussing, this craft is loaded with technology and weaponry. A few repairs—"

"You would draw the attention of those who own this ship?" Yun asked.

Durga pointed to the corpse that Yun and Hannah stood beside. "The owners don't seem to be in any position to complain, unless you hear some kind of muffled groans coming from those rotting hides. They were alone, stranded in the wilderness, and had been camped out there for months. Were any of the dragon kings alive, surely they would not have left useful minions, especially after the death of *Tiamat.*"

"Enlil is not all-knowing," Yun countered. "If our creator, peace be upon him, was not omniscient, then his brother, a pale shadow, could never be so."

Durga's scaled brow arched, as if Yun's comment had kick-started gears working in his mind. Hannah had seen such scheming in Durga's face too many times before. The expression chilled her blood.

If Yun was aware of Durga's plotting, she paid it no mind. "I have seen enough, son."

"I want to search for more of these ships," Durga said. "Think of the power."

Yun looked at the corpses of the Nephilim. "Enough to throw away your freedom?"

"I won't trade my liberty for strength," Durga promised. "But just look—the armor can be retracted. And when it is deployed again, it self-repairs. Throw in the built-in energy guns…"

"We are just looking at more of the same," Hannah spoke up. "Agile aircraft, personal weaponry, communications, we already have all of that. And let's not forget the real power we possess. Is there anything on that ship more destructive than a nuclear warhead?"

Durga grimaced at Hannah's interruption. He gave her a glare that spoke volumes; her mouth was meant only for his pleasure, nothing more. Hannah shrugged off the silent accusation. As royalty, she had duties. Her rank entailed being intimate with all things vital to the safety of the Nagah—hence her presence in the hangar. Examining the spoils of Durga's raid against the Annunaki was just another part of her role.

The angry prince grumbled. *"Tiamat."*

"What?" Hannah asked.

"Tiamat is more powerful than our paltry warheads," Durga said.

"She is dead, as Matron Yun just said," Hannah countered.

Durga pointed to the damaged drop ship. "The skimmer is inactive, but there are still treasures in its belly. Just imagine if we could take the skimmer up to *Tiamat's* corpse. What else could have survived? Improvements on the cobra baths, genetic alterations that could make us immortal as the Annunaki."

Yun's eyes softened, the grief of old losses rising to the surface. "Immortality has no temptation for my old bones."

"What about bringing Father back?" Durga asked.

Yun's sorrow sloughed off her face, replaced by a hard, cold glower. "Do as you will. I'm tired of your ambitions."

The matron pivoted on her heel and strode from the hangar. Hannah glared at Durga.

"What are you gawking at?" Durga snapped.

Hannah shook her head. "I have no idea anymore."

"Was it something I said?" Durga asked.

Hannah's eyes narrowed. "You said that Garuda could just be cloned. Replaced with a look-alike, just as if he were a pet."

"*Tiamat*'s technology could reconstruct my father, atom for atom, cell for cell," Durga explained through gritted teeth. "This would be true resurrection, not the fabrication of a cheap knockoff."

Hannah's lips grew tight. "Do you realize what you're saying?"

"That *Tiamat* can make me a god? As mighty as Enki himself?" Durga answered.

Manticor touched the side of his head. The bodyguard had been standing by quietly, only noticeable when Durga's anger threatened to explode. In his role as protector, he had a backup duty to keep Hannah in touch with news from the rest of the Nagah kingdom. As such, he wore a small earpiece that blended into the shadowy scales on the underside of his cobra hood. "Mistress, sire, communications is picking up a signal inside our frontier."

Durga's eyes widened with alarm. "A signal? What from and who to?"

"From an exploratory team originating from a place called

Cerberus redoubt," Manticor answered. "They're transmitting directly to us, apparently."

Durga took a momentary breath of relaxation, his scaled brow flexing. "Cerberus?"

"Kane, Grant and Baptiste?" Hannah asked. She looked toward the damaged skimmer. "Perhaps they came here because of your prize."

"It's ours now. The humans have no right to be on our land, let alone taking something I fought for!" Durga snarled. "This is our—"

"Silence!" Yun interjected, standing in the doorway she'd exited through only moments before. Just as Hannah had been alerted, so had the queen. She was back, returning upon being informed of the radio activity.

"Mother, damn it…" Durga spoke up, trying to insert his position.

"Don't say another word. The heroes of Cerberus have saved your life, the life of every organism on this planet, on many occasions."

"Humans—"

"Are not a monolithic, single-minded entity. We have threats from their quarter, true, but not all the creations of Enlil are our enemy," Yun explained. "Men are as independent as we are. That is why he created those abominations on your morgue tables. I have made my decision, and we will welcome the three heads of justice with open arms."

Durga glanced toward the damaged skimmer.

"What do you have to hide?" Yun asked.

"Our nation's security," Durga answered. "We are a people under siege by mammalian threats, or didn't the Millennial Consortium's intrusion tip you off, you dim old bat?"

The matron's personal guard bristled at the prince's rude comment, but Yun glared at them. Like Manticor, they were tiring of Durga's posturing, but this was just an argument.

"Yes. They tested you so much. You're not even blind in your scarred eye," Yun replied, sarcasm dripping. "Besides, we have an army, with attack helicopters and assault rifles, and we are one of the few nuclear powers on Earth. The Cerberus explorers are only a handful of people on a peaceful mission."

Durga touched his injured eye. "Damnation…"

"All newcomers are not our enemy, son. Especially these particular arrivals. We owe the existence of our world to them," Yun continued. "They wish to greet us in peace."

"Liars, obscuring the facts to hide their self-serving motives," Durga answered. "Our world is secure because I kept the apes at bay."

"They may not be worthy to you," Yun replied, "but your bitterness blinds you. One error, and you have nothing left but venom, even for your own kind."

"Error? Garuda's murder was an error?" Durga asked.

"Shut the hell up!" Hannah shouted. "Respect your mother, if not her crown."

Durga glared at Hannah, but the tension in Manticor's arms stilled any further response. Hannah looked over her shoulder to her bodyguard. So far, this had merely been a war of words, despite the shortness of temper displayed. However, the princess knew that if Durga lifted a finger in threat against her, Manticor would gladly rip it off the prince's hand. When it came to Hannah's safety, Manticor considered his safety and freedom expendable.

Hannah could see Durga's spark of delight at the prospect of being given free rein to imprison, torture and execute

Manticor, inspiring similar emotional suffering in Hannah. Only the threat of personal injury gave the Nagah prince a moment's pause. Hannah stepped between the two cobra men to diffuse their tension. Her body language let them both know that she would not tolerate their continuing contest of wills.

"Durga, you will take Hannah and Manticor with you to greet the visitors from Cerberus," Yun ordered. "They will be my eyes and ears. Should a conflict arise, they will report whether you are guiltless or a victim of your unthinking, all-consuming bigotry."

"And if Kane and his ilk kill Hannah and her love-struck pet?" Durga said, sneering.

Yun didn't react, except to rest her hand on Manticor's shoulder. It was a calming touch, dulling the insult thrown by Durga. "Then I will not have a grandchild and you will have to find some other Nagani woman to engage in your perversions with."

The words slapped Durga as surely as the bullwhip had scarred his brow and cheek. Manticor folded his arms, the corner of his mouth turning up in smug approval of the matron's verbal torpedo into Durga's dignity. The air in the hangar thickened with the promise of violence. A scream of rage struggled to hatch inside Hannah's throat. If Durga insisted on an altercation, Hannah wasn't certain if she could restrain herself from a few cheap shots to assist Manticor. Her fingers knotted into tight fists.

"Come with me to the communications center, Hannah," Yun called. "Durga, put your toys away and join us when your blood has cooled down."

"Yes, Mother," Durga droned, unsuccessfully trying to smother his disappointment.

"Thank you, Matron," Hannah added. Her scream was stillborn in her throat. The cold war of wills was unresolved, save for Yun's assertion of her matriarchal power.

Hannah and Manticor followed the queen and her personal guard out of the hangar, leaving the embittered prince to calm down.

FARGO LOOKED NERVOUSLY to the other members of the Cerberus expedition as he waited with them. Lakesh caught the anxious expression on the archaeologist's face.

"Worried that Durga will not be the most welcoming of hosts?" Lakesh asked.

"Well, I'm not sure. I mean, I'm certain I put a pretty good crease in his face with my whip," Fargo answered.

"You have a knack for developing deep, loving friendships everywhere, don't you?" Brigid asked.

Fargo shrugged. "That's the risk of doing business, I guess."

"Business? More like bullshit," Grant grumbled. "If you claim you can get on Erica's bad side…"

"Isn't there some kind of big phallic compensation firearm you should be fondling?" Fargo said with a sneer. He didn't quite get the last syllable out before Grant's massive hand wrapped around Fargo's throat.

"Pardon me? Could you speak up?" Grant asked. He held Fargo up with one hand so that the man's toes dangled inches off the ground.

"Grant, you don't wanna kill him," Kane said with more annoyance than urgency. "I know he's a prick, but that's no reason to stink up the temple with his corpse."

Grant lowered Fargo to his feet. "You're lucky that this used to be someone's holy ground."

Fargo coughed, rubbing his tender throat. "Oh, I thank my stars that you are so gentle—"

"Keep in mind," Grant cut him off, "my goodwill does have a limit."

"Right." Fargo coughed. "You're not just the pack animal."

"Not much of an apology, but I'll take it," Grant returned.

Brigid lowered a pair of rangefinder binoculars. The explorers had set themselves atop the roof of the temple in order to limit access by patrols from the forest and to give themselves better visibility of the surrounding region. "I've spotted aircraft."

Grant strode closer to a Stinger missile that he had brought along. If there were multiple armed helicopters, Grant's single shout wouldn't allow him the time to reload the launcher and take down the enemy aircraft. A squadron of Nagah gunships would focus on him, however, giving the others time to escape. It might not have seemed a fair trade, but if the Nagah did try to single Grant out, they would learn that they had picked the wrong prey.

The distant thrum of the helicopters rose in volume. Brigid and Kane swept the horizon, making certain that the approaching aircraft were alone. Lakesh's radio crackled to life.

"This is Hannah, princess of the Nagah, addressing the Cerberus expedition," a woman's voice spoke. Its tone was sibilant, but melodic. "Are you receiving my signal?"

Lakesh knelt by the radio. "We have you, Hannah. We just saw your aircraft come over the horizon."

"Dr. Singh, I presume?" Hannah asked.

"Call me Lakesh," the scientist answered. "Your English is excellent. How did you learn it?"

"India is a multilingual and multicultural nation. The use

of English is a way around provincial and tribal dialects, as well as making it easier to know who our friends and enemies are," Hannah said.

"I presume we are considered friends," Lakesh said as the others listened.

"The Nagah know the debt owed to Kane, Grant and Brigid Baptiste by the whole world," Hannah answered. "The heroes of Cerberus are legendary. Without their efforts, the Earth would have perished many times over."

Kane and Grant shared a conspiratorial grin. Grant's grin dimmed as he brought up a complaint in his inimitable style. "Why can't we meet more groups like this?"

"Can't just be happy with being a big damned hero to the snakes, can you?" Kane asked.

Lakesh glared at the pair, pointing to the radio.

Hannah's voice continued, "The Nagah hear many things, including monitoring your communications and those of your enemies. The royal family is honored by your presence, so much that it sends to you the prince and princess in line with the throne to show our gratitude for your discovery of our kind."

Kane sized up Hannah's acknowledgment, and how it would affect their interaction. Both groups would treat each other with respect, but the Nagah had advanced knowledge of the Cerberus expedition. Except for mythology and specu-lation, backed by the reports of a grave robber, Kane and his allies were in the dark about the snake people.

Still, Kane's point man instinct remained cool and quiet. Except for the flash of psychic awareness, no threats loomed to trigger a fight-or-flight response. Though he was observ-ing the Deathbird gunship accompanying the two transports, it wasn't on an aggressive flight pattern. The armed aircraft were not a threat on the part of the Nagah. The attack helicopter broke formation and stayed far from the temple, out of the effective range of its .50-caliber machine guns.

Lakesh looked at Kane, confused by the separation of the gunship from the other helicopters. "What are they doing?"

"The gunship is for the protection of the royals on one of the transports. Since it is not meant to harm us, it will orbit the temple, alert for threats against their people, but trusting us to not attack the transports, as well as throw in to protect the aircraft in case of danger," Kane explained. "It's a show of submission, akin to when wolves present their throats to an alpha male. They are saying that they are not a threat to us."

Grant broke down the Stinger missile and put it back in its travel case. "Of course, we don't know if those are members of the royal family. They could be lying and this is a trap."

Kane nodded. "True, but your skepticism hasn't kept you from stowing our rocket launcher."

Grant shrugged. "You haven't gotten me killed yet. And you've dragged me through all colors of shit."

Kane chuckled. He turned back to Lakesh. "We'll be all right for now."

"And Durga?" Fargo asked.

"I told them you were here with us," Lakesh repeated, frustrated over the grave raider's anxiety. "They'll tolerate you."

Domi jabbed Fargo in the ribs, just a little too hard to keep Fargo from eliciting a pained yelp. "Stick with us, and maybe you'll get a seat at the table, instead of being stowed with the pack animals."

Fargo glared at Domi but held his tongue. Grant's chuckle reinforced the taunt.

The Black Hawks and their serpentine passengers approached for a landing on the roof of the temple. The next few minutes would confirm whether the Cerberus warriors had formed an alliance or had become ensnared in a den of deadly vipers.

Chapter 8

Durga watched Hannah as she spoke into the radio, conversing with Lakesh. Framed in the open door of the helicopter, she was a vision of serpentine beauty, her face expressing a regal bearing that made her seem fully worthy of being his pureblooded queen. She was a willful woman, prepared to stand up to him rather than buckle under to his authority and his fearful rages. Pangs of respect for her struggled against his grim temperament and monomania, but he fought that admiration back down. Love was not meant for beings as exalted as he was.

Maybe she could have the fire of dignity within her, but petty concerns for lesser creatures doused it, leaving behind only dying embers. Enlil was correct about the Nagah people. The once mighty and proud cobra men had spent far too long huddled beneath the dirt. By mixing with humans, the Nagah had taken on the aspect of worms, pink and soft, instead of commanding the fragile, unarmored mammals with impunity.

The world blurred around Durga, fading out to a white, featureless universe. The sensations of the world disappeared, even though he knew that he was still sitting in the helicopter next to Hannah. He smiled, turning his thoughts into dialogue. Durga had been drawn into a plane of telepathic existence. "I was just thinking about you, Enlil."

"Why do you think I made psychic contact with you?" the supreme Annunaki replied. "You are seeing the truth of my assertations about the feeble peons that surround you."

"I have always known of my dissonance with the other Nagah," Durga answered, frustrated at Enlil's smugness.

"Of course," Enlil said, trying to insert a note of apology into the statement. The bleached-out surroundings began to resolve, filling with color and shape. They took on the semblance of Durga's royal chambers, except that the Annunaki god sat in a high-backed chair. Enlil chuckled as his image settled into the phantom throne. "A comfortable seat you've selected for yourself, Durga."

The prince scratched his chin, looking around. "Hannah might wonder why I'm sitting beside her like a zombie. Do you have a purpose to this visit to my psyche, or do you just want me to look as if I truly am insane?"

Enlil took a long, deep breath, as if to mock Durga's sense of urgency. "What you are experiencing is only the illusion of time's passage. Your mind is expanding the impulse of our communication so as to render our conversation in a manner that it can understand. In reality, what you perceive as five minutes here is a mere flicker of a moment between heartbeats."

"And apparently, I'll need the whole five minutes, since you don't seem to be getting to the point," Durga complained.

Enlil's eyes narrowed for a moment, irritation coloring his features. It faded, a smile replacing the annoyance as it crossed his perfectly sculpted features. "While patience for your inferiors is a sign of weakness, Durga, I remind you that respect for your peers is not."

Durga tilted his head quizzically. "Ah. Calling me your peer. So, have you got something stuck in your craw?"

"I heard the exchange between the interfering apes from Cerberus and your people," Enlil explained, ignoring Durga's sarcasm. "And my own more conventional communications have noted that they are listening to my conversations with the Nephilim."

Durga nodded. "You deride them as inferior creatures, but they are the ones who are walking to us in the open while the god skulks, hiding in the shadows like a frightened rat. On top of that, they come as visitors, while you are attempting to cut deals with the children of one you call a lesser god."

"Those observations are why I call you my peer, Prince," Enlil said. "Just because Kane and his allies are human, there is no reason to underestimate the threat that they pose."

"Unfortunately, my mother is under the assumption that she retains relevance," Durga replied. "Outright elimination of them is out of the question. Those loyal to her would resist any semblance of defiance of her authority."

"So I am not the only god forced to scurry in the underbrush, seeking the allegiance of others," Enlil returned.

"In that case, my apologies for my previous accusation," Durga said.

I was a new, young and brash god once," Enlil said. "Of course, that was aeons ago, before life on your world developed internal skeletons. But I do understand the initial rush that comes with ultimate power."

Durga held his tongue, but his imagination betrayed him, constructing the image of Enlil as a doddering old man, shaking a bony fist, toothless mouth issuing a lecture. "In my day…"

Enlil regarded the psychic effigy, then laughed. "I suppose I deserve that."

"My apologies, sire," Durga answered, repressing a chuckle.

Enlil gestured and the false image froze solid. Cracks spread across the effigy's surface, rending it asunder. Enlil's face darkened, hard eyes locking with Durga. "Remember what I said about respect, brash youth. We can both benefit from our alliance, but it is all dependent on our combined efforts. Betrayal and jealousy tore my brothers from unchallenged command of the skies, giving Kane and his apes all that they needed to thwart us."

"You won't have anything to fear from me," Durga told the Annunaki. He looked at the shattered chunks of the fake Enlil as they faded into the floor of the phantom throne room. "I need you. You need the Nagah."

"And you do not need Kane catching on to you," Enlil warned. "Be on your guard. He is formidable, both mentally and physically. All three of them, Brigid and Grant, are far more capable and cunning than any enemy you've ever faced."

Durga frowned. "I'll watch myself. You do the same, sire. They might already be aware of your presence due to the drop ship that you gave me."

"They can suspect, but it will take a serious misstep on your part to spur them to action against our alliance," Enlil explained. "We have to approach this slowly and steadily. Patience with inferiors is one thing…"

"But waiting to achieve a goal is far different," Durga concluded. "I've waited thirty years for my kingdom."

Enlil smirked. "As I have waited three decades for you."

The throne room disappeared, replaced with the Battle of Sky Spear. Garuda stood clutching a smoking, empty missile launcher. It was only an image, but it loomed over the two conspirators. The Nagah king lowered the empty launcher, relief crossing his face that the repulsion of the Magistrate invasion was complete. A flaming Deathbird spiraled from the sky, smearing the air with its oily smoke trail.

The warrior king turned, looking back to his son, himself a warrior prince, to share a quiet celebratory smile of victory.

Durga felt the powerful recoil hammering up his forearms from the grip handles of the heavy machine gun as he pulled the trigger. Powerful, massive bullets, the same kind that the Deathbirds had fired, tore through Garuda's body. The Nagah king's torso flew apart under the brief storm of shredding slugs. Durga's driver, the only other cobra survivor present, shrieked in dismay at the king's gruesome assassination. The prince leveled a Magistrate's captured machine pistol on the driver, an execution bullet smashing the back of the Nagah's skull.

Enlil strode through the illusion, resting a clawed hand on Durga's shoulder. "My defeat in my old life. Your victorious first step in your ascension. I was unaware at the time how our destinies would be entwined."

"That day, I became the son of a god," Durga whispered, still feeling the wetness of his driver's blood on his face. "As a fallen champion, my father was deified."

"And as the lone survivor and reporter of the events of his death, a glow of divinity transferred to you," Enlil whispered, his voice smooth like velvet. Durga imagined the Western myth of the serpent in Eden, seducing Eve. "The son of a god is himself a god. Which is why your cadre worship you, why they sacrifice their lives for you in battle against the mammals."

Durga had a twinge of fear, discomfort raised by the touch of the Annunaki. At once, he experienced terror and delight. Drunk on psychic energy, body humming with a power that filled him from head to toe, he wanted to swoon into Enlil's embrace. He fought that urge, some instinct keeping him standing.

"I am not that kind of god, Enlil," Durga growled, stepping away from the Annunaki. "Save your sweet nothings for someone else."

Enlil smirked, then affected an innocent glow. "My apologies, Durga. I meant no imposition."

Durga watched Enlil warily. "No, your interest isn't that kind of attraction. I'm the one imprinting homoerotic overtones on our relationship."

"Power," Enlil said by way of explanation. "It's the ultimate aphrodisiac. You would have to be dead not to feel arousal at the prospects of immortality and unlimited power."

Durga smiled, feeling the earphones in the slits on the side of his head. The world began to vibrate, and the warmth of Hannah's skin touched his as they sat in the Black Hawk.

"What are you smiling about? "Hannah asked.

"Meeting legends," Durga said, not quite lying.

"I thought you hated humans, especially Magistrates," Hannah said.

Durga looked out over the forest canopy. "Kane and Grant are no more Magistrates than the Nagah are mere mammals. They have transcended their previous existence, remaking themselves as crusaders for liberty and as explorers of the unknown. Their battles against those that rained tragedy upon the Nagah are the stuff of legend. It took a while, but Mother's words got through to me. I owe them my life."

"Even though they brought Fargo along with him?" Hannah asked. "Even with your face still—"

"My eye? My scar?" Durga inquired as the helicopter

slowed, preparing to land atop the ancient temple. The Cerberus expedition stood, waiting for the Nagah envoys. Durga chuckled, touching his scar. "I think it adds character to my face. Fargo is slime, but he escaped from my ambush. No man has ever done that before. So he's earned my respect. He's also gained a reprieve from my vengeance."

Durga noted Hannah's nervous glance at Manticor. She was confused by the sudden mercy and diplomacy he displayed. The bodyguard watched Durga carefully, hand never straying far from the Pinidad sidearm in its hip holster.

"Smiles, you two," Durga ordered. "We were sent on a mission of peace and unity. Best face forward and all that."

Hannah and Manticor looked at each other in dismay. Durga let them stew in their suspicions. It wasn't as if the princess and her warrior would betray the sudden turn in Durga's attitude to strangers.

Besides, killing the explorers wouldn't do. He needed scapegoats.

KANE, TO ALL APPEARANCES, was relaxed, his limbs loose. To the uninitiated, it would have appeared that he was unprepared for any sudden violence, but to those in the know, from this position he moved like liquid. Not only was he not committed to any specific response by remaining relaxed, but he also appeared to be less of a threat, a useful tactic when there was the potential for a peaceful meeting and the fostering of a beneficial alliance.

The Nagah's airfleet was impressive, and in the reconstructed America, a squadron or two of transport aircraft would prove to be worth their weight in gold.

Just as the Black Hawk helicopter flared for a landing, Kane's instincts buzzed. Something was wrong. It wasn't the

Deathbird gunship. The attack helicopter was still far off, keeping its distance from the temple.

Both Brigid and Grant noticed his tension immediately. Domi picked up on his preternatural reaction to danger only seconds after the others. Kane frowned, realizing that if Domi hadn't noticed a threat with her sharp, feral senses, then perhaps Kane's perceptions had gone awry.

The ex-Magistrate, however, had little cause to doubt his danger sense. It wasn't an immediate menace; there were no indications of a sniper or an ambush. Instead, it was a tickle at the back of his mind, his subconscious feeling that things were out of place.

"What is it?" Domi asked over her Commtact, the only way that the explorers could hear each other over the thump of rotor blades. The added benefit of the implanted communicator was that it allowed them secrecy from Fargo in the noisy environment.

"Something I can't put my finger on," Kane said. "But it can't be anything solid—otherwise we'd have both locked on to it."

"Temples have been responsible for enhanced paranormal visions for you before," Brigid stated. "Perhaps you're having another prophetic episode, like back in Greece?"

Kane's eyes narrowed as he dug into his memories of the past few moments. "It wasn't a vision…more like I heard something. A whisper."

"Like mental telepathy?" Lakesh asked. His Commtact had made him a part of the private conversation, whether he liked it or not. The scientist looked toward Fargo, realizing that their privacy would disappear as the Black Hawk's engines powered down. "You know, direct speech between two or more minds."

"I know telepathy," Kane grumbled. The ex-Magistrate

rolled his eyes, regarding Lakesh coldly. "Give me a break, Lakesh. Balam exposed me to enough of it. Probably screwed my brain up so I can pick up that crap from now on."

"My apologies, friend Kane," Lakesh said. "I meant specifically, did it sound like a two-way conversation?"

Brigid rested her fingers on Kane's forearm in a calming touch. Kane took a cleansing breath. "Not really. It was like catching a fleeting snippet of conversation. I only heard or sensed one voice, so I couldn't tell."

"Between whom?" Brigid mused.

"Quiet. Fargo's wondering what all our mumbling's about," Grant warned. "He could be the one in contact. Or maybe one of the snakes on the helicopter."

"Or both," Kane added.

The Cerberus explorers fell silent at the implication of that threat. Alone, in the middle of the subcontinent, there was no way to tell who was friend or foe, and even with the Deathbird a mile distant, there were enough cobra men on the two transport helicopters to make their lives very bloody and brutal.

"What the hell was all that chin wagging?" Fargo asked. "Because if you guys are planning something stupid—"

"Like traveling with you?" Kane challenged. "Shut up, Fargo. We're not going to war."

Fargo took a deep breath. "Not yet."

That raised a fire in Kane's glare, pinning Fargo silent with the intense gaze. "Just remember, we can leave you here for the Nagah to tear apart. Doesn't matter one shit to me."

Cobra warriors exited the helicopter, flanking two regal figures. Fargo's face paled as he recognized his handiwork in the livid scar and unnatural glare in Durga's eye. The other serpentine figure was smaller, slender and most decidedly female. She was possessed of a deceptively delicate appearance.

Brigid and Lakesh advanced to greet the royal pair while Domi, Grant and Kane stood loose and alert to balance the Nagah soldiers. Quiet pleasantries were exchanged between the humans and their serpentine counterparts.

Durga looked at Fargo for a moment. "So, you brought this one back to me?"

Kane nodded. "Figured that we'd bring you a housewarming present. This was the closest thing to a six-foot rat that we could find."

Fargo's eyes widened in alarm as Durga strode to the millennialist, literally a serpent sizing up panicked prey. After a moment of letting the man sweat, Durga extended his hand. "Well played, Fargo. If any mammal has earned my respect personally, it is you."

Durga tossed a glance to the Cerberus crew. "Present company excluded."

"No offense taken," Lakesh offered.

Kane could pick up a sense of dissonance from Hannah, the Nagah princess. The tall, silent warrior at her side also displayed some confusion over Durga's actions. It was hard to read their exact emotions through their scaled features, but they were put off balance by Durga's behavior.

Lakesh shot Kane a silent but quizzical expression. Kane nodded to the scientist.

No bloodshed was planned for now.

Instead of death, the Nagah handed the companions headsets to protect their hearing from the roar of the helicopter on its way back to the Nagahs' underground kingdom.

Chapter 9

Kane gave Grant a quiet elbow as the Cerberus explorers disembarked from the Black Hawk helicopter with their royal escort. The sharp-eyed point man didn't need his keen predatory senses to notice that one part of the hangar had been quarantined from the rest of the mountainside flight deck. The secluded area was obvious enough with its tall sheets of tarpaulin hanging from the ceiling and cobra men armed with black assault rifles standing vigilant guard over the section. It was a secret, but it was obvious that it was a newly acquired one, because Durga had not had the time or facilities set aside to properly stow it away where it wouldn't be noticed.

What caught Kane's eye were radiation warning signs posted on another secured section of the hangar. Kane was familiar with nuclear power plants, especially considering that atomic generators powered Cerberus redoubt. They'd also encountered other industrialized societies with nuclear-power capability in their travels.

Unfortunately, the hangar appeared too open and far too close to the Nagah population to be a properly secured nuclear reactor. The lead-lined chambers off to the side of the hangar suggested weapons storage bunkers. Radiation and armories could only mean nuclear warheads.

Durga and Hannah hadn't made any fuss about the presence

of the weapons stores, an unstated threat to the visiting humans. The cobra warriors had much more than the venom in their fangs should the explorers from Cerberus show that they were actually enemies. It was a quiet way to convey the knowledge. Durga had watched Kane look directly at the radiation warning label, but said nothing.

Whether the Nagah had the reach to strike at the Bitterroot Mountains was not the question on Kane's mind for the moment. The fact that the cobra men had the power to turn large swathes of the remaining habitable world into lifeless wastelands in a slash of cleansing fire was all that needed to be said. The Nagah had the ability to make any serious conflict with humanity a costly venture, regardless of the final victor.

Durga smiled, then extended a hand to let it rest on Kane's shoulder. "That is no concern to you. I wouldn't want to harm the world we are both sworn to protect."

"I didn't see any aircraft for their delivery," Kane added.

"Astute," Durga complimented him. "We'd have to deliver them the old-fashioned way."

"Deliver what?" Lakesh asked.

"Our defensive munitions," Durga explained.

"No big deal," Kane offered, even though he didn't feel so nonchalant about the presence of atomic warheads, even behind heavily armored doors. He trusted Lakesh to be observant enough to see his discomfort and form a conclusion or two. A slight frown rested on Lakesh's face for a moment, then the scientist pushed it away, continuing to receive the tour from Hannah.

Durga joined Lakesh with that part of the group. Manticor, Hannah's personal bodyguard, lingered back with Kane and Grant.

"Are the humans in this area that much of a threat to warrant those?" Kane asked, nodding toward the nuclear magazine chamber.

Manticor glanced toward the indicated storage area. "Actually, that was a decision by the whole of the royal family. We had located several stockpiles of the weapons, but they were kept under wraps for decades."

"What prompted the claws coming out?" Grant asked.

"*Tiamat*'s presence in the skies above our home," Manticor answered.

"Thought he said you didn't have a means of delivery," Grant said.

Manticor took a deep breath. "Nothing reusable, at least for the great sky dragon."

Kane nodded, not pressing the issue any further. The ex-Magistrate could tell, however, that Manticor was one of the Nagah warriors who would have flown any suicide mission to destroy *Tiamat*. The hooded champion nodded to Kane, a silent message of thanks.

BRIGID BAPTISTE ALLOWED HERSELF to give in to the magnificent expanse of the Nagah's underground home city. The subterranean metropolis sprawled out, according to the proud Princess Hannah, for fifty square miles. The lair was thousands of years old, but the Nagah had preserved it and added to it. Most fascinating to the archivist were ancient murals that depicted elements of the city's millennial history along miles of the several hundreds of corridors. Ancient pictograms adorned the trim along the columns that served as support struts between floors and buttressed walls. This was a much clearer vision of the pictogram script that had been worn down by weather and traffic in the temple. With a much more concise and preserved form, and spotting similar imagery to Egyptian hieroglyphs and Sumerian alphabet symbols, Brigid was able to guess the meaning of inscriptions scrawled beneath the murals.

It didn't provide more than a hint of the Nagah's lengthy history, but it was enough of a taste to intrigue her.

"Are all the columns in the hallways adorned with these writings?" Brigid asked Hannah.

Durga spoke up, stepping between the two women. "The Nagah take pride in the past. We've been able to keep our history alive and vibrant. Most of what is up has been added to remind the newbloods who have joined our family. Stories are repeated on various columns throughout the city."

"And the murals are repeated, as well?" Brigid inquired.

"Only thematically. Artists of different eras depicted events differently," Durga answered.

"Such as the two great dyings," Brigid concluded.

Durga frowned. "Yes."

Brigid nodded. "So, your people were among those that the great flood targeted."

"Enlil was jealous of our devotion to Enki," Hannah interjected. "We would not give in to his rule. And we were not the only ones."

"But it was an effort at driving us into extinction," Durga stated. "It failed."

"Hence, you've remained in hiding since?" Brigid asked. "The subterranean nature of the city kept you safe?"

"Not completely," Hannah lamented.

"The lowest level columns list the names of those who'd drowned when the deluge was directed at us," Durga said.

Brigid nodded sadly. "And the second great dying…?"

Dugra's eyes narrowed. "We had assumed that it was the humans. It was your weapons that wrought much of the destruction. The harsh nuclear winter made life difficult. Then came the mutant hordes. Then finally, the Magistrates took our king. Since then, we've recovered from fate's efforts to render us extinct."

"The newbloods?" Brigid asked.

"Not all who are Nagah were born that way," Hannah answered. "The royal family can trace its lineage back thousands of years, but others are more recent additions to our race. My bodyguard, Manticor, is the son of such converts. He was born true."

Brigid cast Manticor a cursory examination. "Others are not fully converted, at least according to Fargo."

"The remnants of their mammalian heritage," Durga said. "Many who serve in my personal guard are like that. It's not a matter of the time of their conversion, it's just a genetic throwback, something that the cobra baths cannot change."

"Could we see those?" Lakesh asked, curiosity in the scrollwork of the corridors fading. "Those utilize nanotechnology to alter beings on a DNA scale, correct?"

"I'm not sure that would be wise. Without the cobra baths, our people would not have recovered," Hannah said.

Durga shrugged. "I don't see the problem. What damage could they do?"

Brigid picked up the note of skepticism in Hannah's voice, but remained quiet. When they got a private moment, Brigid would point out the incongruities.

The explorers and their royal escort exited one corridor into a vast central hallway. Columns rose a hundred feet to buttress a vaulted ceiling. In the center of the grand central mall stood a twenty-five-foot-tall statue of a crowned cobra warrior. The sculpture wielded a spear that was engulfed in flames. Brigid could tell that the great carving had only been recently added, within the past few decades. She was fascinated by the mechanism for keeping the spear alit, spotting hints of the internal vented pipe that burned natural gas.

"Garuda, my father," Durga said. "This was built to commemorate his victory at the Battle of Sky Spear."

Brigid looked at the carving's face. There was a resemblance between father and son, if the sculpture was accurate. "Purely symbolic, I presume. The sky spear, it's a reference to the antiaircraft missiles used against the Magistrates?"

Durga nodded in confirmation. "We utilized a mix of old Soviet Strella and American Stinger missiles against the modified Apache gunships sent by the baronies."

"You found your own aircraft after that, right?" Kane asked.

Durga regarded Kane. "Once we saw the destructive power of aircraft, we knew that we needed that kind of an advantage."

Brigid cast Kane a furtive glance. The former Magistrate gave her a gentle nod to continue. Brigid caught Durga's attention once more. "When was this excursion?"

Hannah spoke up. "It was thirty years ago. Before I was born."

When Durga rested a hand on Hannah's shoulder, Brigid caught her subtle flinch from his touch. It was the smallest of shrugs, but the reflex told Brigid volumes in a language that required no translation.

Durga continued his Nagah history lesson. "My father

gave his all for our freedom. In the decades since, I have struggled to match his selflessness for the sake of the Nagah."

Durga paused, looking toward Kane, as if to provide a
segue for his next few words. "For a long time, I had a grudge
against the humans because of my father's death. Hannah can
confirm this long festering anger. However, thanks to her
wise, gentle counsel, and the advice of my mother, my fury
at the mammals who caused our people's greatest loss has
cooled."

Hannah turned toward Durga, uncertainty in her expression. "He treated all human intrusion as if they had been sent
to continue the genocidal war instigated by the barons. Fargo
can testify to that."

"Not that the consortium didn't have designs on the wealth
of technology held by the Nagah," Fargo admitted, ending his
long silence.

"The millennialist expedition hid its intentions poorly,"
Durga agreed. He eyed Fargo, his red-ringed eye a baleful spot-
light on the archaeologist, making him squirm. Brigid took a
small measure of glee in Fargo's sudden discomfort. The accusations had flown from the lips of the Cerberus warriors, and
Fargo had an answer for every one of them, each deflected with
skillful ease. However, pinned by the raw, bloodshot gaze of
the hooded cobra man, the condemnations had a ferocious
weight that pressed on Fargo harder than anything before. The
man was incapable of shrugging off the Nagah's glare.

Durga's face relaxed, and he took Fargo's hand in his.
"That is for the past. We have to look to the future, build upon
what has gone before. We both have been handed lessons in
the form of our mistakes. Let us take these lessons and turn
our destiny into a gift, rather than a curse."

Brigid took a deep breath, watching the prince and the tomb robber. If the two were colluding, Fargo certainly didn't show it. The man was paralyzed with fear. What she could see, however, was the grim glint in Kane's eye. Something had triggered his acute senses, but given the nature of this first contact with the Nagah, it would be hours before the Cerberus expedition had a moment of privacy to confer.

There would be a grand dinner after they met with the queen. There was no doubt that introductions with the queen would be long and formal. Though Kane dreaded these kinds of affairs, the dour expression that had seized the tall warrior was not inspired by the potential for death by boredom.

Durga paused as the group reached a tall pair of vaulted doors, wrought in finely carved and polished wood. On either side of the archway stood grim sentinels, armed with black, equally grim rifles. Their eyes gleamed as they eyed the visitors. Brigid noted that these guardians were fresh and alert, and conducted themselves with an intensity that rivaled Kane and Grant when they entered a dangerous new territory.

Durga addressed the party. "These are my mother's public chambers, where she receives citizens and the few visitors who enter our city. Many who step through these door are Nagah, and, without exception, others who have passed through intend to join us by their transformation in the cobra baths."

Hannah nodded, standing beside him. "You will be the first humans to address Matron Yun without intention of transformation. This is the rarest of honors, but hopefully, you will not be the last of the human race to come as friends."

Durga frowned. "The last time…"

A massive thud resounded against the double doors, interrupting Durga's thought. The sudden impact of a body against the wooden panels caught him off guard, and he grabbed Hannah, tugging her aside. A huge crack crawled like a lightning bolt etched in the wood, extending from the center to the top of the arch and to the floor.

The quartet of guardians at the entranced whirled, their rifles up and tracking as they formed a living wall between Durga and Hannah. The sudden racket also prompted Kane and Grant to launch their Sin Eaters into their grasp. Domi and Manticor were only a moment behind the pair, with Brigid also pulling her handgun. Fargo and Lakesh were still bewildered by the sudden burst of activity.

"Mother?" Durga asked, confusion filling his voice.

"Domi, Baptiste, stay out here," Kane said. "Prince…permission to accompany you inside?"

Durga glanced toward Kane and Grant, relief suddenly filling his features. The cobra prince drew his handgun. "Yes, yes, of course! Get those damned doors open!"

A chillingly familiar sound wafted through the cracked door, and Brigid hit the floor in time to avoid being caught by a spray of wooden splinters as an ASP pulse bolt smashed a massive hole in it. The superheated burst of energy had been stopped by the door, but she saw that the wood was easily two feet thick.

Now with a wide-open hole, screams of terror filled the main mall. Behind them, Nagah citizens scrambled, but not too far. Like their human counterparts, they couldn't help but be mesmerized by the horror occurring in their midst.

"Nephilim?" Grant asked, his long, thick arm held out to keep Nagah guardians out of the gaping, smoldering hole in the door. "How the hell did they get in here?"

"The only Nephilim I knew of were the corpses in the hangar," Durga admitted. He thumbed back the hammer on his Pinidad. "But I examined all of the bodies."

Kane's eyes narrowed. "We haven't seen everything yet. Don't jump to conclusions."

"So what should we jump to?" Durga asked.

Kane and Grant shared a quick look, then the two Magistrates hurled themselves at a panel of the broken door. Their combined strength sheared off the cracked piece of wood, and it fell on the body of the Nagah guard who had broken the door. There was no doubt that he was already dead, his crushed skull leaking brains on a broken neck.

The two Cerberus warriors' entrance was noticeable, even through the screams of fear and the sound of firearms and Nephilim blasters.

"Stay back!" Grant ordered the Nagah warriors as he and Kane slipped through the opening. "Cover us!"

Manticor left Hannah's side and crouched, utilizing the broken door as a barricade, tilting his handgun to one side to make certain that he wouldn't jam the weapon on the wood. Brigid grimaced, hating to be left behind, but Kane and Grant were trained professionals. Plunging headfirst into the middle of a blazing battle was what they were trained for and had done countless times as Magistrates.

The former archivist held her ground, knowing that Grant and Kane needed all the room they could get in the royal chambers. Though it sounded like an abattoir beyond the door, Brigid had to hang back, watching. If they needed her support, they'd call for it.

Until then, they needed her to analyze the situation.

A gust of smoke and debris belched out into the central

hall, forcing Brigid to turn away. She blinked particles out of her emerald eyes, tears already washing the orbs clean. Brigid tucked in just behind Manticor, kneeling to keep watch on her partners.

A yellow blast of light speared into a column in the hallway, shattering the stiffer stone structure. The rigid nature of the ceiling support, and the weight it held up, combined to render it more vulnerable to snapping than the free-hanging doors. Pieces of ceiling rained down from above, and Brigid watched in mute horror as Kane leaped on a cowering Nagah moments before a flagstone slammed into the ground.

Kane was nowhere to be seen as the guillotine-like stone chopped the ground.

"Kane?" Brigid called over her Commtact.

Silence.

Brigid couldn't hold back her concern any longer. "Kane!"

Her voice echoed back at her, as if to mock her fear for her compatriot.

Chapter 10

When Kane went through the door with Grant on his heels, he knew that he was plunging into an apocalyptic battle. Cobra-hooded warriors, obviously members of the queen's personal cadre, lay, charred by the intense heat of ASP bolts. The stench of roasted flesh filled his nostrils, while dust swirled in the air.

A figure stood at the throne while two others hauled a limp form away. Kane had never seen the queen before, but considering the slight frame of the captive, he made an educated guess. Kane dropped to one knee, making himself a smaller target and steadying his aim. The Sin Eater roared, launching a powerful 9 mm slug across the space between the ex-Magistrate and one of the kidnappers. The bullet struck home between the marauder's shoulder blades, but the echoing clang of his target informed Kane that the attackers had more than Nephilim weaponry. The smart armor of the Annunaki henchmen meant that only a dead-center hit would penetrate.

Kane adjusted his position with a shoulder roll, firing as he got to his knees again. This time the shadowy figure holding Yun by one arm spasmed. The Sin Eater had cored the attacker, though even through the fog of battle, Kane noted the cobra hood rising from its shoulders.

"Smart metal," Kane informed Grant and the others over his Commtact.

"Got it," Grant answered. Rather than engage in a series of acrobatics to get a better shot, the towering Cerberus warrior adjusted his aim, punching another bullet through the head of the second kidnapper. A bloody geyser of brains and skull fragments erupted, and Matron Yun slumped to the floor.

The third marauder, standing at the throne, turned his fire from a smoldering royal bodyguard toward the two interfering humans. Kane and Grant rushed to reach cover when the ASP hammered out its flaming message. The column that Grant had put between himself and the mysterious attacker snapped under the energy blast.

Grant launched himself from the base of the collapsing stone structure. Though the big warrior's shadow suit protected him from small-arms fire and lacerations, the ceiling coming down on his head would be a bad situation. Grant found himself missing the claustrophobic Magistrate helmet he used to wear as a chunk of rock rebounded off one melon-sized shoulder. Another bit of debris grazed Grant's ear with enough force to break skin, but luckily his headlong charge had protected him from the full brunt of the collapsing roof.

Grant hit the floor in a slide, skidding several feet as more bricks and flagstones struck the ground in his wake. With a deft roll, Grant scurried to his knees, scanning for the enemy who had nearly brought the house down.

The marauder fired another bolt into the air, flagstones breaking off the ceiling.

Kane grimaced as he saw that a royal guardian was still moving, despite a smoking stump where his left arm used to be. Unfortunately, the Nagah sentinel was right beneath the rain of flagstones falling from the ceiling. Kane exploded into action, scooping up the wounded cobra man. Behind him, a flagstone struck the floor hard enough to shatter the marble tiles. A shard of broken marble rocketed hard, glancing off Kane's head with enough force to turn the world around him into a soup of confusion. His normally preternaturally sharp senses were deluged with indecipherable information. The only thing he could do was cradle the injured Nagah to his side and ride out the momentary disorientation.

He heard his name being called and echoing crazily inside his head. Kane looked around, dazzling stars of light fading from where they'd blurred his vision. Grant was trotting up to the throne, Sin Eater blazing toward a stone panel.

"Kane!" Brigid cried. By now, the rolling thunder of blood rushing through Kane's ears had faded enough for him to hear her.

"I'm here," Kane answered, struggling to his feet.

"You didn't answer me," Brigid replied.

"I took a knock to the head saving this guy," Kane explained. He looked at the Nagah who cradled what remained of his left arm. "Can you hear me?"

The royal guard blinked gummily. "Yes…"

"The queen's still here!" Grant bellowed from the throne. He scooped up her slender form into his powerful arms and moved back toward the large double doors.

Durga entered with a dozen cobra soldiers, moving directly toward Grant and Matron Yun. "Blood…"

"That's from my head," Grant admitted. "I took a hit to my head, as well, but it just cut me. She doesn't appear to have any burns or lacerations."

Durga smiled weakly. "Thank you, Grant."

The Nagah prince looked up at the throne. "Why did you move her?"

"There was a passage behind the throne that at least two of the attackers ducked into," Grant explained. "I tried to shoot through, but the marble was just too thick."

Durga took a few steps, but Manticor took the prince's forearm.

"The passage could be booby-trapped," Manticor explained. "I know the urge is to just rush through in pursuit, but there are injured here that need assistance, and the structure—"

Another flagstone dislodged from the roof, as if to punctuate the guardian's point. The slab of rock smashed another crater into the marble floor. Cobra warriors set to work immediately, hauling the wounded to safety.

Brigid stood in the doorway, stuffing her pistol back into its holster as Kane helped his injured ally walk. "Need help?"

"I need a painkiller," Kane admitted. "But I can grin and bear a little headache for now."

"You certain?" Brigid asked.

"If you're worrying about a concussion, I've had them before. I'm not feeling any of the symptoms," Kane responded. "There's others that need help more than I do."

A Nagah medic escorted the one-armed guard to a stretcher, thanking Kane in heavily accented English. Brigid dragged Kane aside and pulled a flashlight from a belt pouch. "Just hold still and let me check."

Kane sighed. "Fine. Thanks."

Lakesh and Domi joined Hannah as other Nagah medics tended to the dazed but still defiant Matron Yun.

"You treat me as if I were dying!" the old snake woman rasped. "Quit clucking after me like hens!"

"Matron Yun, if you don't mind, you should relax," Lakesh admonished.

Yun squinted, looking at the scientist. She also noticed that she was in the shadow of something huge. With a glance she saw Grant towering over her, a vigilant collossus not yet willing to leave her side.

"It's hard to relax when I have a dozen hands poking and prodding me," Yun complained.

"You heard the lady," Grant spoke up. In his best training-officer bellow, he added, "Make a hole and make it wide!"

The command was enough to cause every Nagah within earshot to take a step back.

Yun held up her hand to the big Cerberus explorer. "Thank you."

Grant smiled and accepted her offered hand. "Size has its privileges. I'm Grant."

Yun offered a regal nod of acknowledgment. "I had heard of your legendary strength. I had not realized it extended to such a stentorian voice."

Grant shot a look to Brigid.

"She means you're really loud," Brigid explained.

Grant smiled. "I've got such a kick-ass job. See the world. Meet panterrestrial royalty. Learn new words."

"All in a day's work," Yun added. "You are bleeding."

Grant touched the side of his shaven head. "It's a scratch. I just wanted to make sure you were okay first."

"Don't mind Kane and Grant," Brigid offered. "They're stubborn but essentially good-hearted."

"Brigid, correct?" Yun asked, getting to her feet, offering Grant a chance to sit down. A Nagah medic quickly moved in to attend to the Cerberus warrior. They hadn't had a chance to look at Grant's injury since few of them were tall enough to reach the big human's cut.

"Yes," Brigid answered. She bowed to the queen.

"Grant, the representation of strength. Brigid, the representation of intellect. And Kane, the representation of courage and compassion," Yun noted. "The three heads…"

Kane popped a couple of painkillers into his mouth. He closed the pouch on his belt and swallowed the pills dry. "Sorry for littering your throne room with dead kidnappers, Your Highness."

"A forgivable inconvenience, Kane," Yun stated. "Are you and your compatriot all right?"

Grant rapped his knuckles on his bald skull. "We've both got hard heads. No worries, Your Highness."

"Except for the obvious concerns," Brigid corrected. "Who attacked you?"

"It was hard to tell," Yun answered. "The royal chambers filled with thick black smoke, and the next thing I knew, I had been cuffed by a kidnapper."

"I saw cobra hoods on the two that were manhandling you," Kane said.

"I didn't leave much of a head left on mine," Grant lamented. "But where did your people get a hold of Nephilim weapons and armor?"

Yun frowned. "We have an Annunaki ship, captured only recently by the prince. However, the Nagah military have been guarding it in the hangar."

Durga shifted his stance uncomfortably.

"What is it, son?" Yun asked.

Durga looked around. "Not to cast accusations out of turn—"

"Please. Just say what you mean," Yun cut him off.

"I had heard rumors that some Nagah, recent converts, do

not feel that the current structure of our society is right for them," Durga answered.

Yun let out a long breath. "Yes…the untrustworthy new-bloods, once more."

"I am serious," Durga said.

Yun looked at Kane, Grant and Brigid. "If such is the case, then we have an opportunity to deal with those who would change our ways with lawless violence. We have among us now three who could change the course of such tumultuous times."

Kane stepped forward from the others, the painkillers clearing the throbbing ache in his skull. "Matron Yun, we're not particularly well-known for leaving societies the same way we found them."

"No," Yun replied, "but you do have a reputation for righting wrongs and setting evil to rout. I can think of no one better to aid us in this time of darkness."

Kane caught a glimpse of Durga out of the corner of his eye. The flicker of a smile on the cobra prince's face coincided with a whisper caressing the back of Kane's mind. Durga's grin suggested to Kane that he'd found one of the ringleaders. Kane just wished that he could smother the dread that Durga was using the Cerberus envoys as the catalyst for whatever diabolical plan he had in store.

ONCE MORE, the world faded out and Durga found himself, standing in the wreckage of the throne room with Hannah and Yun, who were impaled vertically on pikes. Their suffering mewls screeched in Durga's ears as Enlil sat between them, reclining in the queen's small throne.

"Do you mind?" Durga asked.

"Mind what?" Enlil asked.

"That's a very distracting image," Durga said, looking away from the sight of the two most important women in his life squirming like worms on hooks.

Enlil chuckled. "For all your disdain, you still care for them?"

"What can I say? I'm not a completely heartless bastard," Durga muttered.

Enlil had banished the images of the two Nagani from the telepathic conference when he turned back to address the Annunaki overlord. Enlil chuckled, shaking his head in disbelief. "You have to be kidding me. You murder your father, force your bride-to-be into sodomy to reinforce your ego and you're plotting to overthrow your mother. And you still have a concern about their discomfort?"

Durga's eyes flashed with anger. "It's one thing to plot murder and betrayal. It's another to hang those people on a shank of steel and listen to them suffer and scream."

"So, killing's easy if you handle it quickly and cleanly?" Enlil asked.

"Just tell me what this is all about," Durga demanded.

"Patience, my prince," Enlil admonished.

Durga was at the throne in a moment, hands wrapping around Enlil's throat. "You're starting to piss me off here, Enlil. Give me a good reason why I shouldn't squeeze your head off?"

"Do you enjoy your heart's beating?" Enlil asked, unaffected by the fingers trying to dig into his trachea.

Durga stepped back, sneering. "What should I be patient about? The weapons you provided my operatives weren't enough to complete the first stage of my plan."

"Your timing was far from ideal," Enlil stated. "With the

presence of Kane and Grant, you could only hope to sow the seeds of an upcoming conflict. Those two humans are notoriously capable of derailing any violence. I warned you about their effectiveness."

"So what do I do in the meantime?" Durga asked.

"You already have a plan B," Enlil countered. "I can peer into your mind easily, remember. You are an open book to me."

Durga grimaced. "If so, then why the surprise at my distaste at your shenanigans?"

Enlil's eyes narrowed.

"What have you got to say, Enlil? I'm standing in the wreckage of our primary scheme here," Durga replied. He kicked at a charred corpse of a royal guardsman. "Literally."

"I'm simply informing you that you will have to find another means to take the power from your mother," Enlil said. "If you act too quickly or harshly, you will draw the attention of the Cerberus interlopers."

"This is where your statements of my being an open book to you ring falsely," Durga replied. "For all your blather of ultimate knowledge, you don't have a clue about what I'm really working at. But for now, I have my pieces in place."

"You're doubting my godhood, Nagah?" Enlil asked.

"I'm doubting your omniscience," Durga replied. "Your power is unmistakable. As is your immortality. But being all-knowing and all-seeing aren't quite working out for you."

"Would you care to elaborate? Or should I make the effort to pry the secret from your mind?" Enlil inquired.

"Let's just say I now have unimpeachable witnesses to the evidence of the conspiracy that I will have to take drastic measures against," Durga responded. "Right now, my mother considers Kane, Grant and the Baptiste woman as unassailable angels of purity and light."

"And it was Kane and Grant themselves who reaped the evidence that you would require to begin a plan of martial law," Enlil mused.

"I hand you a few crumbs, and you believe you are dining on the whole loaf," Durga muttered. "For now, you know enough. I'd rather not have you learn any more, in case the Cerberus people try to pay you a visit."

"How would they know about me?" Enlil asked.

Durga smiled.

"You implicated me in assisting the disgruntled elements you have stirred up," Enlil concluded. "My smart metal armor nodes and the ASP blasters."

"As well as messages to and from you, and graffiti that proclaims that you, not Enki, have been the true forge of the Nagah's greatness," Durga added.

"Your hands are washed clean," Enlil said. "From your concerns for your mother's health and safety, you have proved that for all your flaws, your heart is ultimately in the right place."

"Kane and the others side with me, and together we go after the menaces that would bring down both humankind and the cobra blooded," Durga added. "But when the smoke clears, Kane and his ilk will join Garuda among the lamented dead."

"And I am driven away?" Enlil asked.

"Would it inconvenience a god so much to be worshiped by the wrong name?" Durga countered. "In our time of darkest despair, who better to ride to the rescue than the true lord and creator of the Nagah?"

"In person?" Enlil asked. "The Nagah would know that no Annunaki craft would be in Earth orbit."

Durga laughed. He pointed to a large screen summoned into the telepathic conference between the two conspirators. On it, Enlil appeared, a news ticker crawling across the screen, announcing the contact between Enki and the Earth across the vast gulf of space.

"Hyperspace transmissions are not possible, even for the Annunaki," Enlil warned.

"You know that. Would the rest of Earth's population be aware?" Durga asked.

"There is a reason why the humans refer to the sneakiest of their ilk as snakes," Enlil surmised. The Annunaki grinned, his needle-sharp teeth gleaming in the throne room. "A twisted little ploy. But what would make you feel that the Cerberus warriors would help you in your plan?"

"There is a dead starship in Earth orbit. Damaged, ruined, but still stocked with the treasures of extraterrestrial technology. Technology that you would like to recover in order to restore your dominion," Durga said. "The Nagah rebellion will be eager, even anxious to get hold of it for you. And Manticor, the rival for my bride's affections, has already planted the seed of our ability to reach *Tiamat*'s corpse."

"Another unassailable witness, this time for the humans." Enlil laughed. "Clever."

"So, Kane and his people will seek the fastest way to the bowels of *Tiamat,* armed and ready to expect trouble. They will go on a desperate mission to plant nuclear munitions in the heart of the great ship, in order to deny the rebels their prizes," Durga continued.

"And in the process, they will sacrifice their existence in a flash of atomic fire," Enlil concluded.

"Perhaps my book is open to you, Enlil," Durga said.

"Not quite, but once you started explaining your ploy, I was able to read ahead," Enlil noted. "Naturally, in the race to reach *Tiamat,* the bogeyman Enlil will be defeated."

"The Nagah are not quite aware of the rule, if you don't see the body, they aren't dead," Durga responded.

"Keep up the excellent work," Enlil said.

The telepathic contact broke off, and Durga had to repress his grin. If the grand old god knew what was really in store, Enlil would be seeking the sanctity of mountains to hide his head. The Annunaki had no love in the prince's heart. For too long, the Nagah had been outcasts, hunted to near extinction.

Soon, millennia of wrongs would be righted, against both man and Annunaki.

Chapter 11

The quarters for the six humans were roomy enough for them to find their space comfortable, even though the denizens of Cerberus made sure to exclude Fargo from their current conversation.

As Fargo sulked in his corner of the suite, Kane began informing the others of the nuclear capabilities he suspected the Nagah of having.

"Nothing that can't be loaded onto an improvised orbital rocket, perhaps similar to that the Chinese used to have along the coast," Kane said. "As far as I can remember the history of conflicts in this area, India and Pakistan both had short-range nuclear missiles. Enough to toss a warhead about five hundred miles across a border."

"The conflict was over this very region," Brigid added. "The Kashmir has been claimed as sovereign territory by both nations."

"They didn't have much by way of a program," Lakesh explained. "There were not any autonomous human space flight programs, though they did have success with launching satellites."

"We're working under the assumption that the only ones involved in giving the Nagah space travel were India's humans," Grant said. "According to the history lesson we were given, Enki gave the Nagah the task of watching over humanity, guarding against future abuses by Enlil and his faction. With *Tiamat*…"

"Sound reasoning, except that Durga seemed very concerned about maintaining guard on the captured skimmer," Brigid said.

"Could be a trick," Domi countered.

"Why?" Lakesh asked. "He seemed genuinely upset by his mother's attempted kidnapping, and the betrayal of his own citizens to an overlord."

"I just don't trust him. He made his own people jumpy," Domi explained.

"I noticed that Hannah flinched every time Durga touched her," Brigid replied. "Manticor also expressed some disbelief in Durga's benevolence."

"Manticor also indicated that the Nagah had some form of manned craft set up for a suicide run against *Tiamat*," Kane added.

"Well, in 1993, the Indian government had developed a Polar Satellite Launch Vehicle," Lakesh mused. "Its orbital payload was around 3200 kilograms, but its maximum height was 660 kilometers. To reach *Tiamat* and return…"

"It was a one-way trip," Grant corrected.

Lakesh frowned. "So if the overlords had been inspired to act against the Earth…"

"*Tiamat* would have eaten the PSLV like a peanut," Brigid replied. "Kane and Grant can attest to the firepower on her hull, dedicated to point defense."

"A nuclear explosion would still have jarred her," Lakesh mused.

Grant shook his head. "Like shooting a Sandcat with an

arrow. You'd need an insanely lucky shot to guarantee anything."

"As it stands now, though, it looks as if the warheads are designed for defensive use," Kane suggested. "Reconfigured to be deployed by helicopter."

Lakesh shook his head. "Even a Deathbird couldn't fire a missile powerful enough to remain outside the atomic detonation's blast radius."

"Who said anything about shooting?" Domi asked. "Land in front of the advancing army, cover the nuke with a small layer of dirt, then fly away. Detonate when the approaching force is within a mile or two."

Domi splayed her hands in an approximation of a nuclear explosion. "Flying fast, the helicopter would be out of the blast radius in a few minutes, right?"

Grant nodded in agreement. "Back in the seventies, that was one of the plans between the Soviets and the Americans in Europe. The plan was to leave behind atomic demolition charges. The Red Army would roll on through the areas where their tank forces could maneuver easily, and small-yield nukes would be set off after being planted like that."

Domi grinned. "Grant comes up with some fun history lessons."

Fargo looked up from his journal. "You've got a strange sense of fun."

Domi's good mood deflated as she regarded the archaeologist. "I liked him better when he was sulking in the corner."

Kane looked at Fargo as if he were a diseased rat. "He'll probably figure this out soon enough anyway. I picked up another flash of psychic conversation."

"Psychic conversation?" Fargo asked, one eyebrow rising.

"I'm sure the Millennial Consortium has data on psi-mutie powers," Kane replied dismissively.

"There's some evidence, but the high command is skeptical of it," Fargo answered. "Really, there hasn't been much contact, and the scientists in charge are too busy looking for reliable technology to enforce their rule to go hunting for rumors and myths."

"But they sent a small army to investigate a corner of the subcontinent?" Lakesh asked.

"The snake people were only a legend. However, ancient records of Indian facilities surfaced, and after running into two or three emptied redoubts, we knew that someone had to have taken the goodies within," Fargo replied.

"The rumors of underground snake men had some factual basis," Lakesh said.

"Underground war base chief in their minds," Fargo emphasized. "I was surprised that they were utilizing helicopters."

Domi shrugged. "They don't wear a lot of clothes, but so what? I'm barefoot half the time. I still get my molecules shot halfway around the planet in the mat-trans."

"They maintained a low profile, even while flying to greet us and return us to this facility," Brigid added. "They don't want to be seen. A stealthy existence is paramount to their survival, especially given their interactions with both humankind and the overlords."

"Durga appeared quick to downplay his hostility toward humans," Lakesh said. "He could have simply stated that his attack on Fargo's group was defense against hostile raiders."

Fargo snorted in derision. "Self-defense. More like a man throwing bricks at an ant mound."

"This all could just be a ploy to make Durga look good while he's eliminating any competition for rulership of the Nagah," Grant spoke up. "The queen took a good hit to the head, and being taken hostage would have given Durga every validation to turn this whole underground city upside down."

"We got in the way of that, though we did find another corpse left behind in the throne room, also sporting Annunaki gear," Kane added.

"Leaving a false trail?" Lakesh asked. "That could backfire."

"Not if the pace of events prevents a rational examination of the evidence," Brigid said. "Tyrants have utilized manufactured threats in order to justify their power base before."

Fargo pursed his lips as he listened to the Cerberus group. Kane decided to take the bait. "Got an opinion on this?"

"If you have suspicions of a conspiracy, then what are you doing sitting around thumbing your asses over it?" Fargo asked.

"And here you thought he didn't have any useful input," Grant grumbled.

"It's best to be patient, and give Bry and the rest of our support staff a chance to give us everything we need through electronic scanning," Lakesh concluded. "If we discover anything that might help prevent a takeover of any kind, we'll turn it over to the proper authorities here."

"You guys heard that the Nagah have been monitoring your frequencies. That's how they learned so much about you," Fargo protested. "What's to keep them from hacking your Commtact signal?"

"Encryption," Brigid returned. "And now that we know where to look, and that we're monitoring the low-profile AM band transmissions that the Nagah are using to keep from being heard, thanks to the monitor we left back in the temple, we'll be kept up to date."

Fargo nodded. "Right. Well, I don't want to be thrown in irons when they discover you're spying on them."

Domi nonchalantly began to pick her stubby fingernails with her knife, ruby-red eyes locked on the archaeologist.

Brigid spoke up. "It's a passive system, so if anyone does discover it…"

Domi grinned.

"All right, all right," Fargo grumbled. "Annoying bullies."

There was a knock at the door. The Cerberus explorers and their companion paused at the sound. They hadn't been expecting anyone this soon and were surprised by the intrusion. Kane rose to his feet and answered.

It was Hannah and her bodyguard, Manticor.

"We're sorry to interrupt," Hannah said. "We just want to make certain that your recovery is coming along well."

"We're fine," Kane answered. "What about the royal guardsman I rescued?"

"Can we come in?" Hannah asked.

Kane stepped aside, allowing the Nagah representatives into the suite. Manticor dipped his head to get through the doorway, the same as Grant had done when they first settled in. Hannah waited for the door to close before speaking again.

"Guardsman Coral will recover, though the loss of his arm will prevent him from returning to active duty as a protector," Hannah answered.

"Why can't the cobra baths be utilized to regenerate his limb?" Lakesh asked.

Manticor tilted his head. "They are just for turning man to Nagah. Regrowing severed limbs?"

"We have a theory that the cobra baths are nanomachine suspension. Lakesh here is over 250 years old," Brigid explained.

Hannah blinked in disbelief. "But I thought Lakesh had been preserved by means of suspended animation."

"I was, for about a century," Lakesh answered. "Then I had transplants and cybernetic organs implanted in my body to extend my lifespan."

"Hence your blue eyes," Manticor offered.

Lakesh nodded. "Astute."

"It's my job to be aware of little details," Manticor answered. "The slightest thing out of place could mean the difference between life and death for Hannah or any of the rest of the royal family."

"Too bad you weren't present in the royal chambers," Kane mused. "Were you two aware of the secret passage behind the queen's throne?"

"It was a secured escape route," Manticor explained. "From her throne, Matron Yun would need to cross only ten feet to achieve cover in the event of an attack."

"What about on the other side of that escape hatch?" Brigid asked.

"We had lost contact with the sentries watching the egress end of the corridor," Hannah told them. "Both warriors were found with their throats torn."

"Torn?" Lakesh asked.

"Cobra fangs," Domi interjected. "Much quieter than using an ASP blaster."

"That would take a considerable amount of aggression, wouldn't it?" Lakesh inquired.

Manticor sized up Lakesh, then turned to Kane and Domi. "I'm just going to demonstrate something. This is not meant as a real attack…"

"Real att—" Lakesh began. In a flash, Manticor had pinned Lakesh to the wall, his lips pressed to Lakesh's throat. The scientist's blue eyes were wide with horror. Domi had her Detonics .45 half drawn, but Kane's hand was on her wrist.

"Good Lord!" Lakesh exclaimed. Manticor stepped back, lowering the scientist to the floor again.

"We can't run much faster than a standard human, but within a few yards, we are deadly quick," Manticor explained.

Lakesh rubbed his neck. "But wouldn't another Nagah have the same reflexes?"

"You were able to dodge my slap back at Cerberus?" Domi asked, holstering her weapon. She eyed Manticor warily.

"My apologies," Manticor offered.

She nodded to him.

"Domi has a point. The aggressor generally has the advantage in a situation like this," Kane explained. "By the time the victim realizes he's under attack, the fangs are already in his neck. Especially at short range. And since the conspirators were using their natural weaponry, it was quiet and quick."

"I would have thought there would be some immunity to your own species' venom," Lakesh mused.

"The killing factor was not venom but the fangs tearing the jugular and carotid arteries," Hannah corrected Lakesh. "Their throats were torn, they weren't killed by venom."

"But wait, we were talking about regrowing limbs and the cobra baths," Manticor interrupted. "And we're looking at a 250-year-old man who doesn't look much older than forty."

"My youth was restored via the use of a process similar to the one that converts humans to Nagah," Lakesh answered.

"So the cobra baths could be reprogrammed to another purpose?" Hannah asked.

"Absolutely," Brigid answered. "Provided the proper interface."

"Do you have that kind of interface?" Hannah pressed.

Lakesh shook his head. "No. But Enlil did, back when he went under the identity of Sam."

"Sam?" Hannah asked.

"Enlil reincarnated himself in several forms. The most recent of which was the artificially aged son of one of our regular opponents, Erica van Sloan," Lakesh explained.

"The dragon bitch who made damned certain I couldn't cut a new deal with the Millennial Consortium," Fargo interrupted.

Manticor glared at the archaeologist. "You will keep a civil tongue in the presence of the princess of the blood. I will not warn you a second time."

Domi chuckled. "Fargo, you'll have to tell me your strategy for making such warm, lasting relationships."

Fargo obviously contemplated a response to the albino woman, but Manticor's warning was fresh in his mind. He folded his hands into each other, interlacing his fingers.

"Enlil," Hannah said slowly, turning the word over in her mouth. "We had just been speaking of him. In regards to the skimmer that Durga had discovered."

"The nanomachines, as you call them, are Annunaki technology?" Manticor inquired.

"Not exclusively," Lakesh answered. "But Enlil, both as Colonel Thrush and Sam, had considerable experience with them. It's no stretch of the imagination that Enlil still possesses a facility with that technology."

Manticor and Hannah looked at each other.

"What?" Brigid inquired.

"Durga spoke of using the skimmer to head to *Tiamat* to gather information," Hannah said. "He said that the Annunaki still had treasures on the corpse of the ancient ship."

"A programming interface, perhaps?" Manticor asked. "Because he also mentioned reconstructing Garuda from his interred remains. If a variation on our cobra baths could rejuvenate you and undo 210 years of aging."

Lakesh nodded. "But how would Durga even know what to look for?"

"Would you?" Hannah inquired.

Lakesh shook his head. "Then again, my field of expertise is high-level mathematics and quantum physics. Brigid would have a better clue, but only because she and the others have been on Colonel Thrush's ship."

"Enlil has another craft?" Hannah asked.

"Staffed by android and cybernetic duplicates from alternate universes," Brigid answered. "But that craft doesn't exist in this timestream anymore. Enlil wouldn't have access to it."

"So his only hope would be to return to *Tiamat*," Hannah mused.

"Not his only hope," Lakesh said. "There are caches of ancient Annunaki technology that have been deposited around the globe. Including potentially here in your city."

"That's one thing I wanted to ask you," Brigid interrupted. "What is the power source of this city?"

"The catacombs are warmed by thermal vents that reach deep into the Earth's crust," Hannah said. "The process is very low pollution. We utilize standard fatty oils from livestock to provide candles. More recently we constructed a small fission reactor that generates electricity. If there had been another form of power for the city, its secrets have been lost in antiquity."

"Not if there's someone walking around now who was alive when this place was built," Grant said. "Like Enki or Enlil."

Hannah frowned. "You seem to be fairly loose with the implication that Durga might be in collusion with your enemy Enlil. How do you know you can trust us?"

Kane clapped his hand against Manticor's bicep. "Like your guardian said. Small details can mean the difference between life and death for those we care about. Just how has Durga been acting out of character?"

"Demonstrations of understanding that he is not known for," Hannah pointed out. "Especially his forgiveness of Fargo. Durga fumed for weeks after he was scarred."

"I'm glad it took months for me to reach Cerberus, in that event," Fargo spoke up. "Gave him time to forget most of his anger."

Hannah's lip curled. "He loves his red eye now. It makes him more intimidating."

"I have another question, if you don't mind," Brigid said. "Your relationship with Durga…"

"We are only promised to each other. Durga cannot marry me until the matron steps down as queen," Hannah explained.

"It is a safety measure, to prevent Hannah from taking action against Matron Yun," Manticor added. "There is less temptation for intrigue."

"You don't look happy about that," Domi spoke up.

Manticor fell silent.

"Considering that you're not married, I'm wondering…" Brigid continued.

Hannah shook her head. "Durga is not a kind prince."

"Why put up with it?" Brigid asked.

"Some things are worth giving up if it means protecting something else," Hannah answered. She fought the urge to glance back to her bodyguard, but it didn't work. It was only a flicker of peripheral vision, but she still made contact.

"Do you know why Durga could be changing his public views?" Brigid asked.

"Your presence," Hannah answered. "And I'm not certain Durga received that skimmer in the way he told us."

"Handed over on a silver platter?" Kane inquired.

"We have corpses in storage. The Nephilim suffered gunshot wounds, but the old legends state that they are soulless and mindless minions," Hannah said.

"It would not take much for them to stand still and die at their master's command," Manticor replied.

"You people seem so certain of these speculations," Fargo mentioned. "What if you're wrong and Durga really is correct about a faction of Nagah willing to throw in with the Annunaki?"

"We're not acting on our suspicions," Kane said. "Unlike the consortium, we don't go off half-cocked. We need to be sure about what truly is going on before we take action."

Fargo took a deep breath, his face screwing up with inner turmoil.

"What?" Kane asked. "The bathroom's that way if you gotta take a shit."

Fargo's eyes narrowed. "He cussed in front of your princess, hoodie."

"He did not say anything derogatory toward women, hairless ape," Manticor answered.

Fargo ground his teeth. "Listen, Durga might be a lot of things, but I know he's not in with the Annunaki."

"How so?" Grant asked.

"Because…" Fargo said.

"That's no answer," Domi snapped, frustrated with the archaeologist. She looked at Lakesh. "Let me loosen his tongue up a little bit."

"Because the deciding factor for going after the Nagah's stockpiles of twentieth-century technology was that the consortium had been told to by one of the Annunaki," Fargo confessed. "We'd get the equipment to further our aims of controlling North America, and they would get the means to rejuvenate *Tiamat*."

Kane shook his head in disbelief. "When are you idiots going to learn that you can't make deals with the overlords?"

"Don't lump me in with them. I was told to go and act on my rumors," Fargo protested.

"Which of the overlords did you deal with?" Brigid asked.

"I'm just an errand boy, and besides, they all look alike," Fargo said.

"You knew enough about us," Grant snarled.

"Well, yeah. Because I'd actually run the risk of encountering you," Fargo replied. "You don't skulk behind the scenes, and being explorers yourselves…"

"Fine. So an overlord wanted the Nagah out of the way?" Lakesh asked. "They sent a small enough force."

"The old gods' information about us was based on outdated intelligence," Hannah said. "When the barons sent their soldiers against us, they inflicted heavy losses among the truebloods. Garuda was only one of many, though his struggle was the most heroic."

"In the thirty years since, thousands have been added to the ranks of our race," Manticor said. "Part of Durga's plan to reinforce the population against another genocidal attack."

"Durga's plan?" Brigid asked. "But he told us about his distrust for the newly converted."

"Without the newly converted, there would be less than five hundred Nagah in the world, rather than the ten thousand who now exist," Manticor replied. "The calling went out for pilgrims to come and be raised to an elevated status."

"Rejuvenating *Tiamat*," Kane muttered. "So instead of going to her for these treasures, there must be something beneath the city."

"Ancient pictograms?" Brigid asked. "I don't know the Nagah's written language."

"It's based on Hindi," Hannah said. "The scrollwork is an archaic form. And besides, all of the sections are repeated."

Brigid nodded. "You mentioned that during the tour. Is there anywhere else where there might be a control panel? Perhaps near the cobra baths?"

"A control panel?" Hannah asked. "There are primary controls for the cobra baths, but they are not like the pictograms. We simply pour the solution into a vat, the pilgrim enters and is transformed. Then the vat is drained back to the main storage."

Brigid frowned.

There was another knock at the door. It was a Nagah warrior who entered, bowing. "Forgive my interruption, but Prince Durga requests the presence of the humans and Princess Hannah. There has been another incident...."

Chapter 12

On the way to the hangar, Kane was quick to notice a scrawled creed on one wall.

"Enlil the Redeemer," Lakesh translated from Hindi. "So much for the mystery of who is causing the disturbance among the Nagah."

"But how much of this is Enlil, and how much of it could be our other option?" Kane asked, not wanting to say Durga's name in the presence of the Nagah warrior sent to retrieve them.

The hallway to the hangar had been barricaded. Cobra men wielding assault rifles were poised and ready to charge into the flight bay. Wisps of smoke twisted through the archway, and the familiar stench of explosions and torn bodies reached Kane's nostrils.

Durga paced back and forth, kept out of the line of sight of the hangar by anxious bodyguards. If looks could kill, Durga would have laid out his Nagah defenders with a glance. With the arrival of the envoys from Cerberus, Durga's mood improved somewhat. At least the cobra prince would be able to talk with someone.

"What happened?" Kane asked.

Durga grimaced as he heard gunfire rattle far behind him. The chatter of automatic weapons was swiftly punctuated by the sizzle of an ASP blaster, and the Nagah leader's eyes narrowed. "We've got two pieces of information. One is that their goal is to get the skimmer operational. The second is that the group's title is the Fist of Enlil."

"Three if you count their current location," Kane grumbled sardonically.

"If knowledge is supposed to be power, then why do I feel so fucking impotent?" Durga griped. He took a deep breath and let his frustration bleed out in a long, sibilant exhalation. "Apparently they started a fire using helicopter fuel. In the confusion, a group of the insurgents managed to rush the skimmer and take it over."

Kane looked at Grant and Brigid. Already the archivist's mind seemed to be grinding out the minutiae of the hangar's layout, her perfect memory of the flight bay rolling across her mind's eye. Grant knelt and pulled a dry-erase marker from his pocket, marking off a map on the tile floor.

"Is that to scale?" Brigid asked. "I seem to remember more aircraft on the west side."

"I'm just doing a rough for now," Grant replied.

"Would you prefer I do the mapping and leave you free to delineate approach vectors?" Brigid inquired. She looked at Durga. "It'd have been easier if you had a command post set up."

"The Enlil followers only struck a few minutes ago," Durga replied. "It's not as if I have tents, maps and tables in my back pocket."

"That's all right," Kane said, trying to soothe Durga's frustration. "Besides, this is just preliminary work. We don't have the specifications on the part of the hangar where you put the skimmer."

"That's why I'm using the erasable marker," Grant said. "And that, Brigid, is why the layout doesn't look to scale for you."

Brigid nodded. "All right. Sorry."

Grant rose to his full height, looking down at the map. "So, how many little Fists are hanging out at the skimmer?"

"My men didn't have a chance to count. There were at least two weapons firing on the guards, as well as burning fuel," Durga said. "With the fire and the smoke, an accurate assessment was impossible."

"It's probably not more than three Nagah," Kane noted. "They moved quickly and made use of a good distraction. Are there any soldiers in there?"

"We have them on the radio, but they're pinned down," Durga explained.

"That's what the recent bout of shooting was," Kane said.

Durga nodded. "They're trying to get a closer look, but apparently the skimmer's weapons are active. Why the Nephilim didn't use them when we found the craft…"

Kane interjected a thought, hoping to see if Durga would give away if he were involved in the scheme. "Perhaps the reason you found it was because Enlil wanted to supply his followers. You bring in an operational skimmer with cosmetic damage and a dead crew…"

Durga's brow furrowed in thought. His hood flexed as he appeared to analyze Kane's suggestion. He started to take a few steps toward the hangar entrance, but his guards interposed themselves, keeping him out of the line of fire. "It doesn't make any sense that way. I had Nagah soldiers protecting the ship. No one was even supposed to be behind the tarpaulin."

"Did you have guards stationed inside the ship?" Grant asked.

Durga rubbed his forehead for a moment. "No. I had called for a complete quarantine of the area. Do you mind?"

Grant handed the cobra prince the marker. Durga knelt and drew an addition onto Grant's diagram. "See, that part of the hangar was away from the weapons magazine. Just in case the skimmer might have some form of transmission that compromised the safety of our explosives."

"The tarp also would obscure someone approaching from another portion of the hangar, wouldn't it?" Brigid asked, looking at the quarantined section.

"There is no entrance on the other side," Durga stated.

"Air vents?" Brigid inquired. "Repair access tunnels?"

Durga grimaced. "I don't buy the air-vent theory. Have you ever tried crawling through one?"

"Have you?" Brigid asked.

"As a child, I played in them. My bodyguards always found me because the walls of those vents are fairly inflexible, and any weight on them would create loud banging sounds," Durga explained. "We might have serpentine features, Ms. Baptiste, but we're still limited by our bipedal nature and our physical mass."

"So, a repair tunnel or another form of secret passage akin to the queen's throne room," Brigid suggested.

Durga frowned. "That's another thing that's confusing me. Mother's escape route was a very closely guarded secret. Only those entrusted with her protection knew of that corridor."

"So Enlil has contacts within the queen's guard, or former guard?" Kane inquired.

"It's possible," Durga said. "Not to accuse those currently protecting her. We lost a half-dozen good warriors in that attack, with another three wounded badly enough that they can no longer fight."

"Washouts?" Grant asked. "Back when we were Magistrates, we had one or two who just didn't cut it. We only recently encountered one who turned to banditry."

Durga shrugged. "I have my duties. But I will run this past the head of the Matronal Guard. He's more familiar with the Nagah under his command than I could be."

"Fair enough," Grant said with a nod.

Kane looked toward the hangar again. "Any idea if they damaged any of your aircraft?"

"Why would that be a factor?" Durga asked.

"To prevent pursuit," Kane said. "Especially if they want to take the skimmer out."

Durga nodded. "They have the ship's guns working. Maybe they know how to fly it."

Durga punched the palm of his hand in frustration. "I wanted to get the skimmer flying again."

"To see if *Tiamat* had anything worth salvaging?" Brigid asked.

Durga glanced at Brigid. "Is it wrong to want your father back?"

Kane frowned, having something in common with the cobra prince. "No."

Durga watched Kane's face for a moment. "My sympathies. That's the thing. I want to use the cobra baths to their fullest power. Somewhere on *Tiamat* is the means to interface with the liquid and program it for other purposes."

Brigid dropped her bomb into the conversation. "I have a theory that the cobra baths already have a form of programming interface. And it utilizes cues based upon the pictogram alphabet that carry your city's history."

Durga swallowed, looking at Brigid. "What do you mean?"

"There has to be some form of control panel utilizing the pictogram language displayed in the carvings in your city," Brigid said. "This control panel then can give the nanomachines new orders."

Durga rubbed his flat, armored nose with a clawed thumb. "So, all this time, for the past thirty years, I've had the ability to resurrect my father? I just didn't know where the controls were."

"If the pictograms were copied from an original template accurately," Brigid added. "The carvings would serve as a form of Rosetta stone."

Durga looked confused for a moment. "Oh, the tablet discovered in Greece. It said the same thing in Greek, and two other languages. Linguists were then able to extrapolate the other two languages from what was known of Greek."

Brigid nodded.

"It's hard to imagine the caves you've lived your whole life in possessing any hidden secrets," Durga said. The prince shook his head. "That doesn't matter. Right now, we've got the people who tried to kidnap my mother threatening our lives."

Kane and Brigid locked eyes for a moment. The prospect of power already in his control had taken Durga's mind off the worries of armed killers in close proximity to nuclear weapons.

"You're right. If they take a shot at the storage magazine, there's a chance that they could crack the containment on your warheads," Grant offered. "The last thing we need is radiation, or worse, particles of plutonium getting airborne."

Hannah looked surprised at Grant's comment. "Why would that be more dangerous than the radiation? And shouldn't we be worried about the warheads detonating if they use an energy weapon on them?"

"The explosives used to create a nuclear reaction are relatively inert," Lakesh explained. "They detonate through electrical impulse, not heat or impact. The real danger is in the form of the fractured plutonium core. The airborne particles, if inhaled, will deliver a far more lethal dose of radiation than a conventional leak."

Hannah frowned. "And how did you know we had nuclear weapons?"

"When we came through the hangar, the radiation warning symbols gave it away," Kane said. "Durga was giving us a bit of a backhanded threat, but an understandable one."

Hannah glared at Durga for a moment. "Showing off our nuclear weapons?"

"It wasn't as if I opened the doors and let the humans fondle them," Durga growled. He turned to Kane. "You've had experience with the weaponry of the skimmers. Could they cut through three inches of armor plate and radiation shielding?"

Kane shook his head. "It'd take a long concentrated blast. When the overlords came after us, we had defenders able to take cover behind rocks, and the energy blast duration was very short in general."

"They have the time if necessary," Durga said. "How about the vulnerability of the skimmers?"

"They can be taken out with a Stinger missile," Grant offered. "They really don't have anything that a Deathbird doesn't have, except for speed and transatmospheric capability."

Durga waved one of his Nagah commanders forward. "Have warriors stationed outside the cave entrance with antiaircraft missiles. If they try to make a run for it, we'll blow it out of the sky."

Durga returned to the improvised layout that Grant had

drawn. "Someone get me the plans of the hangar, too. I want to know how they slipped in."

Brigid looked at the layout, then held out her hand. "Give me the marker."

Durga handed it back to her, then watched as she began sketching a smaller, more finely detailed version of Grant's map. She began drawing in crosshatch marks along the walls, measuring the distance between them. She then used that distance to extrapolate two more entrances in the section of hangar that Durga had filled in on the other map.

"What are those?" Durga inquired. "Vents?"

"No. Like you said, if we tried making an entrance through the vents, we'd make enough noise to turn it into a deathtrap," Brigid replied. "These hatches in the walls are access points to the pipe system honeycombing the underground city, if your facility is anything like our headquarters."

"Right, the utility tunnel system." Durga nodded. "Electrical, fuel, water. I remember now. I played hide-and-seek in there as a boy."

"How much room is in there?" Grant asked.

Durga looked the big Magistrate over. "Not enough for you."

Grant shrugged. "How about Kane?"

"It'd be a squeeze," Durga said. "But he could make it."

"Is there any way to enter the hangar's utility tunnels from inside here?" Kane asked. He looked over toward Domi, who seemed to be fidgeting. "What?"

"You'll need some backup since Grant can't scurry through without you," Domi offered.

"I know you want to come, but remember what you volunteered for," Kane told her.

"Right. Keeping Moe safe, and making sure Fargo doesn't get out of line," Domi answered. She sighed. "But going by yourself…"

"If Kane can do it, I can," Brigid interjected.

"Fair enough," Kane said, sounding a bit reluctant. "We'll need our gear bags, though."

Durga nodded. "I can have soldiers pick them up. It'll cut down on the time. What's your plan?"

Kane took the marker from Brigid, then knelt.

DURGA KEPT HIS THOUGHTS shielded as he watched Kane and Brigid slip into the utility hatch. He personally handed the flame-haired archivist the stubby little Copperhead submachine gun through the hole. "Be careful, you two."

She nodded in response.

The woman disappeared down the utility tunnel, and Durga stepped back. A Nagah technician sealed the hatch, then left the prince to stand watch.

A smile curved his scaled lips. Enlil might have had the ability to monitor his thoughts, but Durga doubted that the telepathic communication resulted in a deep mind probe. Certainly, there were moments when obvious thoughts manifested themselves. They were simply surface reactions, flights of whimsy influenced as much by the Annunaki as Durga's own imagination.

It was a risky ploy, pitting the Millennial Consortium, the Annunaki and the Cerberus explorers against one another. If it hadn't been for Durga, then the Millennial Consortium wouldn't have known a thing about the Nagah's supplies of technology. Durga had convinced the millennialists that they were working in the interests of a lone overlord. Since the fall of *Tiamat,* the surviving Annunaki had abandoned the ideas of alliance with their brethren. As such, the Millennial Consortium was interested in keeping any contact with the remaining overlords secret from their brethren.

That level of paranoia allowed Durga to manipulate them. The consortium was looking out for its own interests, and it would take advantage of any offer of allegiance. The chess game was also being played by the Annunaki against the consortium, as the millennialists had found themselves at odds with one another, such as in the conflict that had left Fargo high and dry.

Durga could tell that even Kane and his allies were hedging their bets. They had kept Fargo close by, even going so far as bringing him back to India. The Cerberus warriors wanted every advantage they could get in case Fargo was manipulating them.

Durga cursed himself for letting his interest in the nanomachine interface dominate his thoughts in a crisis situation. He hoped that he had recovered, but he doubted it. The games of intrigue and the laying of conversational minefields were too complex. Durga had stumbled, but apparently not enough to take Kane's mind off the situation. He hoped that his minions in the Fist of Enlil could do some damage to the former Magistrate and his female ally, but he doubted it.

After watching the fluidity that Kane had displayed while storming the royal chambers, Durga was certain that he would prevail even against Nagah warriors wielding Annunaki technology. Even without the extra grenades and weapons drawn from their gear bags, Kane was a formidable combatant with swift reflexes and a steady gun hand. Anyone slower and weaker would have been killed by the falling debris, while

Kane had not only kept himself alive, but rescued a crippled royal guardsman. That kind of skill gave Durga pause.

The Nagah prince was a fighting man, trained in marksmanship and unarmed combat since he was a child. Across three decades, he had led his soldiers from the front, staring his enemies in the eye as he killed them. That kind of experience was hard won, but Durga wondered if it would be enough to best Kane if the time came.

There were other advantages. Durga's natural reflexes and his venomous fangs might provide him the edge needed. Even so, the prospect of sending the Cerberus warriors up to *Tiamat* in the improvised orbiter, then detonating a nuclear warhead to kill them was an attractive plan. Durga was not an old man, but the years were starting to catch up with him.

The best part of Durga's machinations was that he had managed to draw in Enlil. The overlords were not forgotten in their efforts to eliminate the Nagah. Between humankind and Annunaki, the cobra folk had been driven nearly to extinction on too many occasions to count. Pulling Enlil into this conflict was more than just icing on the cake; it was a chance to eliminate the mightiest and most resourceful of the overlords. Nagah observations of the Cerberus missions indicated that Enlil had resources not only buried in archaeological troves around the Earth, but also possessed a ship and a crew of robotic duplicates that traversed the universe.

If Enlil grew desperate enough, he might revitalize his links to the assemblage of Colonel Thrush and the pan-dimensional craft.

While not possessing the world-shattering firepower of *Tiamat,* it was a resource that Durga would be helpless to act against, even with a quiver full of nuclear weaponry.

Enlil had to be stopped now, which entailed use of the Cerberus rebels. Kane and his allies would be all too willing to strike such a blow against the leader of the Annunaki. Though they would be wary of Durga and on the watch for his manipulations, the opportunity that Durga presented would be too juicy a morsel to pass up.

The Millennial Consortium had also assembled another expeditionary force in the months since Fargo had been repelled. This group was composed of hundreds of soldiers, bandits and coldhearts who'd been recruited with the promise of murder and pillage. The consortium welcomed the prospect of gaining an arsenal of nukes. Even in an atomic-war-ravaged Earth, the power to shatter an army with a single shot was too good to pass up. The environment was already heavily damaged, so the consortium could be far more casual in its use of the hugely destructive munitions either defensively against rival armies, or in the form of global blackmail.

The thought of such a government gave Durga a bitter taste in his mouth. The humans were much too willing to destroy the world all over again for just a sliver of power. Pitting Cerberus against the consortium, backed by the might of the Nagah, would give Durga just the opportunity he needed. Not only would the conflict weed out officers more loyal to his mother, but the millennialists would also be crippled in their international reach.

The rumors of recruitment that reached Durga's ears let him know that their resources in Asia had been taxed to the limit. With a cadre of some of their finest officers thrown into the mix to ensure success, the consortium was in an all-or-nothing end run against the Nagah.

Durga finally arrived back at the barricade that his warriors had built to contain the insurgents in the hangar. Grant had assembled a massive rifle and was getting ready to provide support to Kane and Brigid when the time came.

"There was another exchange of gunfire between your boys and Enlil's toadies," Grant told him.

"Did we lose anyone else?" Durga asked, letting genuine concern slip into his voice. The Nagah prince knew that severe losses to his nation's population would make his rule that much more difficult. His ploy required the elimination of leaders, not those who would be considered cannon fodder.

"No. A couple of the men were wounded by shrapnel," Manticor explained. "But they'll be fine."

"Good," Durga said. "When Kane and Brigid get into position, you'll tell me?"

"Sure," Grant answered, adjusting the scope on his rifle.

Durga nodded. "All right. I have to confer with some advisers in the meantime."

Grant's face flickered with a moment of suspicion, but he returned his attention to the hangar.

Suspect all you want, Grant, Durga thought. By the time you're aware enough to do anything, you'll have been swept away by the whirlwind.

Chapter 13

In the claustrophobic confines of the utility corridor, Brigid followed Kane. They navigated their path by Brigid's instant memorization of the twisting route thanks to the plans provided by Durga's people and multioptic visors that granted them night vision via infrared illumination. The Cerberus pair spoke low as they moved, their Commtacts amplifying even the softest of whispers.

"Durga took your bait," Kane offered. "Which explains why we're being given the go-ahead to derail his attempt to hijack the skimmer."

"What makes you think that?" Brigid asked.

Kane paused, waiting for Brigid to direct him in the tunnel. She pointed the way, then continued speaking. "Because he's given us help to come in behind his own cultists."

"According to Fargo, one of the Annunaki was interested in unseating the leadership of the Nagah," Brigid said. "Add in the fact that Durga would be implicating Enlil in this insurgency…"

Kane shook his head. "No. That doesn't fly. Using Enlil as a scapegoat does nothing in terms of lessening any alliance they have. Enlil loves the fact that he is one of the most feared beings on this planet. And despite a few minor differences, all of the Annunaki look alike."

"So Durga passes off his sudden beneficiary as some other overlord?" Brigid asked.

"Enki himself," Kane suggested. "Once the Nagah have been harrowed enough in conflict with those willing to follow Enlil, they'll cast about for a more comforting friend. And given that Enlil is hardly sociable—"

"Not to mention that Enki wouldn't have to be present to give Durga all the information he requires to upgrade the cobra baths' interface," Brigid interrupted.

"No," Kane said, thinking about Brigid's addition. "Good point." He paused and looked at a hatch. "Okay, we're here," he whispered.

Brigid examined the utility hatch. It was designed as a safety mechanism against a burst pipe unleashing gas. Not only was it airtight and soundproof but it was also securely placed so that opening it would take an effort. The clamps around the ring, fortunately, were undone. The hatch was slightly ajar, and Kane pulled Brigid back.

"What?" she whispered.

Kane shook his head and focused the illuminator on his multioptics, scanning for trip wires. His point man instinct was correct once again as he spied a gossamer-thin thread stretched across the hatchway. Brigid's lips tightened into a bloodless line as she saw the booby trap.

Kane took out his combat knife and followed his half of the trip wire. Brigid, opening a pocket multitool, examined her side. The walls of the tunnel were not smooth, and there was a raised lip around the hatchway. In the shadow of that lip was a packed worm of plastic explosives, and the trip wire had been hooked into two pencil-thin detonators. Any pressure on the line would trigger an electrical charge through their bodies, so that even if one of the detonators had been pulled loose, the arch of high explosives would unleash a guillotine blade of force that would carve anyone trying to get through the hatchway.

Kane indicated that he found one detonator. Brigid pointed out hers.

Kane used his combat knife carefully, cutting into the puttylike explosives, releasing the section that the detonator was anchored in. The trip wire grew slack, and Kane carefully sliced the slender thread connecting the two now that it was no longer taut. As soon as he did that, Brigid carved the detonator on her side out of the plastic explosives, then peeled the pliant material off its trigger.

Kane smirked in the darkness, pulling down the wadded explosives, packing them into a soccer-ball-sized lump. He then attached a longer section of slender cord to the pencil detonator. Brigid arched one eyebrow as she watched him insert the rearmed pencil detonator into the doughlike mound. Once that was done, Kane imbedded his grenades into the mass of explosives.

"You are a dangerous bastard," Brigid whispered.

Kane repressed a chuckle. "You can flirt with me later."

He anchored the end of his cord to a pipe, though he knew that the slamming hatch would do the job in pulling the pin on his improvised explosive device. He handed the blob of demolition to Brigid. "I'll take care of the hatch. You stuff this through."

"Will the panel protect us?" Brigid asked.

"It should. The explosives aren't shaped into place, and there's plenty of room for the overpressure to escape," Kane answered. "Any shrapnel or debris launched by the detonation won't get through this steel."

Brigid held the ball. "Give the word."

Kane rested his hand on the hatch's handle. With his other hand, he counted down on his fingers. Reaching one, Kane threw the door open and Brigid hurled the improvised bomb out. There were two Nagah right in front of the door who looked down in surprise as a gray-white ball of putty with grenades stuck in it rolled out between them. One exclaimed in surprise that someone was in the hatch, but Kane yanked back hard on the door, slamming the metal shut.

Moments later, the wall shook, dust knocked loose as it flexed. The metal plate buckled under the explosive force, but as it flexed, it still managed to shield Kane and Brigid from the deafening roar and the lethal concussion of the blast. Kane pushed on the hatch, but it was stuck in place.

"They're distracted," Grant said over the Commtact. "The skimmer moved about five feet with that firecracker."

Kane braced his back against the pipes, Brigid pushing in next to him in the same position. They didn't need to talk to coordinate their actions this time. Their four feet hammered the hatch out of its frame with a well-timed kick. Smoke swirled as the falling panel dropped through it. The cloud was thick, but nothing moved within the smoke. Kane went through, muzzle first, searching for targets. He looked to his right and saw that one of the Nagahs who had noticed their momentary intrusion was a pulverized slab of lifeless flesh stuck to the wall. The other was nowhere to be seen in the restricted visibility of the skimmer's hangar.

Brigid slid out of the utility tunnel on Kane's heels and they switched the modes on their multioptics, searching for a setting that would allow them to peer farther than an arm's length in the postexplosion confusion.

Kane stopped adjusting his visor as he heard feet scrape on the concrete floor. Ragged breathing accompanied the footsteps and Kane whirled, pushing Brigid out of the way.

One of the dazed cobra men stumbled forward, jaws distended and fangs flashing with feral fury. Thanks to the jarring effects of being caught by Kane's improvised bomb, the Nagah's assault had none of the blinding speed that Manticor had demonstrated only minutes before. Kane reversed his fighting knife and drove it like an ice pick through the cobra man's lower jaw, the point pinning the mandible to his trachea. Blood gushed through the double wound, and the snake man twisted the knife out of Kane's grasp.

Brigid's Copperhead snarled, 4.85 mm bullets pummeling the chest of a second Nagah insurgent. The high-velocity projectiles perforated the humanoid's rib cage, shredding his heart and lungs. "Put the optics on setting seven."

Kane shoved his optics up onto his forehead, then dragged Brigid out of the way of a hissing stream of stinging venom. "Maybe later."

The Sin Eater bellowed out its deadly message at the cobra man who had launched the spray of blinding poison. Kane's bullet tore through the head of the Nagah, cleaving his skull in two.

A thunderclap sounded on the other side of the hangar. The roar of Grant's rifle was followed by the sprawl of a shattered worshiper of Enlil as the snake man succumbed to a powerful bullet. The skimmer's engines hummed, starting to rise for takeoff.

The craft fired a bolt toward the entrance to the city, its energy blast creating a cloud of debris that elicited a grunt of dismay from Grant.

"You hit?" Kane asked over the Commtact, rushing toward the swiftly closing ramp descending from the bottom of the ovoid craft.

"Just covered in dust. Keep that thing from leaving," Grant snapped back.

Kane dived onto the ramp and scurried into the skimmer. Brigid was hot on his heels, her slender form slipping through the shrinking opening that would have snagged the broad shoulders of the Cerberus warrior.

"You're gonna catch a missile if you stay on this ride," Kane complained.

"So are you, so let's stop the bus," Brigid returned.

Kane didn't have the time, nor the inclination to ask what she meant by "bus." The skimmer rose higher, and the Cerberus pair burst into the cockpit, where a solitary Nagah sat at the controls of the ship. Kane leveled the Sin Eater at him. "Land this thing, now!"

The Nagah looked back over his shoulder, eyeing the high-tech machine pistol only inches from his face. "Shoot me, and we crash."

Kane took a quick glance at the monitor screen. "We're not high enough for it to matter."

The pilot's fangs swiveled down as his lip curled. Before the cobra man could lunge and spear those venom-filled barbs into Kane's arm, the ex-Magistrate pulled the trigger, blasting a cavernous wound through the Nagah's face. Blood and greasy blobs of brain vomited onto the monitor. Kane whirled and scooped Brigid tight against his side as the skimmer lurched in midflight. The ovoid ship no longer had a steadying hand at its controls, and it flipped sideways, shattering the rotors of a Black Hawk transport.

Brigid, tucked tightly against Kane's chest, was shielded from bone-breaking impacts as the two people bounced into the ceiling, then were thrown hard against the wall of the control room. Their bodies flew away from each other as the skimmer skidded to a halt. "Kane!"

"I'm right here, Baptiste," Kane grunted.

"Are you hurt?" Brigid asked, crawling off her partner.

Kane winced. "Just a few bruises. Like Grant said, Mags are a hardheaded bunch. Besides, I took most of the hit against my shoulders."

"You only just got over being smacked in the head by a rock a while ago," Brigid complained. She looked at the tossed corpse of the Nagah rebel. Unlike the group that had attempted to kidnap the queen, he wasn't wearing Nephilim armor, and had only a standard handgun stuffed into his waist sash. "Enlil must have been stingy with his toys."

Kane sat up, then slipped his Sin Eater back into its forearm holster. "Since when has the old bastard ever been any kind of generous?"

"When he's attempting to overthrow a hidden society?" Brigid asked.

"Kane? Brigid? You all right in there?" Grant's voice boomed over their Commtacts.

"What did the queen call his voice?" Kane asked, wincing from his friend's bellow.

"Stentorian," Brigid answered.

Kane cleaned out his ear on the side of his head that the

Commtact was implanted on. "That Latin for 'busting my eardrum'?"

Brigid laughed. "Close enough."

"Well, excuse the hell out of me for worrying about you two," Grant complained. "Any prisoners on that silver egg?"

"No," Kane said. "What about the other insurgents on the ground?"

"Whoever you didn't take care of tried to run and were burned down by some pissed-off snake soldiers," Grant explained. "Not that I blame them. The good guys lost some more people."

"We're not here two hours, and already we've got a civil war with the death toll in the double digits," Brigid said, exasperated.

Kane indicated that Brigid turn off her Commtact. "It's not our fault."

"I never said that it was," Brigid replied. "But what proof do we have that Durga is setting this whole thing up?"

Kane looked at the Nagah corpse in the pilot's seat. "Even if we'd taken one of them alive as a witness, it probably wouldn't do much good. Durga seems smart enough to have supplied these idiots through a cutout."

"So, back to square one, except for a few extra bruises and some ringing in our ears," Brigid sighed.

"Durga will make a mistake," Kane answered. "And when he does…"

There was a banging on the hull of the skimmer. It took a moment for Brigid to touch the interface for the command panel and open the hatch and deploy a ramp to the ground. Durga and the others were outside, looking at the pair. Kane held Brigid's hand as he lowered her down the ramp. Then, grabbing the lip of the hull, he somersaulted to the concrete.

"Sorry about the helicopter," Kane apologized.

"Grant lost contact with you," Durga said. "We were worried more about you than a hunk of machinery."

"Feedback in our Commtacts," Brigid lied. "We had to break contact before the whine melted our ears off."

Durga smirked. "I think you'd look better without ears, Brigid."

Brigid raised an eyebrow, then laughed it off. "Thank you, but I prefer being a mammal."

Durga shrugged. "Just keep in mind that as king, I'm allowed to have a queen *and* a consort."

Brigid looked at Kane, who was doing a remarkable job of concealing the jealousy on his face. She smiled and walked away from the Nagah prince.

Durga turned to Kane. "She's not interested?"

"Nothing personal," Kane answered. "She's got a prior commitment."

Durga nodded. "Ah."

Kane bowed his head, then walked off to join Brigid. He said a quiet "Thank you" to Durga under his breath. Any compunctions that Kane still had about punching the suspected conspirator into a messy pulp vaporized the moment he turned his attention toward Brigid.

Suddenly the back of Kane's neck prickled, his danger sense, warning him about an error he had made. Kane looked back at Durga, who stood, smug satisfaction on his face, surrounded by a dozen fellow Nagah who would be able to corroborate Kane's barely contained jealous reaction to Durga's flirtations with Brigid. Cold dread speared into Kane's heart, as he realized that as surely as the Cerberus rebels had manipulated Durga before, the prince had returned the favor.

Whatever purpose Durga had for getting on Kane's nerves, it was not going to be for the sake of boosting the cobra prince's ego. Most likely, Durga had a frame in mind, and Kane had stepped right into the provocation.

Kane remembered when he was a Magistrate patroling Cobaltville. The number-one reason for murder in the ville was jealousy.

Kane grimaced as he watched Durga. I just gave you all the motive for an assassination. And after the Magistrates' attack three decades ago, you have to have a Sin Eater to make the attempt a perfect frame.

Durga entered his mother's bedroom. Matron Yun was fussing, giving her nurse a hard time and had apparently gotten dressed against her orders. Durga chuckled as the poor caretaker shook her head in dismay.

"Son, what brings you here?" Yun asked.

"I came to inform you of the details of the most recent incident," Durga answered.

"Yes, yes, my guards filled me in on the details. They call themselves the Fist of Enlil, and they attempted to hijack the skimmer," Yun griped. She looked at the robes she wore. "I wish I could be more presentable to the heroes of Cerberus."

"You look splendid, Mother," Durga said. "But you really should give yourself more time to recover from your previous ordeal."

Yun glanced at Durga out of the corner of her eye. "Who are you and what have you done with my son?"

"I'm myself," Durga replied. "I'm just worried about you."

"Usually you're impatient with me." Yun sighed.

"Usually I am. But only because you treat me like a bitter,

vengeful brat," Durga answered. "But this time, you're actually allowing me to do what I do best."

Yun took a deep breath. "My city has come under attack, and like it or not, you are the warrior prince of the Nagah. When it comes to wreaking vengeance, you are the finest."

"You don't appear very proud of that," Durga noted.

"It's hardly a respectable vocation, murdering for a cause," Yun said.

"Even if that cause is the survival of our species?" Durga asked.

Yun's eyes narrowed. "The forces against us have always failed at that task."

"Not for the lack of effort," Durga countered. "And if it hadn't been for my efforts at recruitment—"

"You've recruited new blood to our race, but at the same time, you treat them as secondhand citizens," Yun cut him off. "Why?"

Durga frowned, then turned away from his mother.

"Durga, why would you work to alienate the very people you've brought into our lair?" Yun asked.

"Back in the twentieth century, in the United States of America, blacks and hispanics faced enormous bigotry. How they weren't good enough. You know what most of them did?" Durga asked.

"The best of them worked to prove their detractors wrong," Yun said. "That's a horrible way to inspire your people."

Durga looked to her. "And yet, the Nagah have the finest craftsmen, the bravest warriors and the most patriotic of citizens. I may speak ill of them, but when they excel, I am also there to reward them."

Yun shook her head in disbelief. "Why can't you just be a

nice person? Your subjects, what you do to the woman who would be your queen…"

"Hannah is a strong woman. The forge I am putting her through will only increase that strength."

Yun blinked, then turned back to the bed and sat on it. "I'm getting tired of all of this. I thought I had raised you better."

Durga smiled at the queen. "You raised me? Garuda did that job. He taught me to walk in his shoes. He made me into a warrior. He made me into the son of a god. And I've lived the past three decades trying to maintain that deification."

"You are insane," Yun said.

Durga chuckled. "I'm still the one you're counting on."

Yun swallowed a sob as the Nagah prince left her alone in her chamber.

Chapter 14

Devon Lan crouched in the shadows, watching the Nagah warriors lower their antiaircraft missiles, noting that they seemed to have been in a position to prevent the escape of some brand of flying machine. Whatever crisis there had been, it was over, and the cobra soldiers were given the go-ahead to return inside.

Lan relaxed, returning his silenced Calico machine pistol to its slung position over his shoulder. At first, he couldn't quite believe the serpentine appearance of the Nagah, but there they were, men with all the armored scales, folding fangs and neck hoods of a cobra. Then again, Lan was aware of other things that would have been impossible during his employ as a Millennial Consortium paramilitary commander. The visage of the snake men was imposing, however. The cobra was legendary around the globe for being a deadly serpent. Its attributes, combined with that of a human being, added up to a walking nightmare that turned his bowels to ice. Throw in the well-maintained small arms and heavy weapons that the creatures possessed, and Lan realized that the hundreds of Southeast Asian and Indian pirates and bandits he'd recruited for this combat expedition were a necessary burden.

Nguyen, one of his highest-ranking recruits, knelt next to

him, lowering his binoculars. The Vietnamese pirate's beard managed to conceal most of the scar tissue that covered his cheeks and jaw. Compared to Lan, a Eurasian man raised in the wilds of North America, Nguyen was a wiry, hardened thug. Lan had thought that his experience with the consortium's military had made him tough, but Lan's smooth, round face belied an almost gentle demeanor compared to the rugged pirate. "I thought that you were on a fool's errand."

"Those hangar doors are huge," Lan said. "And according to Fargo's final report, they had three transport and utility helicopters in pursuit of him."

"Three aircraft are a lot to search for one man," Nguyen replied.

"The expedition we'd sent before was large. Around sixty men," Lan answered. "Fargo wasn't the only fleeing prey, though he was smart enough to play dead."

"So why isn't he with us?" Ngyuen asked.

"The board of directors did not feel he would be best used in this manner," Lan said. "He has to earn his return to the consortium's good graces the hard way."

"By being our target marker," Nguyen muttered. "Hell of a way to redeem yourself."

"That's not my concern," Lan replied. "Come on, let's get back to the rest of the force."

Nguyen nodded. "I'll take the point."

Lan nodded, appreciating the Vietnamese man's willingness to avoid trouble. The man was a predator, like the rest of the four hundred thugs that Lan's millennial officers led. But he was a stealthy hunter, not some wild maniac willing to throw his life away just for a cheap thrill. The map of the lessons Nguyen had learned was literally etched into his face, visible even through his thin black beard. The pirate mercenary led Lan back along the path that they had taken to the front gates of the hangar, a route that had been handed down from the consortium's contact.

Apparently, an Annunaki overlord was supplying the millennialists with all the information they needed to blindside the Nagah on their home ground. The advance intelligence included patrol routes and angles of approach. Lan had a healthy dose of skepticism telling him that this information was too good to be true, but the directors informed Lan that it was his place to confirm the usefulness of the supplied data. If it proved viable, then Lan's job was to make use of that knowledge to increase the lethal power of their assault on the snake people.

Anyone or anything capable of putting up a fight was to be exterminated.

Toward that goal, the millennial expeditionary force had been supplied with crates of grenade launchers and SIG AMT assault rifles, as well as their signature Calico sidearms. Some of the raiding army brought their own heavier artillery, literally. Nguyen's crew had a pair of man-portable mortar units, munitions launchers reverse engineered from Japanese knee mortars. With the ability to hammer the hangar with high-explosive rounds, Lan felt confident that he'd be able to negate the air force of the Nagah.

Without the ability to maintain air superiority, the cobra folk would lose their greatest advantage on the grounded consortium assault.

Lan was glad to get back to his lines. The supreme commander of the assault force, a former Magistrate named Christian, had spread the small army across several small pockets under the forest canopy.

Christian stood well over six feet tall, a towering pillar of strength who managed to keep the assembled thugs in line with just the force of his will. His reddish hair conformed to his blunt skull.

"Report," Christian ordered gruffly.

Lan looked back toward the Nagah's mountainside hangar. "All information has been confirmed correct. We located three patrols, but did not engage. There was also crisis-level activity at the hangar doors."

"What kind?" Christian asked.

"Nagah had surrounded their own hangar doors, and had rocket launchers ready to engage an escaping aircraft," Lan reported.

Christian nodded. "Fargo said that he was going to infiltrate the Nagah's ranks once more with the assistance of the Cerberus group. However, it does not follow that Kane and his people would try to steal a helicopter to escape. Especially after having been in there for only a few hours."

"You have confirmation of their presence?" Lan asked.

"Bader has been monitoring all communications in the area," Christian explained. "Lakesh made arrangements for a pickup. We sent another scout party to that location."

Lan frowned. "Did we see what they had?"

"They left behind a couple of heavy weapons," Christian said. "A rocket launcher, a heavy antitank rifle and a medium machine gun, as well as a communications relay."

"Have we been able to listen in?" Lan asked.

Christian shook his head, frustrated. "No. They have the signals encrypted. It's just a relay, transmitting to a satellite, and presumably back to their headquarters. However, during the period of time when you described the Nagah responding to a crisis, there were no signals being beamed toward Cerberus."

"They'd have been looking for assistance if they were attempting a breakout," Nguyen concluded. "So, there's something else going on here."

"The Nagah have broadcast that a terrorist group calling themselves the Fist of Enlil attempted to steal a captured skimmer from the hangar," Christian said. "It could be disinformation, but that's not likely."

"Enlil?" Lan asked. "Did the directors state who our Annunaki benefactor was?"

Christian shook his head again. "Negative. It's possible that even they don't know. But when you get handed a gift, you make use of it."

"And there's nothing to indicate that the terrorists are actually linked to Enlil, right?" Nguyen asked.

"Apparently they know enough to fly a skimmer," Christian said. "Right now, the entire city is on lockdown, a curfew to keep conspirators from doing their work in the shadows."

Christian smiled. "With the Nagah military and police distracted with internal troubles, we'll have the perfect opportunity to hit them unaware."

Lan smiled. "When the Nagah soldiers were returning to base, we saw a perfect entrance to make our initial strike."

"They won't know what hit them," Christian said smugly.

THE DIMINUTIVE DOMI MOVED swiftly through the utility tunnels in the Nagah metropolis, her compact size allowing her to snake along the access corridors almost as fast as if she were running. On the other end of their Commtact link, Lakesh guided her movements.

The Cerberus adventurers had only two known quantities on their side that would not betray their skulking to Durga— Princess Hannah and her bodyguard, Manticor. They too suspected that Durga was involved in some plot to turn the cobra people into a dangerous threat.

Domi paused as she noticed a hatch down the tunnel was open. A snake man entered the pipe and turned away from her, heading toward a new location.

"Domi?" Lakesh asked over her Commtact. "You've grown silent."

The hatch clunked shut, echoing down the access pipe. Domi kept her voice low. "Someone else just crawled into here with me."

"A repairman?" Lakesh asked.

"No. No light, no toolbox. I'm following him."

"Beloved, that's too risky. What if he notices you?" Lakesh protested.

"Always wanted cobra-skin boots," Domi replied, scurrying after the mysterious Nagah.

"Domi…"

Lakesh stopped. The slender thread of a radio signal kept them connected, but it was not a strong enough leash to bring the feral young woman back to him in the event of an emergency.

Domi crawled through the darkness, her multioptic visor allowing her to stay on the snake man's trail.

DURGA HEARD THE TAP in his den and moved swiftly to the hatch. It was Hedin, a former member of Durga's personal guard, now promoted to the rank of colonel in the Nagah Defense Force. Hedin crawled out of the access hatch, pushing a pair of active night-vision goggles off his sloped, scaled forehead.

"Did anyone follow you?" Durga asked, closing the hatch but not securing it, in case Hedin was required to make a swift exit.

"No. I'm sorry that the Fist's effort to acquire the skimmer failed, but you gave Kane and his allies all the access they required to foil the plot," Hedin stated.

"The skimmer's irrelevant to our plans for now," Durga replied. "We have the means to access the knowledge of Enki, so that plundering the other Annunaki's secrets is no longer necessary."

"What?" Hedin asked. "But won't Enlil be frustrated that we're deviating from the plan?"

Durga shook his head. "Enlil won't be a factor in this. You see, the carvings we've so lovingly copied around the city are more than just historical reminders. They may be the key to understanding Enki's programming for the cobra baths."

"How did you find this out?" Hedin asked.

"It was the archivist Baptiste. She's had experience with studying the language of the old gods and feels that the pictograms are part of a control interface," Durga stated.

"But they're just symbols carved in rock," Hedin said.

Durga smiled. "Somewhere in the mechanism of the cobra baths is a true control panel. We can then direct the nanomachinery inside of the baths to do whatever we want them to."

Hedin nodded in appreciation. "Immortality is a fine prize. But right now, we have another, more pressing concern."

"The consortium is in place?" Durga asked.

"A patrol caught movement, but were unable to determine if it was an intruder or local fauna. I had one of the trusted take a closer look at the trail, and he reported that it was indeed two humans who had come within yards of the hangar entrance. They returned back down the same trail, escaping notice this time, and returned to where we suspect the humans have set up their staging grounds," Hedin said.

Durga retrieved a map. "Give me the exact locations."

Hedin marked off the positions of the trail and where their trusted scout had trailed the intruders to. "It was a company-sized unit, approximately forty to sixty men. No vehicles, and the base is well camouflaged."

"Only one company?" Durga inquired. "I was hoping that the consortium would have learned from their prior mistakes. When I informed them of our position and military strength…"

"It's not necessarily just that one unit," Hedin interjected. "On the way back to his normal patrol route, the scout spotted evidence of another unit. It was a faint glimpse, and had he not wanted to attract attention by his absence, he would have investigated it further."

Durga looked at the suspected second unit's position. "They're sticking to the thickest parts of the forest. Very hard to see from the air, and the ground is relatively uneven, allowing them to keep out of sight of our patrols."

Durga made seven more circles in similar areas to the two known consortium positions and smiled. "Nine times fifty…"

"Close to five hundred soldiers, if all the units are of the same size," Hedin said. "We could be looking at a devastating attack."

Durga smiled. "That's what we want. The matron is under the delusion that because we have made friends with the humans from Cerberus, all of humankind can be considered a potential ally. I've worked too hard fanning the fear of the hairless apes to allow a trio of heroes to flush that all away.

It's time to start consolidating the trusted soldiers so they won't become cannon fodder."

"I've already begun that," Hedin said. "As it is, we will lose a lot of good fighters."

"We have a new advantage, thanks to Kane," Durga countered. "We have the skimmer and its weaponry."

Hedin managed a weak grin. "You realize that this is a betrayal of our oath to defend the Nagah and keep them from harm."

"What greater harm can there be than having our fangs plucked?" Durga asked. "We are on the path to becoming weak worms. We need to inform the citizenry that we have to use our venom against the hated mammals."

"And having the humans make the first strike is all the justification to launch a brand-new crusade," Hedin said. He sighed. "And what about the Cerberus people?"

"They are enemies of the Millennial Consortium. They will not mind going after a group of murderers with dreams of tyranny. They've clashed many times before," Durga said. "Have they been monitoring our communications?"

Hedin nodded. "The trusted ones have been broadcasting misinformation that will get them into position to make the moves we want them to."

"I'll get in touch with my men in the Fist. We'll need a good distraction tonight, and I want the security forces on full alert. This way the consortium will make their move," Durga replied.

"This will be worth it?" Hedin asked. "All of this?"

Durga looked at his desk. A glance to one side showed that the hatch was cracked ajar. His eyes narrowed, and he put his finger to his lips. Hedin's face showed a flash of panic, his hand dropping to the handgun on his hip, but Durga shook his head.

A gunshot in Durga's office would attract too much attention, especially with the presence of a military officer who was supposed to be acting independently of royal influence. Hedin grimaced, realizing that their secrecy had just made them even more vulnerable to a spy's attention. Durga frowned, accusation that Hedin's insistence on not being followed was wrong. Hedin condemned himself, guilt flooding his being. He moved his hand to the dagger in his belt, and Durga nodded.

DOMI HEARD DURGA GO SILENT and drew her cheek back from the hatch. The open door had been noticed, and she knew that it was time to go. Her slender, muscular limbs drew her along immediately, scurrying through the tunnels like an albino spider. Every handhold moved her along another few feet as she counted down the beat of moments before the two conspirators moved to investigate the cracked hatchway.

There was a creak of metal, and Domi twisted down a side tunnel, yanking her feet out of sight as a lamp blazed along the floor. She saw it, her multioptic picking up the illumination from Hedin's active night vision.

Domi kept herself tucked in tightly, not moving, holding her breath.

There were whispers down the way, but she couldn't make them out. She thought that perhaps she could have called Lakesh, but if the low voices of the conspirators reached her sharp ears, then there was no way that she could make a peep while they were present. The hatch remained open, the hushed conversation continuing unabated.

Domi checked the depression she'd squirmed into, and

while pipes extended through this passage, there was no room to squeeze along them. There was another passage on the other side. If Hedin were to crawl back this way, there was a chance that he'd notice her.

"Domi? Domi? Answer me," Lakesh called in her ear. The vibrations of her lover's voice rattled in her ear, carried by her jawbone.

Domi gave a guttural cough to respond, barely loud enough to be heard outside of her own head.

"Domi, just speak," Lakesh pleaded.

The glow of Hedin's night-vision illuminator disappeared and the whispered conversation of the conspirators faded. The hatch closed, and Domi twisted out into the repair tunnel. "I'm fine, but I didn't want anyone to hear me talking to you."

"I know," Lakesh said.

"They didn't want anyone to know what they were talking about, otherwise they wouldn't be skulking about like thieves," Domi said, reaching the next intersection before the hatch moved again. With a dive, she made it out of sight.

"Like you?" Lakesh asked.

"You already knew I was a shantytown rat when I first came to Cerberus," Domi answered. "These snakes are supposed to have a hint of nobility, right? So why is Durga talking about how he gave the consortium a chance to strike at the Nagah?"

"His plan is to incite his people into a war," Lakesh answered.

"So what can we do?" Domi asked. "We let the consortium attack, innocent people will die."

"No, we can't allow it, but Durga was too clever not to

mention exactly where the troops are, in case anyone was indeed listening," Lakesh grumbled.

"Then call Bry. The Nagah know that we're going to watch them back," Domi said. "So we have satellites in the skies looking down on this place."

"Right," Lakesh answered. "Just come back. I'm getting worried that someone else will find you. And then there's this distraction that Durga wants to arrange…"

"I'm on my way," Domi replied. "Just let Kane know. Okay?"

Chapter 15

Lakesh paced in the Cerberus exiles' suite, looking at Kane. Disappointment colored the scientist's face as he digested what Kane had just told him. "You let Durga get under your skin enough to give him an excuse to blame you for taking a shot at him?"

"We're looking at someone who has managed to get the consortium past his own country's defenses, and convinced them that he was an Annunaki himself," Kane answered. "Plus, I didn't think that it would matter."

"Everyone makes mistakes," Brigid spoke up in Kane's defense.

If anything, her support made Kane feel more uncomfortable, embarrassed that the feelings for her had compromised him. "We can save the lectures for after we deal with the consortium."

Lakesh nodded. "Correct, friend Kane. Besides, I've had my missteps in the past, as well."

Kane grimaced, remembering how he and Lakesh had argued when he first came to Cerberus. The scientist had been the chief archivist at Cobaltville, and it had been Lakesh's machinations that had branded Kane, Grant and Brigid as seditionists against the barons. Once they had been ostracized, they were hunted and marked for death.

The truth of Lakesh's manipulations had driven a rift between Kane and Lakesh that had taken years to heal. Only the fact that the society they had rebelled against was corrupt, ruled by unearthly monsters, even before the siren call of *Tiamat* had altered their fragile hybrid forms into their true nature, had forced the two men to respect each other in their shared struggle against the true manipulators of the world.

It was a small embarrassment that Kane found himself regretting a disappointment to Lakesh. That it involved a display of affection for Brigid was doubly damning.

Kane shoved his guilt aside, a headache pounding just behind his ears. "So does Bry have the coordinates of the consortium forces?"

"Yes, ape," Lakesh said, his grin spreading, needle sharp teeth showing behind his lips.

Kane blinked in disbelief, then realized that his pain was the signal that his perceptions were being altered. With a grimace, Kane reached out and grabbed Lakesh's cheek. Digging his fingers into the flesh, he felt it go soft, peeling away from reptilian skin. Under tatters of rubbery flesh, Enlil grinned at Kane.

"It's really too bad that the actions taken in one of these telepathic conferences don't occur in the real world. It would have been amusing when you awakened to see Lakesh's face bleeding all over the floor." The Annunaki chuckled.

"So, when did you get into telepathic communication?" Kane asked.

"I'd found a little trinket in one of my older caves. It allows for instantaneous conferencing that could reach around the globe if necessary," Enlil said. "Unfortunately, since my brothers and I are not on close terms after Lilitu's escapade, its utility is limited."

"If that were the case, snake face, how come I keep hearing the hum of it when you talk to Durga?" Kane asked.

Enlil raised an eyebrow, smirking in admiration. "Balam keeps speaking highly of your intellect. He spent a long time touching that mind of yours. This is an interesting little realm."

Kane folded his arms. "So, what are you in here for?"

Enlil grinned. "Seeing what you've learned so far."

Kane nodded. "Trying to probe my mind. But you just said your trinket was just for communication."

"That's true. But you never know. You might want to spoil things for Durga, especially if he seems to be acting against me," Enlil said. "He's not your friend."

"What gives you the delusion that I want to suddenly be your buddy?" Kane asked. "If either of you stabs each other in the back, it's all cake for me."

Enlil chuckled, walking around the memory image of Brigid Baptiste. His talons reached out to caress her, but Kane snatched Enlil's wrist. Kane dispersed his memory of Brigid, fading her into nonexistence.

"See? Even when you're not saying a word, you betray your deepest concerns and wishes," Enlil gloated. "Just the thought of me touching your beloved little archivist spurs you to physical violence. This kind of information is worth its weight in gold."

"Thoughts don't weigh a thing," Kane corrected.

Enlil shook his head. "A figure of speech, smart man."

"As if you didn't know in the first place," Kane muttered. "As if it's some big secret that Baptiste and I have feelings for each other."

"Your discomfort with those feelings makes you vulnerable to manipulation," Enlil said. "How many times have you undertaken perilous odds to ensure her safety?"

Kane remained silent.

"So, what were you talking about? The consortium in the area?" Enlil asked.

"You tell me Mr. Telepathy," Kane answered.

"Well, I do remember you asking if Bry had their coordinates," Enlil mused. "Which means…"

"Which means Bry's using our satellites to look for the consortium in the Nagah's back yard. You know, the others are going to wonder why I'm sitting there drooling," Kane warned.

Enlil laughed. "Good. Maybe your allies could stand to consider you mentally unstable. After all, how sane can you really be if you're attempting to usurp the very being who created your race?"

"Pretty damned sane, because you haven't proved you're responsible to run your own species," Kane said. "So, I'm afraid I'll have to ask you to cease and desist and retire to the nearest available parallel dimension."

"Oh…are *you* a god?" Enlil asked.

Kane smiled. "Remember our first dustup on *Tiamat*. I was the one who walked away from that fight. Your ass ended up at the bottom of a pyramid. I don't know if that makes me a god per se, but if I can kick your ass, I'm pretty sure that I can tell you to get the fuck out of my universe."

Enlil sneered. "Why are you insisting on being so difficult, Kane? Just relax your mind and let me see what Durga's up to."

"Do your own chores, snake face," Kane growled.

Enlil's grimace was accompanied by a flash of his eyes.

Kane tensed at the sight. Suddenly, a massive tendril, like the point of a sharpened log, burst from the floor, rocketing toward Kane's heart. The Cerberus warrior lunged, leaping out of the path of the spearing limb, feeling it rush like a freight train past him.

In the moment of reprise as the lethal point tried to slow itself and turn back toward Kane, he could see that Enlil's face was contorted with effort.

"What's wrong, Enlil? Take too much energy to try to kill me with your superior—"

The trunk of the tentacle flexed off to Kane's right, and he spun, hands rising. The log-thick point rushed up, but Kane braced himself, grabbing the tip. The impact made his shoulders feel as if they would pop out of their joints, but he knew that the battleground he was on was entirely in his mind.

Though the lethal barb shoving against Kane was a product of a psychic assault, the death it would bring was very real. The "physical" pain he endured was an indication of the strain that Kane felt as he fought off Enlil's lethal effort. The point pushed, but the muscles in Kane's arms rippled. He could feel the sweat pouring down his face.

Teeth gritted, Kane tried to shove the deadly spear tip away from his heart. If the shaft penetrated Kane's chest in this war of the wills, then his heart would be stopped. He could only imagine how things were going in the real world with his body.

"No more smart…uh…comments, Kane?" Enlil asked.

"Trying to…come up…with a…phallic joke," Kane replied, grunting. "Over…compensating?"

"You'll tire," Enlil growled, his eyes blazing, growing brighter the harder the deadly tentacle tried to plunge into Kane's heart. "And once you weaken…"

Another pair of hands appeared out of nowhere. Kane recognized their deep chocolate hue. To his right, Brigid threw her shoulder against the point. She glanced at him.

"C'mon, Kane, just breathe for me," she said.

The tentacle writhed, its trunk splintering, fissures ripping along its sides. It continued to push, but instead of Kane weakening, Enlil seemed to be fading. The Annunaki's lips moved, a string of curses issuing under his breath. The tendril disappeared, and Kane felt a pair of strong hands compressing his chest, someone else's lips on his.

"I said breathe, Kane!" Brigid said, rising from exhaling.

"He's waking up!" Domi exclaimed.

"Grant, get off my chest," Kane growled.

"You stopped breathing, asshole. We were giving you CPR," Grant complained, leaning back.

Kane rubbed his sore breastbone. "Stopped breathing?"

"It looked like you were suffering a seizure at first, and then your breath stopped and your pulse faded," Lakesh explained. "What happened?"

Kane sat up. "Enlil. And it's confirmed—he has a means of psychic communication with Durga, but whatever it is, it's fairly limited."

"It almost killed you," Brigid said. "Fairly limited?"

"He was putting as much strength into killing me over our telepathic link as my body was putting into fighting it off," Kane answered. "The moment you two pitched in to save my life, my psyche felt it, and the added strength helped me shrug it off."

Kane took a few deep breaths, recovering his strength. His breastbone felt as if he had been punched in the heart by Grant, but given the recent chest compressions, that impression wasn't far from wrong. He licked his lips, tasting Brigid for a moment, cursing that he hadn't been conscious to enjoy the moment. "Enlil is curious about what we know about Durga. That's where his main limitation comes in."

"He couldn't read your mind," Lakesh concluded. "So, he could be talking to Durga, but not aware that Durga has other ploys."

"Correct," Kane said. "Which keys in to why Enlil didn't know about the consortium's presence until he heard me talking about it."

"What did he hear?" Brigid asked, watching him warily.

Domi handed him a glass of water and Kane drained it. The cooling liquid made him feel a little better. "When he initiated the psychic contact, I was asking if Bry had the coordinates of the consortium forces."

Lakesh tilted his head. "We were talking about our mistakes. You rubbed your eyes, and then immediately collapsed in a seizure."

Kane frowned. "Immediately? I'd only just felt the headache when Enlil started speaking."

"How long did his psychic attack seem to last?" Brigid inquired.

Kane frowned. "Call it two minutes before you two assisted me."

Grant nodded. "You'd begun struggling, and after about the same amount of time, you stopped breathing. We took your pulse and began CPR."

"And how long was Enlil's conversation with you?" Brigid asked.

"Three or four minutes," Kane said, calculating. "So the telepathic interaction could only seem, to an outside observer, like it was only occurring in a moment."

Brigid nodded. "Which is why you'd only heard a snippet of a whisper. You could sense the communication, but it moved at literally the speed of thought."

"So, Balam's mucking around, talking to me mind to mind, did leave me sensitive to very near psychic phenomena, but Enlil's communicator worked like a speed dump," Kane mused. "When I caught the conversation, I heard the whole thing, but it was put on extreme fast forward so I couldn't understand it."

Grant helped Kane to his feet. The ex-Magistrate's legs felt rubbery, but his heart didn't seem under undo strain, despite the heart-attack-like reaction his body suffered at Enlil's psychic assassination attempt.

"What's to keep Enlil from trying to stop your heart again?" Domi asked.

"From the look on his face, he was feeling nearly the same shit he was putting me through," Kane answered. "Another attempt might not work and could backfire on him. Enlil hates my guts, but not enough to burn up his body in the effort."

"Sit down and let me get a listen to your heart," Brigid ordered. "You were as close to dead as you can get. I want to make certain that nothing's weakened."

Kane was about to protest, but the worry in Brigid's eyes cut through to him. "Good idea. I wouldn't want to suffer a coronary in the middle of kicking the consortium's ass. Oh, before I forget, did Bry find those assholes?"

"The satellite picked them up on infrared," Lakesh said. "We have the coordinates."

"You two stay here," Grant offered. "The rest of us will take this to the queen. She's allowed me to have an audience with her whenever I want."

Kane smirked.

"What?" Grant asked.

"Shizuka's going to be jealous of your new girlfriend," Kane chided.

Grant's eyes narrowed. "The queen appreciates the man who personally saved her life. And you should thank me. I was going to do the chest compressions *and* the mouth-to-mouth all by myself."

Grant shook his head and marshaled Lakesh and Domi out of the suite. Kane started to peel out of his shirt when Fargo cleared his throat.

Kane glared at the archaeologist.

"Don't stop on my account," Fargo replied.

Kane was about to take action when Brigid grabbed Fargo by the collar of his shirt. She shoved him through the door, then slammed it shut.

Kane sat down on a sofa, doffing his shirt. When he set the top down on the cushion beside him, he saw that Brigid was going through her gear bag, pulling out a stethoscope. A smile crossed his lips. "You know, I make a lousy patient."

Brigid looked at him. "Just don't talk during the examination."

Kane nodded. "Right."

Brigid cupped his chin, then planted a chaste kiss on his lips. "That's for being jealous over me. Just don't get any ideas that we have to paw each other like we're in heat."

"Miles to go before we sleep," Kane replied. He added in a softer tone, "Together."

Brigid smiled, winking at Kane's addition to the poetic phrase. She pressed the stethoscope to his heart, and Kane took a deep breath, closing his eyes.

THE QUEEN LOOKED AT GRANT, then back at the map coordinates that Lakesh had marked.

"I wish that we had the ability to print out the satellite imagery," Lakesh said. "But we've never seen the need for that kind of communications setup in the field."

"That's perfectly fine," Yun replied. "You've given us both the location and estimated troop counts in each case. Durga would have wanted more proof, but I have no cause for disbelief."

"But Durga seems to have control over the military, doesn't he?" Grant asked.

"Durga has his own personal guard and expeditionary force, but the bulk of the Nagah military is kept deliberately away from being under the control of any one official," the queen responded. "I'll present this to our advisory council, and we'll mobilize a preemptive strike against the forces massed on our frontier."

Grant nodded. "I wish that our Mantas had some firepower or transportation capability."

"Fortunately, our air force has no such limitations," Yun replied. "Though, if they are aware of our air-assault capability, we should engage in a more stealthy approach."

Grant smiled. "We'll pitch in with that."

Domi nodded. "It's been a little too quiet for my tastes."

Lakesh lowered his head as if to look at the map, but Grant could tell that he was restraining an incredulous reaction to Domi's statement. She'd barely escaped being murdered by conspirators who'd detected her presence. Still, Grant sympathized with her. Domi was a woman of action, and the menace of the consortium would provide her with plenty of that.

Kane and Brigid were escorted through the queen's chamber door by two of Yun's guardsmen.

"Apologies for being late," Brigid said. "Kane had a psychic incident with Enlil."

Yun looked up, meeting Kane's eyes. "Is this true?"

"Yes," Kane answered. "Apparently Enlil is not aware of the presence of the consortium, but according to Fargo, the consortium did have the support of an Annunaki overlord who provided them with a route through your territory that avoided detection by your military."

"Yes, Lakesh and Grant informed me of this," Yun replied. "However, if it were an Annunaki overlord, he would have to have his own telepathic powers to plot a course through our defenses."

Kane took a deep breath, looking around the room. "Enlil's psi-mutie powers don't work that way. At least in terms of mind reading."

"Whatever device Enlil used to project his thoughts is primarily for communication. He tried to kill Kane, but the psionic feedback was strong enough to cause Enlil physical distress in the attempt," Brigid added. "I have a theory that delving into the memories of a human requires similar mental effort."

"Enlil's amplifier wouldn't be able to pick up more than surface thoughts, not deep-down knowledge," Yun agreed. "Not without causing mental harm to whoever he scanned. It would not be a subtle effort, especially since these projections are at range."

"Chances are Enlil isn't within a thousand miles of the Nagah's city," Kane replied. "As to caring about whether his mind-probe victims were harmed by the attempt, I doubt it.

He's only seeking to do this stealthily. In fact, Enlil appealed to my suspicions of your son."

Yun's eyes narrowed, her lips pursing at Kane's statement.

"My apologies, Your Highness," Kane said.

Yun managed a lopsided smile. "I would not delude myself that the heroes of Cerberus would not notice a few discrepancies in my son's behavior. I always hoped that he would prove to be the noblest of kings, living up to his father's image."

"I take it he has not?" Lakesh offered.

"Far from it," Yun replied. "This will be one of his backward ploys. Despite the rules separating government and the military, Durga is one of the few who has the knowledge to have delivered this menace to our doorstep. And once they make the first move, he will be able to rally the Nagah nation into bloody conflict against the consortium."

"And since the consortium has operations around the world, that means going all over the planet, and fighting a whole lot of humans," Grant grumbled.

"It has been his goal," Yun said. "He is a bitter man. He was a bitter boy, as well."

"Our condolences," Lakesh offered.

"Thank you," Yun said. "I would, however, prefer to keep this betrayal secret. There's no telling who my son has contacts with inside the military."

Kane nodded. "Which is why I would like to launch our preemptive strike right now. Domi, I know you'd love a shot at the consortium, but I need you and Lakesh here to deal with the insurgent operation Durga's planned."

"He's betrayed us to the humans and has organized a cult of Enlil worshipers to revolt against us?" Yun asked. "If one attack fails to inspire martial law, the other will surely succeed. I have birthed a monster."

"I'm good at taking out snakes," the albino woman said. "And Lakesh has given me the name of the military officer who's in charge of the crazies. Give me the go-ahead, and I'll do what I do."

Yun nodded to Domi. "If you could take the traitor alive, I would appreciate it."

Domi smiled. "He'll be able to answer questions."

"I'll request that Lakesh stay here in my chambers. He will help explain the situation to General Kimerra with me," Yun replied. "When that is over, I'll call an emergency council meeting."

"Good," Kane said. "That will give the three of us time to put the consortium's forces off balance."

Yun smiled to the Cerberus warriors. "I pity the millennialists and their pawns. May Enki smile upon your efforts."

Kane and his allies left the queen's chambers. It was time to go to war.

Chapter 16

The radio on Durga's desk crackled, distracting the Nagah prince from the daily paperwork of running his part of the Nagah royal government. Even as he schemed and plotted to overthrow the old regime and install himself as a god and to reforge his race into a crusading force that would scour the globe of the Annunaki's taint and to subjugate humanity, the drudgery of everyday life still burdened him.

Durga picked it up, and heard a voice he hadn't expected over the airwaves.

"Durga," Enlil rasped on the other end.

"No telepathic conference?" Durga mocked.

Enlil's frustration was evident in his tone. "Shut your fool mouth. The more we converse, the more likely that the Cerberus folk will hear us."

"No, really, what's wrong, Enlil?" Durga asked, trying to sound concerned.

"I tried to deal with the human, Kane," Enlil admitted. "Let's just say that my telepathic potential enhancer is no longer operable. Are you aware of the consortium forces camped near the hangar entrances to your subterranean city?"

"What!" Durga exclaimed. Fortunately, he was as surprised by Enlil's knowledge as he would have been at the presence of the human army. Durga swiftly lowered his voice, hovering over the radio. "The consortium, here?"

"It looks as if they have a second crack at you. I conferred with my personal contacts within the organization, and they claim that they are receiving information from one of my kind," Enlil told him. "There is a 450-strong force, armed with rockets, light artillery and grenades ready to breach your lair."

"Blood of my father," Durga cursed. "Can you assist? I have my own rebels poised to engage in activity tonight."

"I suggest you call them off and concentrate your energies on dealing with the consortium. They are not known for their gentle touch when thwarted," Enlil offered. "As for any assistance I can provide, all I can do is inform. Even with the speed of my few remaining skimmers, I will not be able to engage them before they are due to strike at dawn. Besides, how would you be able to explain my intercedence on the behalf of the Nagah?"

"The Fist of Enlil is to take over our city in your name. You are claiming your rightful place by dispelling the human rabble," Durga replied.

"You have a contingency for everything," Enlil complimented him. "You've lived so long among the fallible that you are prepared for disaster at every turn. I wish that I was so accustomed to dealing with failure that I had such foresight."

Durga smiled at Enlil's backhanded compliment. "Such is the burden of perfection, sire."

There was a grumble on the other end as the sarcasm struck Enlil. "I have to disconnect. The enemy may be listening."

Durga shut off the radio with a chuckle. That last barb had bitten the Annunaki overlord hard. He wished that he could get into instant communication with Hedin, but his self-imposed discipline of operational security meant that such blatant displays were forbidden. Even the encrypted radio communications between Enlil and Durga, as had been done before Enlil had discovered his telepathic projector, had to be kept at a minimum to foil eavesdroppers.

He contemplated his options, but kept calm.

There were too many things that could go wrong. Certainly, the Cerberus warriors had the information with which to interfere with the consortium, but thanks to his taciturn conference with Hedin, if they had been spying on him, they wouldn't have known of the Fist of Enlil's exact plans. Durga had hoped to keep what little the humans knew to a minimum by discussing with Hedin in Hindi, but with the addition of Lakesh to their expedition, that layer of secrecy was penetrated.

The two irons Durga had in the fire were now hot enough to strike, and yet they depended on the ability and the trustworthiness of the Cerberus envoys. All of the information that Durga had gathered on them told him that they would possibly be able to derail everything.

Durga's intercom beeped again. It was his mother's line. "What is it?"

"I am summoning the advisory council for an emergency meeting," the queen informed him. "Our allies from Cerberus have warned us of an impending threat."

Durga nodded. "I'm on my way."

The situation was straining the tapestry Durga had woven, but there were a few points of slack that still allowed the Nagah prince a shot at victory. The first was that the very presence of the human assault force would drive the Nagah to want to strike back against the Millennial Consortium. The battle's outcome would be far different, but it would still provide the provocation for a global war of extermination against the millennialists. The second was that even a failed assassination attempt would give the cobra folk a reason to distrust other citizens who opposed efforts to secure the safety of their people.

Enlil had mocked preparation for failure, but Durga's web of deceit was well strung so that even if threads were torn, others would take up the slack.

Durga went to meet with his mother and the emergency council. He pitied their feeble efforts to bring about a new golden age. Blood would be shed, and after this meeting, he was certain that the son of a dead god and a living queen would evolve into a blood-drenched, torn-eyed crusader.

All it would take would be the death of that queen.

"ONE HUNDRED AND FIFTY to one odds," Brigid Baptiste spoke up as she, Kane and Grant stalked through the Kashmir forest toward the Millennial Consortium. "I know we make it a habit to butt heads with gods on a daily basis, but unless you have a good plan, we're not going to do much."

"Don't worry, Baptiste," Kane answered. "I know I'm not a one-man army."

Brigid looked at Grant, but the big man shrugged. "Don't look at me."

"Says the man who once literally tackled a Deathbird and won," Brigid said.

"And they don't have attack helicopters," Grant added with a grin.

Brigid sighed. "You know, Kane, my statement was an invitation to be informed of your brilliant stratagem that will make the odds equal."

Kane shook his head. "There's no way to even things up

against the consortium's force. We can go toe-to-toe with beings like Maccan and Enlil because, even if they have incredible power, they are solitary individuals for the most part. As such, we can outthink them by working outside their usual strategies and perceptions."

Kane took out a map and pointed out a discrepancy in troop strength at some of the consortium's positions. "Artillery units. Three of them."

"They'll be used to provide both cover for the initial charge and to literally tear open the hangar," Grant added.

"So their assault plan hinges on the power of those heavy guns," Brigid said. "We take them out, and they'll be thrown off their game."

"Looks and tactical acumen," Grant stated. He glanced at Kane. "A lady like that doesn't come along every day. Oughta marry her."

Kane's face tightened, but he ignored Grant's crack, much to Brigid's obvious relief. He handed out Copperhead submachine guns with grenade launchers attached to their muzzles. He also gave his two partners a trio of rifle grenades that would snap onto the end of the barrels. "The plan's simple. Fire your rounds at the ammunition stores at each of the artillery sites, then we fade into the jungle. The stacks of shells and powder should be large enough for even you to hit from three hundred yards, Baptiste."

"That's the range of these things with the grenades," Brigid said. "But with the density of the trees, I don't think we'll have the luxury of being that far back."

"No, but the closer you get, the more likely you are to be hit by your own shrapnel. And if the detonating ammunition doesn't get you, then responding patrols of consortium troops will," Kane emphasized. "I'm giving you three shots because there's a possibility that we could miss, and we could end up having to face down an overly aggressive response team."

Brigid nodded. "Shoot, and don't stick around."

"No heroics, Baptiste," Kane admonished.

"Why can't you just tell the lady to be careful?" Grant asked him.

Kane shrugged. "I've got an image to maintain."

"Well, it's an image the whole damned world can see through," Grant complained. "I know you two keep telling yourselves that there's a time and a place for everything, but stop putting on a charade as if you don't care. I'm a pretty damned patient man…"

Grant paused as both Kane and Brigid snorted, trying to contain laughter at that comment. He glared at them, giving the two people the hairiest eyeball he could manage. He continued, "I'm a patient man, and I can damned well understand not throwing it all to the wind to form the beast with two backs. I can respect that. But be honest with your friends and with each other, okay? Sexual tension is only interesting for so long, especially with Kane turning down some truly hot stuff like Erica, Hera and Fand in the past few months."

Kane and Brigid shared a glance.

"Plus, it's not only forcing us to ignore the elephant in the room, but it's also an insult to me and Shizuka and Domi and Lakesh that a working partnership and a healthy adult relationship can't be maintained by two people who have proved themselves equals for the past five years," Grant explained. "That's how Enlil ended up in your head, nearly killing your dumb ass, Kane. You were so distracted by Lakesh chewing you out, and all because of a flash of jealousy for Brigid…"

Kane whirled in reaction to some threat, and Grant fell

silent, recognizing his friend's point man instinct. The big man grimaced, silently going through a regimen of self-reproach over allowing himself to get caught up in a rant that had obviously been held at bay for months. The trio slipped into the shadow of a large, thick tree. Through the forest canopy, they were able to hear the hum of an engine.

"Another skimmer," Brigid whispered. "It's an unmistakable sound."

"At least it wasn't a patrol stumbling upon my relationship guru lecture," Grant sighed with relief. "Unless those ships have super hearing…"

"Enlil told me that he didn't have any personal assets within a thousand miles of here," Kane grumbled. "That proves a lie."

"Not necessarily. It could be another of the surviving Annunaki," Brigid suggested.

"Either way, I'm going to have to thank him for the divine intervention," Kane replied. He slid his multioptic visor into place.

Grant and Brigid followed suit. Whereas the standard Annunaki skimmer was a gleaming, smooth-skinned ovoid, this particular craft looked more as if it had been thrown together with random patches of metal and fiberglass. On one large fiberglass panel facing the trio, was the stylized symbol of a featureless man. The blank-faced figure held a cornucopia horn in one hand and a sword in the other.

The Millennial Consortium obviously had managed to salvage an Annunaki drop ship. Unlike the cosmetically scarred craft that the insurgent Nagah tried to steal from Durga, this one had actually suffered severe damage, but the technocrats of the consortium had the resources to return it to flying condition, albeit without the flawless metal hull typical of the original Annunaki design.

The multioptic visors were working at their maximum telescopic magnification to examine the hovering ship, and the trio looked long and hard to determine if the skimmer's weapons had been salvaged, as well.

If not, there was no doubt that the consortium would have been able to improvise a new armament package for the salvaged ship. Its presence was obviously to provide air support for the ground army's rush against the Nagah stronghold, just in case the children of Enki were able to mobilize a few of their Deathbirds.

The question that dominated the minds of the Cerberus trio was whether the salvaged skimmer was alone or were there other craft in the area?

Either way, Kane swiftly dismissed the idea of shooting the skimmer out of the sky.

"We'll give away our position, and without the element of surprise, we can't cripple their artillery column," Kane said. "But now we know that the enemy has its own eyes in the sky. If the sensors on those things are akin to what we have on our Deathbirds, the forward-looking infrared won't be able to see an adult human through a tree trunk. Even if a small part is poking out around the side, if you keep low and don't allow too much of your body to be exposed, you can be mistaken for native wildlife."

"The scanners were good for the area around Cobaltville because of the flat desert. Here in the forest, you'd need a ground patrol and seismic sensors for reliable observation," Grant added.

"If it weren't for the fact that the consortium's army hasn't been staging for long enough to set up those sensors, I wouldn't have put it past them," Brigid noted.

"The skimmer does make things a little more difficult," Kane suggested. "While it wouldn't be able to stop us from hitting the artillery sites, the skimmer will be able to respond and could catch one of us out in the open."

Grant looked at his Copperhead, then the trio of explosive shells he had for the stubby weapon. "I do have an idea."

Kane frowned. "You know I hate it when you want the enemy to get target practice on you. Besides, you're forgiven for the relationship advice."

Grant flipped Kane the finger. "I like living too much to let a skimmer beat me up over a pang of guilt."

"How will you make certain that the consortium ship will come after you?" Brigid asked.

"Simple. The two of you coordinate your attacks. The skimmer will be put on alert. After a sufficient pause, I pop my target and linger just enough to draw its attention," Grant said. "Maybe two magazines from the Copperhead will do the trick. Once he comes down on me, I plunk a rifle grenade into the skimmer."

For all of his brute strength and simple, down-to-earth manner, Grant was an intelligent man who had decades of experience with dangerous situations. Survival not suicide was his nature, and if he had calculated a means of destroying the consortium's airborne advantage, then it was quite likely he would succeed.

But like all the members of the Cerberus crew, Grant was human and fallible. One mistake, especially with an alert and hostile millennialist force looking for reprisal, and he could end up seriously injured or killed. Kane told him as much.

"You get bumped off, who's going to be our guiding mentor in the realm of healthy adult relationships?"

"Well, that's the other bit of genius to my little ploy," Grant said with a sigh. "You two shoot first, and then instead of retreating back to the Nagah's subterranean city, you come and back me up. I'll have my hands full dealing with the skimmer, in case you forgot."

"And here you thought he was being noble," Brigid grumbled.

"Sensei Grant, your student in gripe-fu may just be about to graduate," Kane commented.

Grant smiled. "As it should be when you train at the feet of the master. Come on, those artillery sites aren't going to blow themselves up."

PRINCESS HANNAH, ACCOMPANIED by her faithful bodyguard, swiftly entered the emergency advisory council chamber where other members of the royal family and the elected citizens of the parliament had assembled. Hannah always felt self-conscious about bringing Manticor along with her to parliamentary hearings, simply because average Nagah citizens had been entrusted by their government with the right to self-defense.

Hannah had a small dagger and a flat little pistol tucked into her belt sash, but Manticor's intimidating size and strength created a fearsome impression whenever she encountered one of the citizens. The queen, with her royal cordon, was a genuine treasure to the society, a keeper of ancient knowledge that she spent her lifetime passing on to others. The intricacies of royal intrigues had made a personal army a necessity for someone of her stature.

Hannah warranted a protector simply because she was betrothed to the last full-blooded prince descended from the royal lineage.

I'm only worth protecting because I'm sleeping with the future king, the princess thought bitterly.

At the same time, she relished Manticor's company. There was no denying the affection the two Nagah shared, but because of her position and the promise of her marriage to Durga, neither of them could act on it. As such, the development of their relationship was platonic. Manticor could be counted on for endless conversation. As well, except for a few uncomfortable moments when Hannah was bathing in the lagoon, he did not proffer her any special treatment that she didn't feel she warranted.

They could laugh with and at each other.

He kept her from feeling completely alienated or an object of pity because she was a creature on a pedestal. It was a sense of connection that she cherished.

She took her seat, Manticor sitting beside her. The bodyguard didn't tuck himself up against the conference table, leaving himself room to respond if danger arose. It was a chilling thought that Hannah allowed herself, especially in the wake of prior assaults by the Fist of Enlil.

The emergency advisory council meeting would be a juicy target for the troublemakers. However, the sight of Durga coming through the doors with his personal guard relaxed her.

Durga was a conniving bastard, she thought, *but he was not suicidal.*

With Durga present at the meeting, she felt a little safer.

She smiled to Manticor. "We're in the safest place in the whole of the city."

Manticor looked doubtful, but held his tongue.

Hannah slid her hand into his under the table, their fingers intertwining. Manticor's lips drew tight at the gentle contact between them.

"We have a chance," she whispered.

Manticor allowed himself to smile. "Wouldn't that be nice?"

Durga passed the pair. From his vantage point, he couldn't see their clasped hands, but there was a knowing smile on his lips. Hannah felt the tender moment evaporate.

A clatter in the hallway spurred Manticor to untangle his hand from Hannah's. He tensed, rising to his feet, hand falling to the grip of his pistol.

The torso of one of the queen's guardsmen, shorn off just before the ribs and trailing flames, smashed through the doors in the wake of an ASP blaster strike.

The emergency council rose as one, screams filling the air as the worshipers of Enlil followed the severed body into the meeting hall, their energy weapons spearing yellow tongues of blazing death.

Chapter 17

Domi gauged the approach she would take against Hedin. The Nagah colonel had two soldiers standing beside him, guarding him in his office. Though Domi was willing to cause crippling pain and permanent injury to the traitorous colonel, someone who had condemned himself by his own actions in leaving the cobra people vulnerable to the predatory consortium, the two soldiers could have been innocent, honest men simply doing their job.

With a lunge, she popped open the access hatch in Hedin's office, the heavy steel door smacking one of the soldiers across his knees. The snake man howled in surprise at the impact. Domi's swift form lunged through the opening, and she hooked both hands behind the bodyguard's neck. She folded her knees up to her chest, turning herself into a deadweight around the cobra soldier's neck, toppling him off balance. Before she hit the floor, she twisted herself, dragging her opponent's face to a jarring impact with the hard tiles.

A grunt of pain filled the air as the breath left the unconscious Nagah's lungs. He flopped limply as Domi spun out from under his settling form.

The other cobra soldier reacted with lightning speed, lunging at her with his fangs extending savagely. The venom-dripping barbs lashed the air close to Domi's shoulder, barely avoiding contact with her shadow suit. Domi jammed her elbow deep into the crook of the Nagah's neck, hitting the juncture of nerves that was vulnerable to such impacts in humans. Grant's lessons in martial arts versus anatomy apparently also applied to the snake-modified humanoids as the soldier froze with temporary pain. The momentary paralysis wouldn't last long, so Domi followed up the attack with a knee to the sternum.

Fetid breath exploded from the Nagah's lungs, and his legs folded beneath him. The collapse was swift, and Hedin's stunned protectors weren't going to be rising soon.

Domi turned in time to see the Nagah turncoat reach into his holster for his gun. The snake traitor's speed was as fast as his serpentine counterpart's, the draw coming so fast that the feral woman couldn't get out of the way of the 9 mm round that Hedin had launched. Fortunately, the shadow suit gave her enough ballistic protection that Domi would only suffer a fist-sized bruise covering her porcelain-white ribs. The savage side of her gave Hedin a silent thanks for removing all need for restraint by shooting. The gratitude, however, was verbalized in an animalistic snarl as she bounded over Hedin's desk. Though Domi wasn't much more than one hundred pounds, giving up another seventy-five to Colonel Hedin, it was the size of the fight in her, not her size in the fight that mattered. One hundred pounds of muscle and sinew plowed into Hedin, driving him hard against his bookcase.

Tomes jarred from their shelves, raining down on the heads and shoulders of the two combatants. Domi felt the corner of a heavy hardcover tear her scalp as it bashed into her head. Hedin grimaced, trying to peel the wiry combatant off him, but Domi ignored the rain of books and Hedin's struggles. She fired off knotty fists into Hedin's sides, her knees smashing against his inner thighs and groin. The Nagah conspirator took advantage of his natural weapons and flung his mouth wide open, intending to drive his fangs into Domi's neck.

The outlander whipped her forehead into Hedin's lower jaw, a head butt that bounded his skull off the bookcase for a second time. A statue toppled off the top of the piece of furniture, the bulk of its weight coming down hard on Hedin's shoulder before it finally drove Domi off him by thumping into her chest. Staggered by the sculpture's fall, the two combatants swayed for a moment, eyeing each other for an opening. Hedin coughed, having taken the worst of the punishment, though Domi's bone-white hair was tinged pink where the book had cut her scalp.

"That was you spying on Durga and me," Hedin snarled. He whistled as he spoke, blood and spittle drooling over his lower lip.

"Yup," Domi answered. One part of her wanted to say more, but her throat was constricted, her vocabulary reduced to monosyllabic responses by a rush of adrenaline. The feral woman's ruby-red eyes regarded the snake man with an almost glowing rage in the confines of the office. Hedin swallowed, grimacing. One of his fangs twitched and folded back up, but the other had been driven through his lip, snapped in two by the force of Domi's head butt.

Hedin grimaced, feeling the sharp point of his broken fang poking out of his jaw. He'd been reduced to a messy slur, but his curse was easily understandable. "Bitch."

Domi charged forward, her head and shoulder crashing into Hedin's stomach with enough force to lift the snake man. The bookcase, not meant for this kind of abuse, finally collapsed, shelves torn from their moorings as Hedin's and

Domi's weight combined to break at least two of them. Hedin howled as splinters gouged his back and the sandwiching force of the albino outlander and the immovable shelf broke ribs.

Hedin collapsed to his knees, curled over. He was breathless with pain, his golden eyes gleaming with fear of the savage little human who had manhandled his bodyguards and him as if they were garter snakes.

"I surrender," Hedin coughed, barely able to speak.

"Where did Durga want the Fist of Enlil to strike?" Domi grunted, struggling to ask the question despite her predilection for blunt, simplistic speech while her adrenaline raced.

"They…act when…emergency council meet to…consortium," Hedin grunted. Agony forced tears from his eyes, bile and blood pouring from his lips. "Guts…on fire."

Domi keyed her Commtact. "Moe! The council!"

"Beloved?" Lakesh asked on the other end. She heard him grunt in surprise. "Dear God!"

Domi whirled, knowing that she was needed at Lakesh's side. Hedin reached out, holding her wrist.

"Please…medical…"

Domi kicked Hedin in the side of the head, a crunching blow that might have been lethal. The albino warrior didn't care. The man she loved was under attack, and she didn't have time to waste dealing with the traitor who'd arranged to endanger him.

MANTICOR EXPLODED FROM HIS SEAT as the assassins entered the chamber. He quickly assessed them as they came through the door, his Pinidad pistol pinging 9 mm rounds off the leader's smart-metal armor. The first few, though wounded by grinding their way through royal guardsmen, were so well protected by their bullet-resistant second skins that they continued to battle on. The corridor stunk to high hell as bodies burned and shattered torsos exposed the stench of shredded internal organs.

Others in the fighting group swarmed in behind the armored Nagah, serpent men wielding conventional AK-47 assault rifles that hammered out their deadly beats. Though the citizens and the guardians of the royals had handguns, the swarm of murderers was at least twenty strong, lead by a formation of nearly invulnerable killers armed with body-roasting energy weapons.

He spotted one of the Annunaki-armed assassins raise his arm toward the queen's position, and Manticor opened fire. The bodyguard wanted to hit the turncoat cobra in the head, but the killer's head was protected by an armored shoulder, and what bits he could hit were only the flared hood between head and neck. The salvo of rapid-fire rounds distracted the killer, though, and Lakesh's .45 tore a grisly cavern through his head.

Unfortunately, the snake man's dying reflex unleashed a blast into the ceiling. Manticor grabbed Hannah and threw her under a table as chunks of masonry and mortar rained down from above. A rock smashed into Manticor's forearm, jarring the weapon from numbed fingers.

Hannah pulled a small Walther PPK, thumbing back the hammer. She saw that Manticor had coiled to go get his pistol, when she grabbed his wrist. "Where are you going?"

"Lost my gun," Manticor replied. "Stay down and don't shoot. That puny little popgun won't do anything."

A searing pain lashed across Manticor's legs, burning fire that numbed him even to the breaking of his nose on the tile floor. He could hear a screech of horror somewhere in the distance, through the maelstrom of trauma racing through his central nervous system. He reached up and found his hand clasped tightly in Hannah's.

The crazy girl was still shooting despite his warning not to, brass flying from the breech of her tiny PPK. Her teeth were gritted in quiet fury.

"Manticor! Manny, hold on!" Hannah screeched. She sounded as if she were yelling through a door, despite the fact that she was kneeling right next to him.

Her pistol locked empty and she hurled it. With a lithe leap, she grabbed at Manticor's fallen Pinidad and rolled over, blazing away at one of the unarmored cultists, perforating a line of bloody blossoms on the attacker's chest from sternum to forehead.

Manticor sighed. "My girl can take care of herself...."

"Manny, no! Don't pass out!" Hannah screamed at him.

She clutched his hand tightly, and Manticor hung on. As always, she was his anchor, but this time, she was keeping him from slipping into the void of oblivion.

MOHANDAS LAKESH SINGH WAS NOT a hardened warrior, despite the dangers he'd faced in the war against the forces that struggled to pry humanity's destiny out of its own hands. When the corpse of the energy-blasted royal guardsman hurtled through the meeting room's doors, Lakesh didn't have the instincts or reflexes to pull his sidearm from its spot in his holster. However, the recovery of his youth had restored his courage and strength of will and he didn't give in to blind panic.

"Dear God!" Lakesh exclaimed as the Fist of Enlil cultists, some of them bleeding where their smart-metal armor had been pierced by guardsman fire, poured into the emergency council's chamber.

"For the true creator!" one snake man bellowed, swinging his ASP forearm blaster toward the queen. Lakesh pulled out the Detonics as fast as he could, but he knew that his draw would not be fast enough to protect Matron Yun from the incinerating energy launched by the assassin. He thumbed back the hammer, cursing his slowness, wishing he'd spent more time training with firearms.

The Nagah who would assassinate the queen found himself jerking as 9 mm bullets pinged off his armor. Manticor was firing half the magazine of his Pinidad into the center of the killer's torso. Sparks flashed on the skin-conforming metal. Lakesh had seen Nephilim ignore glancing strikes by rifles, and the only sidearm that had proved effective against the alien alloy was the Sin Eater with its extraheavy 240-grain slugs. Considering that Lakesh had seen Kane and Grant cripple Deathbird assault helicopters with extended bursts from their Sin Eaters, the folding machine pistols were the equivalent of forearm-housed rifles.

Still, Manticor's opening salvo distracted the Enlil-following assassin from Matron Yun. Lakesh centered the front sight of his pistol on the insurgent snake man's face and pulled the trigger. The killer's unarmored head seemed to fold in on itself as the .45-caliber bullet smashed his nose and burrowed out the back of his skull. A spear of golden fire stabbed into the ceiling, blowing tiles, brick and mortar everywhere. A rain of debris poured from the roof, and Lakesh lurched toward Yun.

"Matron! Get down!" Lakesh bellowed. An assault rifle chattered down below as more conventionally armed insurgents joined the fray. He watched in horror as one of Yun's protectors threw himself into the line of fire. The Nagah's scale-armored chest exploded in crimson as heavy-caliber rounds smashed through his reptilian skin. Other guardsmen turned over the queen's table, tucking her down behind it. Lakesh fired more shots at the attackers, but suddenly he was surrounded by dozens of snake men and women, all of them armed. What had been an insurgent strike had devolved into a two-way gunfight as free citizens and bodyguards entered the fray.

The smart-armored insurgents continued to hurl their ASP bolts into the advisory council, each energy blast searing gaping holes in serpentine flesh.

Lakesh's Detonics was empty, the slide jammed back on a depleted magazine. He tore out the old clip and fumbled, looking for a new one. He'd started the fight with seven shots, and the only one that had made a difference was a shot at a distracted murderer whom Lakesh had aimed at for all of two seconds. The rest of his return fire was wild, and Lakesh wasn't certain that his bullets hadn't inadvertently struck his Nagah allies from behind as they scurried for cover.

A royal guardsman hauled Lakesh to the floor, tucking him next to Matron Yun. "Stay the hell down!"

Lakesh was about to thank the Nagah protector when the guardsman spasmed under the body-drilling impacts of a dozen rifle rounds. The snake man's blood exploded from his body, spraying Lakesh and painting him a grisly crimson.

The table rattled as the line of automatic fire raked across the tabletop. Lakesh crawled toward Yun, because even though the thick wood gave them some protection, it wouldn't last forever. He reached out for her hand.

"Come with me! We need to get out of here!" Lakesh urged.

Yun scooped up a handgun, a sneer of defiance on her face. "I shall never see the fall of my nation, for I will die in the final effort."

"Let's hold off that last-ditch stand by finding something harder to hide behind," Lakesh snapped.

Yun's lips drew tight. Lakesh remembered all the times Cerberus had been assaulted, the helplessness he felt when he witnessed the deaths of people who were his friends. That impotence was written on the queen's face, and as much as he could sympathize with her, her protection was a duty that he could not shirk. He lunged forward and tugged on her arm, pulling her toward a stone column.

The heavy wooden tabletop exploded in a spray of splinters just as Lakesh was about to push Yun behind the protective shaft of marble. Needle-sharp fragments prickled Lakesh all along his left side, and only natural reflex had kept one splinter from gouging out his eye. Yun grunted under the wave of wooden shrapnel generated by the ASP-bolt-shattered table. Lakesh reached out again, half blind, to continue to get Matron Yun to cover when a follow-up spray of rifle fire plucked several gouges along his arm.

Yun writhed under the hail of murderous lead, and Lakesh cried out, as if he could scare off the grim specter of death before it took Yun away.

Arm hanging limply, Lakesh's grief-filled cry failed in its task.

Matron Yun slumped against the stone column he was trying to hide her behind. Her blood smeared the white marble as she slid bonelessly to the floor.

Numbed, Lakesh turned to look at the renegade Nagah as they cheered at the fall of the queen. The pistol in Lakesh's right hand rose and he scowled, aiming at the murderers, even as they turned their attention to the interfering human among the ranks of their leadership. An ASP blaster glowed with its predischarge energy. The .45 barked, a spark flashing on the Enlil-follower's chest armor. The smart metal deflected the bullet, and the battered assassin seemed too punch drunk to be concerned by the impact.

Lakesh growled, knowing that he was going to die.

Suddenly, a blur of pink and black launched through the doorway. In the clarity that comes with heightened adrenaline from a near death experience, Lakesh's eyes locked on the hurtling form of Domi leaping on the blaster-armed assassin. Her scalp had been torn, blood turning her short spiky hair a flaming pink.

Domi's face was twisted in a rictus of rage as she rode the armored Nagah to the floor, holding on to a handle that was jammed into the back of his head. Lakesh couldn't imagine why a Nagah would have a handhold stuck in his skull, but as Domi twisted off the dead snake man's back, he recognized the pommel of Domi's fighting knife.

The feral woman left her blade lodged in the skull of the insurgent cobra, the pistol in her other hand blazing fire. Where Lakesh had been given a little bit of experience with the compact .45, Domi moved as if she were born with it as a part of her arm. At arm's length, she planted bullets in the face and throat of a second of the Nephilim-armored Nagah, killing the heavily armed assassin in a cloud of free-floating blood, muscle pulp and facial bones.

A more conventionally armed insurgent tried to follow the lithe, savage woman as she whirled like a tornado in the midst of the killers. The snake man opened fire, but Domi had already abandoned the air where his bullets went. Instead of killing a human, the turncoat cobra riddled the chest of one of his allies. As he tried to bring his assault rifle to bear on the albino woman, Domi lunged in, pushing her handgun as if she were a fencer and the .45 her sword. A blossom of fire lit up the rifleman's face from below, his heart cored by a fat slug flattened by the force of its passage through his breast-bone.

In the space of seconds, Lakesh watched the woman he loved slaughter four murderers with a speed and savage grace that took away his breath. The pistol in his hand was forgotten, and he didn't even realize that he stood as still as a statue until Domi disappeared behind the weapon's slide, her thighs wrapped around the neck of a fifth killer.

Lakesh lowered his gun as Domi's thighs scissored the hooded insurgent's head. An ugly crunch of neck bones filled the air, the punctuation mark on the murderous assault on the advisory council.

Nagah citizens, the survivors of the terrible attack, watched as Domi staggered to her feet, blood red eyes looking around the meeting hall. Except for the heaving of her lungs making her shoulders rise and fall, she looked as if she were carved from obsidian glass, thanks to the midnight-black hue of her shadow suit. Blood had seeped down her forehead and cheeks, turning her hair and face a shade of crimson only slightly less intense than the ruby fire burning in her eyes.

Silence reigned in the council chamber as the shell-shocked survivors held their breath and tried to determine whether the wild thing standing before them was finished with her task of bloodshed or if her rage was unabated.

"Domi," Lakesh whispered.

The woman's face weakened, her anger gone, replaced with concern as she saw Lakesh's arm and face soaked with blood. The scientist only just realized that he had to have looked as frightening as she did, then dismissed the thought. Domi was a force of nature that had just single-handedly exterminated an assassination squad. "Moe?"

Durga rose shakily from cover. His gun was empty, its slide locked back. Bullets had lacerated his shoulder. Lakesh struggled to his feet, only able to use one arm to assist his efforts to stand. He trotted down the stairs to join Domi who wrapped her arms around him, burying her face in his chest.

"You…saved us," Durga whispered. "Those maniacs could have killed all of us."

Lakesh could feel Domi trembling against him, hear her choking down a sob of worry over his bloodied condition. "The queen…shot…"

Durga's eyes widened. "Mother?"

"I tried…I failed," Lakesh murmured. He looked at the column, reddened with the lost queen's blood.

Durga whirled, then ran up to where Lakesh was looking. The prince cupped his mouth, eyes pained as he looked down on the bullet-ravaged corpse. For all the suspicions that Lakesh had possessed about the Nagah prince, he knew the cold truth that no son should have to see a parent violated by the horrors of gunfire.

First Garuda, now Yun. Though the losses were separated by decades, Lakesh could see that Durga was hit hard by the grisly demise of the queen. He almost felt ashamed that he was going to present the evidence that the prince was behind both the impending threat of the Millennial Consortium and had been the force that organized the Fist of Enlil. Lakesh tried to fight his shame aside, but the heartbreak in Durga's eyes was hard to beat.

"Are you okay?" Domi asked softly. "Moe?"

Lakesh looked down at her. Her ruby-red irises were matched by the swollen, tear irritated veins of the whites of her eyes. Tears left her cheeks glistening.

"Talk to me, please?" she asked.

"My arm hurts," Lakesh admitted reluctantly.

Domi looked to Durga. "You have to say something."

"His mother was just murdered," Lakesh replied, his voice cracking. The furrows cut in his forearm and bicep were reminders of his failure to protect the queen.

Domi pulled reluctantly away from him. "The prince, in association with Colonel Hedin, conspired to make this attack possible. The queen sent me to bring Hedin before this council!"

Shell-shocked, confused citizens looked at Domi.

"You fucking *ghouls!*" Durga cursed. "You're accusing me…"

Durga trembled with rage and Domi tensed. Lakesh felt a twinge of panic in his heart, seeing Domi put aside the vulnerable, compassionate child and allow the cold fury to return.

"It's true," General Kimerra spoke up. "The queen left these orders with me. We were called to respond to an attack by the humans of the Millennial Consortium. Already Kane, Brigid and Grant are out there trying to hamper the consortium's army, but we as a council have to agree to mobilize our forces!"

Durga glared at Kimerra, then glanced back to Lakesh and Domi. Lakesh had cast aside his fear, standing as backup to his diminutive lover.

"You hear this kind of paranoid ranting?" Durga asked, a sob cracking his voice. "My *mother* is lying in a pool of her own blood, and they want me arrested? They want the control to throw the lives of our soldiers away in an attack on a human army?"

"Come off it," Domi growled. "If Hedin can't confess, I'm sure he left behind enough notes to prove your ass is guilty!"

Durga hissed, fangs snapping down. "Quiet!"

The blast of a handgun into the air broke the tense tableau. All eyes turned to Hannah as she stood over the limp, legless form of Manticor. The smoking gun in her hand faded as the focus of attention as hard, angry eyes burned with seething fury.

"The queen has been murdered, and her son is guilty," Hannah hissed. She looked toward Manticor, the harsh rage flickering, replaced by a moment of hollow-souled sadness. Returning her attention to Durga, she aimed Manticor's pistol at the prince. "As the next in line of leadership, I demand justice. Destroy the consortium's army, hang Durga and his conspirators, and the failures from Cerberus will be made to pay for their fumbling ways!"

Durga, Lakesh and Domi all shared a frightened moment as the beautiful, vicious princess's compassion shattered like glass, leaving behind a gaping hole where reason used to rule.

Chapter 18

Kane had sneaked within fifty yards of the ammunition stockpiles for one of the consortium's artillery nests. A quartet of mortar tubes was aimed toward the Nagah hangars in the distance, stacks of fat shells resting in crates. The ex-Magistrate was aware that the millennialists could pump out those high-explosive rounds at the rate of five per minute per tube. While a combined total of twenty shells in a minute from one firebase didn't sound like much, each of the deadly mortar projectiles packed a pound of high explosives. With the added firepower of the other two artillery nests, the 81 mm and 120 mm tubes had the power to carve a swathe of destruction through even the heavily armored panels that protected the hangar.

Given the number of crates of ammunition, this particular firebase had the potential to sustain its rate of fire for close to half an hour. It wouldn't require more than thirty seconds to hammer the hangar entrances open with the rain of thunder. The remaining ammunition would target the depths of the hangar and alternate exits from the Nagah stronghold. With almost all exits to the outside world hammered shut by a wave of thunderbolts, the cobra folk wouldn't be able to fight back while hundreds of savage pirates, bandits and mercenaries poured into their midst.

Kane also realized the purpose of the salvaged, refitted

skimmers. The small flying saucers were able to slip through the wreckage of the hangars, able to hover within the confines of the building, providing vital air support. He'd seen and reported to Brigid and Grant, the presence of a second skimmer. This particular craft's armament was highly visible, the long barrels of .50-caliber machine guns bristling through a jury-rigged gunport. The twin Fifty was a menacing piece of ordnance that could chew through stone walls and armor plate as if they were soft clay. Against snake soldiers defending their home, the dual-mounted machine guns would be like a scythe to grain.

Nagah bloodshed would be horrendous if they could not find a way to eliminate the skimmers.

Kane conferred with the others over his Commtact. "Grant, when you bait your trap, I'll take up the slack on the second skimmer."

"That's if the consortium's pilots are stupid enough to commit both of their skimmers to chasing my ass down," Grant returned. "Besides, the range on those Fifties is measured in miles, well out of reach of our puny little grenade launchers."

"Puny?" Brigid asked. "Grenade launchers?"

"Only three hundred yards," Grant answered. "Even without the beam weaponry of a normal skimmer, the pilots could hang half a mile up laughing at us as they poured bullets down like rain."

"If they're both armed with Fifties," Kane offered. "We didn't see any guns on the first consortium skimmer."

Kane heard Grant sigh, getting ready to deliver another morale-destroying pronouncement when Lakesh's voice came over their Commtacts. "Friend Hannah, please. We did our best to save the queen."

Lakesh's words hit the Cerberus trio like a splash of ice water, chilling them all to the bone.

"Lakesh?" Kane asked. "What's wrong?"

"Punishing us for her death won't bring the queen back," Lakesh continued. He obviously was transmitting to Kane and the others without the knowledge of the Nagah. There was a tremor of fear in his voice.

"Hannah?" Grant asked. "I thought that Durga was the big plotter here?"

"Please, perhaps we can provide assistance to Manticor…" Lakesh began.

"Manticor's down," Brigid said. "And we could tell that Hannah had affection for him. Her pain must have driven her to distraction."

"Distraction?" Grant asked. "The snake bitch probably has Lakesh shitting in his pants and has the backing of the Nagah council to lynch him. That's not distraction, she's bug-fucking nuts!"

"Grant," Kane admonished. "Why can't things ever go simply?"

"Look out!" Lakesh shouted. "Durga's getting awa—"

There was the meaty sound of an impact, then silence from Lakesh's communicator.

"Fuck!" Grant snapped. "Did they just kill him?"

"You let Durga slip away, but you assholes can punch a peaceful, wounded scientist," Domi spoke up. "You dropped your Commtact, Moe."

Kane sighed with relief. Domi had taken over the running commentary to keep him and the others informed of their situation. At least Lakesh and Domi were on the same page with that strategy, and were resourceful enough to transmit their signals.

"So what do we do now?" Grant asked. "Maybe the consortium's attack would give us the chance to get Domi and Lakesh back."

Kane grimaced. "If Hannah and the Nagah weren't essentially good folk put into a shitty situation, I'd say let the damned snakes squirm. Lakesh and Domi are family, even if Lakesh and I don't particularly act like friends. But if we let the consortium go through with its assault, innocent people are going to die. And that's not how we work."

Grant grunted in disgust. "Shit can't ever be black and white."

"Baptiste, if you have your shot, you'd better take it," Kane said. "On three…"

There was the sudden sound of crashing foliage over the Commtact rather than Brigid's answer. Kane tensed, finger poised over the trigger of his grenade launcher. "Baptiste?"

"Kane!" Brigid growled through gritted teeth.

"Shit!" Grant cursed. "Light it up, Kane!"

In the distance, a grenade launcher thundered its deadly single shot.

Things were going to hell in a handbasket. Kane triggered the launcher on the end of his Copperhead, then took off to Brigid's aid. The concussion wave of the high-explosive grenade amid hundreds of rounds of artillery shells buffeted the ex-Magistrate as he sliced through the forest, praying that he wasn't too late for Brigid's sake.

THE MILLENNIALIST TUMBLED as Brigid pivoted out of his path, utilizing some of the empty-hand techniques she'd picked up from Kane and Grant over the years. The millennialist's arms were spread wide as he sought to capture her in a bear hug. The smelly, bearded man with the scars on his face caught the heel of Brigid's palm in the nose, cartilage and bone popping under the impact. Blood gushed from Nguyen's nostrils, his head snapping back in surprise.

Stunned but not deterred, the Vietnamese pirate lunged again, this time lashing out with a hard fist. Brigid sidestepped the punch, winding her arm around Nguyen's extended limb. An epithet exploded from the millennialist's lips as Brigid turned, using Nguyen's weight against him, her pivot dumping the man down a slope with a crash and snap of foliage.

"So much for the quiet way," Brigid muttered. Off in the distance, a thunderclap split the air. She whirled to see a fading pillar of fire roll skyward, the flames dying out as they ran out of fuel to burn.

Kane had already taken out one artillery site. Brigid was running behind the curve and she scurried to the top of the rise, retrieving the Copperhead that had been knocked from her hands in Nguyen's attack. Thirty feet down the slope, the scar-faced pirate chattered angrily in Vietnamese.

Her time to take out the second artillery site was running down, and she shouldered the Copperhead. The extra weight of the rifle grenade had thrown off the submachine gun's balance, and she adjusted her aim so that the shoulder-fired bomb would reach its target, not fall short. With an extra hard kick she was unaccustomed to, Brigid launched her grenade toward the ammunition stockpile. As the explosive arced toward the emplaced mortars, she saw the movement of men in the long grass and between tree trunks, thanks to her multioptic visor's night vision.

Brigid adjusted her aim, leveling the Copperhead at the advancing consortium mercenaries when her grenade dropped in among the mortar shells. A blinding flash forced Brigid to squint, her visor's light amplification blazing a bright neon green as it tried to process the fireball. A heartbeat later, a rush of air and thundering noise tackled the former archivist like a predatory cat, knocking her to the ground and beating her ears mercilessly. Flattened in the dirt, she saw flaming limbs and torsos tumbling in the air overhead. She realized that it had to have been the hired pirates who were manning the artillery site, their bodies torn asunder by proximity to the earth-shaking detonation.

Able to suck in a breath after being rattled by the shock wave, she blinked as the world returned to darkness. Brigid struggled to sit up, stunned by the force of the massive explosion. Her ears rang, and her head hurt like hell, but she'd survived the blast, while the men who had been summoned by her attacker were not so lucky.

Brigid struggled to her feet, and discovered that the concussion force had torn the Copperhead from her hands. She looked frantically around for it, knowing she didn't have more than a few moments to find it. If she couldn't get it, then she'd have to rely on her 9 mm pistol.

"Lose something, bitch?" Nguyen growled, holding the fallen Copperhead in his hands.

Brigid dived sideways as the muzzle flashed, a pair of 4.85 mm bullets glancing off her hip. She was thankful for the ballistic protection properties of the shadow suit, but knew that if she hadn't leaped for cover, the angle of attack on the Copperhead's rounds would have been sufficient to penetrate the high-tech protective polymers. Skidding in the thick brush, Brigid ripped her pistol out of its holster.

Nguyen cursed, sweeping the long grass and bushes with the remainder of the weapon's 35-round magazine, but the bullets passed over her prone form. The crackle of the weapon gave Brigid something to focus on, and she cranked off three shots at the millennialist pirate.

More curses salted the air, and Brigid emptied her slim little pistol. She wasn't hitting anything, but she was keeping the millennialist from transferring to another weapon and continuing his attempt to murder her. She bit her lip and dumped the empty magazine from the little handgun, stuffing home a fresh one. She hoped that her adversary didn't have anything heavier than a pistol of his own.

Something thumped into the grass off to her right, and Brigid's most powerful weapon, her mind, recognized the sound of a grenade landing. With a lunge, she tumbled down the slope where she'd thrown her attacker. Gravity and the lubricating qualities of wet grass and mud accelerated her away from the deadly radius of the grenade's shrapnel barely in time, bits of shrapnel poking into her shadow suit like needles, but stopping just at the skin.

It was as irritating as hell, but a lot better than those bits of notched wire slicing through her suit and churning through her internal organs. Her butt and legs had been peppered with the splinters of wire and grenade shell, boots too thick to be penetrated by the decelerating fragments. With a tumble, Brigid flopped into the mud bottom-first.

Nguyen scowled from his vantage point halfway up the slope, but Brigid had landed right in his line of sight. The Vietnamese pirate's handgun was a beast of a weapon that would probably knock a hole in Kane's old Magistrate armor, let alone her sleek shadow suit. She fired uphill at Nguyen, the first round plucking at the man's thigh. The pirate missed his first shot, as well, a beefy slug kicking up a gout of mud where it struck inches from Brigid's head. She pulled the trigger on the little 9 mm again, but in her dive to escape the grenade, the pistol had been bound up with long, tough grasses and clogged with mud. The trigger was spongy as the action froze.

Nguyen chuckled and thumbed back the hammer on his hand cannon. "Jammed?"

"Go ahead and gloat," Brigid snarled in defiance.

"I will." Nguyen laughed.

A bolt of black lunged into view, heaving Nguyen into the air. A bloody point of steel jutted through the pirate's chest, and finally the grim wraith behind him was recognizable.

Kane hurled the corpse aside, the throw wrenching his blade out of the corpse's back.

"No, motherfucker," Kane answered Nguyen's final boast. "You're never gloating again."

Kane slid down the slope in a controlled skid. He stopped to scoop up Brigid's fallen Copperhead. As he extended his hand to Brigid to help her up, Grant's voice was audible over their Commtacts.

"I'm pinned down by a patrol near my target!" he announced.

"We're on our way!" Kane called.

DURGA NEVER LOVED Hannah more in his life, and if he weren't fleeing to ensure his freedom, he'd have gone back and kissed her hard. As it was, he was positive that the next time she saw him, she'd do her best to drop all the fires of hell on him. Manticor looked in a bad way, and there was never any doubt about Hannah's affection for Matron Yun. In response, the princess had snapped in an emotional burnout of epic proportions.

Hannah's rage, directed at Lakesh, gave Durga the sliver of opportunity to escape.

That's right, Durga thought as he squirmed out of the utility tunnel access hatch. Forget the horror of your own mother sprayed all over the architecture.

A wave of nausea rocked him, and he remembered Enlil's taunting nightmare of watching Yun and Hannah pinioned on giant skewers. Their unnatural writhing on the stainless-steel spikes was the first solid mental image he had of their end. Before the telepathic conversation with the Annunaki overlord, he glossed over the end of their existence in his plotting.

Yun would have died of old age. Or her body would have been cleaned up, a serene expression settled onto her face after the coroner prepared her to be viewed by Durga. And Hannah? Maybe he could have ultimately persuaded her to see things his way, to accept that a strong Nagah nation needed to be forged by the fires of conflict with the two races most determined to render the cobra folk extinct—human and Annunaki. A cleansing war would safeguard the Nagah from further reprisals, and maybe, down the line, coexistence with the mammals could be reestablished.

There were hints that Hannah was starting to come around. Her rage at Lakesh and Domi's failure to stop the death of the queen was deep and genuine, a driving force that Durga had merely attempted to duplicate in the wake of his assassination of Garuda.

Maybe by the end of the day, Durga would have the opportunity to mend bridges with her. He'd grant her exalted standing in the new Nagah order, and even be so magnanimous that when he promoted her to second in command, he'd do everything in his power to return Manticor's legs, either through cybernetics or a reprogramming of the cobra baths to allow cellular regeneration.

It had been one of his dreams to utilize the nanomachine technology to do far more than turn humans to cobra beings. He wouldn't have resurrected Garuda, but the idea of being able to restore brave minions to full health despite horrific injuries would have the dual effect of increasing his people's affection for him and keeping his army of magnificent warriors in peak condition. Durga paused in a corridor, tempted to either return to his own office, where he would be surrounded by loyal guards, or to head to check on Hedin, his fellow conspirator.

What Domi had said, however, left him with the belief that the Nagah colonel wouldn't be in any shape to assist, even if Hedin could still breathe.

Durga froze as he turned into the hallway leading to his office. Fargo stood in the middle of the corridor, his coiled whip in one hand, his fat revolver clenched in his other fist. The millennialist archaeologist stood, his body bladed toward the Nagah renegade prince. The man had gone from bullied and harried innocent to ready for battle, a cruel smile carved into his face beneath hard, determined eyes.

"What the fuck do you want?" Durga asked.

"The assistance of the overlord who let us in the back door," Fargo replied. "The consortium could be good friends if you let them."

Durga flinched. Obviously if Lakesh and the others were aware of his betrayal of the Nagah to the consortium, then Fargo was in on the trick. "Who would really believe that?"

Fargo looked behind him nervously, then locked eyes with Durga. "I did. Twice. Once when they recruited me, and then when I said that I could redeem myself in their eyes."

Durga chuckled. "So you're not exactly the best spokesman to recruit me. Right now, Kane is softening up your friends, and I'm certain you were supposed to engage in sabotage within this city."

"I managed a few things, thanks to all the distraction you've been providing," Fargo answered. "The devices I've improvised can either assist you, or they could help the consortium."

"But not Kane and the others?" Durga inquired.

"Why should I help them?" Fargo asked. "They've threatened me enough."

"Which means when the Cerberus interlopers return, they'll want a piece of both of us," Durga stated. "Preferably the heart."

"You join me, I join you, it really doesn't matter," Fargo said. "I need help and so do you."

"And you would have an ally against the consortium," Durga added.

Fargo laughed. "The Millennial Consortium is a franchise, not a monolithic force. The board of directors engage in intrigues against themselves. I've got sponsors who still love me."

Durga looked behind him. This conversation was going on too long. "Then why?"

"I just need to know if you still have a grudge," Fargo answered.

Durga walked past Fargo, grabbing him by the bicep to drag him along toward his personal command center. "Chatting in the open is not a good idea at this time. As for the eye, fuck it. I've got two, and I can still see out of both of them. We're good."

Fargo breathed a sigh of relief as the pair entered Durga's

suite of offices. Nagah soldiers loyal to the prince were scurrying around, setting up barricades to repel angry factions looking for revenge against their leader. "So, how are we going to keep everyone from jumping down your back? I mean, you've got a small army, but so do they. And they've got the Cerberus people on their side."

"Propaganda is a powerful tool," Durga answered. He headed directly to his office. The sound of rifles and handguns being loaded clattered behind Fargo, sounding like the metallic rain that had preceded a prior massacre. Dread hung over Fargo.

"Propaganda, when you've been implicated in offing your mother?" Fargo asked.

Durga went to his desk and typed into his personal computer. The prince pulled up a voice modulation program, then inserted a microphone into a USB port. He hooked the computer to his intercom and typed in a control function on the keyboard.

"What's that?" Fargo asked, confused.

Durga smiled at his new partner, then spoke into the microphone.

"This is Enki, your god, returned to you. My children, your greatest trial is at hand as my brother's worshipers and the human race are striking at you from two angles."

Fargo swallowed, chilled by the thunder of an Annunaki overlord's voice reverberating over the intercom system. It was a convincing charade. He remained silent as Durga continued.

"Only my counsel, children, can save you from extinction!"

Chapter 19

The chatter and debate sparked by Hannah's assumption of leadership following the assassination of Matron Yun faded as the multitonal voice of an Annunaki overlord filled the air. "Only my counsel, children, can save you from extinction!"

Domi looked up from securing Lakesh's bandaged arm in a sling, her stomach turning at the sound of Enki's speech. "Moe, does that mean we're as fucked as I think we are?"

Lakesh glanced around the meeting room. Nagah citizen representatives choked back tears of relief and joy around them. Though pained and a little clammy from his flesh wounds and the beating he took from Hannah, all that discomfort faded as he analyzed the reactions of the cobra folk. "Crudely put, beloved, but yes. If it's Enlil posing as his brother, or if it's some other ploy of Durga to save his skin, we're going to have an uphill battle. This society has already been fractured by the events of the past few days. With the reverence of their creator guiding their actions, we'll be dealing with religious fanaticism."

"So, skeptics will be our buds," Domi concluded. "Never enough of them around to dispel a conspiracy theory."

"Or to confirm it," Lakesh added. He looked toward Hannah. Waves of doubt and confusion rippled through the assembled Nagah as the princess tended to the badly wounded Manticor. An ASP bolt had shorn his legs off above the knee, but the intense heat of the energy had cauterized the stumps so that Manticor wasn't losing blood.

As it was, the crippled bodyguard looked delirious. Though the cobra folk didn't sweat, the luster of his scales was dulled, and Manticor's jaw hung slackly. Hannah, torn between Enki's speech and her wounded bodyguard, looked to be in enough doubt that Lakesh thought she'd be receptive to what he had to say. Her authority was their only hope to quell the confusion wrought by the return of an overlord.

It would be a gamble, however. Blame for the death of the queen hung on Lakesh, despite his best efforts. The added injury of Manticor had strained Hannah's compassion to the breaking point, so much so that she'd waved a gun in Lakesh's face, then struck him so hard it knocked off the external plate of his Commtact.

"Domi, help me carry Manticor," Lakesh said.

"But you've only got one arm," Domi said.

Lakesh looked at his wounded limb as it hung in the sling. Deep furrows where bullets had scored his forearm and bicep left it in paralyzing pain, and if he exerted too much strain on it, he was certain to bleed through the bandages. It was worth it, though, if he gave Kane and the others a safe haven when they returned from dealing with the Annunaki. "I've got a healthy arm yet. Just help me."

Domi nodded, and the two people raced to the princess and her wounded protector. Lakesh hooked his uninjured arm under Manticor's, letting the crippled Nagah's weight rest on his shoulders and legs. Domi's wiry, compact strength slipped under Manticor's other side, and despite her diminutive size, she took most of the burden.

Hannah's eyes were a turmoil of anger and hesitation. She

kept her handgun aimed at the floor this time. Lakesh didn't want a repeat of the pistol-whipping he'd received before.

"What are you doing?" she asked. Her voice was as taut as a garrote.

"We're getting Manticor someplace comfortable so I can stabilize his condition," Lakesh said. "I'm not a doctor, but even I can tell that he's going into shock from the loss of his legs. He might not be losing blood, but the trauma of getting limbs burned off could be too much of a strain on him, no matter how conditioned he is. The fact that he's easily as strong as Grant is probably the only reason Manticor's still alive."

Manticor nodded groggily, a weak smile on his lips. When he spoke, it was as if he were in a drunken stupor. "Exercise… prayers…vitamins…"

Lakesh looked back to Hannah. "Listen to his voice. He's not going to make it if you insist on reining in these people. He needs attention now."

Domi's ruby eyes locked with Hannah's. "They already forgot you. Enki, or whoever, has their attention now. Help us."

Hannah fired a shot into the ceiling. "Citizens! Citizens, we cannot afford this distraction! The enemies are at our door!"

"Silence, blasphemer!" came the challenge from across the meeting hall.

Hannah lowered her gun, her gaze falling on Manticor as he hung between Domi and Lakesh. Lakesh shifted as he secured his grip on Manticor. "Dearest Hannah, please. Together we can restore sanity, but his life is at stake."

Hannah whirled in frustration, tossing aside a chair that was between Manticor and the door. Nagah danced out of the path of the tumbling furniture as she led the way to the door. "Damn you, worms! Let the wounded through!"

Snake men and cobra women looked at the princess with widened eyes. Her seething rage was an emotional whip, scattering them so that Lakesh and Domi could carry Manticor out of the abattoir. Lakesh grimaced, not because of the weight of his wounded ally, but because he recognized the angered impatience, the same dialogue that Durga had used about the rest of the Nagah.

Perhaps the princess had an opportunity to be pulled back from the abyss, but Lakesh worried if she should slip. He kept silent, carrying Manticor to safety.

GRANT LURCHED AGAINST THE SIDE of the tree trunk as a sheet of consort'um mercenary fire tore through the forest after him. The impact of bullets on the trunk shook leaves loose from the upper branches, and birds squawked as their nighttime perches were disturbed by the war among the humans. The smoldering remains of the mortar tubes he'd blasted were lit from behind by burning grasses that also illuminated the men who hunted Grant.

The ex-Magistrate had purposefully missed the ammunition stockpile with his initial shot. The artillery launchers would be hard to replace; he wanted to save the big blast for when the skimmers came in for the kill. Unfortunately, instead of the airborne ships, Grant was faced with dozens of gunmen who had scrambled to protect the last of their thunderous punch.

"The skimmers are pulling to about a mile of altitude," Kane informed Grant over his Commtact. "We're not going to get a shot at them, but they'll be able to rain down on you."

"Where are you?" Grant asked.

"A little bit above your position," Kane answered. "Call it fifty yards."

"I'm a few yards away from Kane," Brigid answered. "You left your intended target alone."

"And the goons are staying far away from it," Grant complained. "Our first two big hits taught them to avoid being caught in the blast radius."

"Hang on," Kane said. "Domi, Lakesh? Where the hell is the Nagah air force?"

"The advisory council's too busy to authorize them to take action now," Domi answered.

"Where's Lakesh?" Kane asked.

"Lakesh lost his Commtact when Hannah smacked him one."

"So what is the council busy with?" Kane asked.

"Someone who sounds like one of the snake faces just made an announcement over the intercom," Domi growled. "Sorry, Manticor."

"What happened to him?" Kane asked.

"The insurgents blew off his legs," Domi told him. "We're getting him someplace comfortable. He's in shock."

"Who sounds like an Annunaki?" Kane asked.

"Not sure. Might be Enlil, or it might just be Durga," Domi said. "Either way, people are getting religion around here. And not the turn-the-other-cheek style."

Grant grimaced at that news. "Who do you have on your side?"

"Hannah's here," Domi answered.

"Ask her if any Deathbirds are ready to go," Kane told her.

Grant grimaced. "Doesn't matter. We've still got the skimmers in the air. They're too agile, even with the damage they've suffered. The guns the consortium put on 'em will just be too powerful."

"The skimmers and their larger counterparts are controlled

via a mental energy interface," Brigid suggested. "Domi, ask Lakesh if he could try that."

Domi repeated the question, then answered Brigid. "He says he'll do his best."

"Tell Hannah that we'll do what we can, but those skimmers are small enough to fly into the underground passages. And with the weaponry that the consortium's packed onto them, hundreds could die," Kane warned.

"We're on our way to the hangar," Domi said. "Just hold out a little longer."

"All right, we'll soon have air support," Grant said.

"Provided Lakesh doesn't get them all shot out of the sky," Kane suggested.

Grant squinted, keeping watch to see if the mercenaries were aware of his presence. "It doesn't look like they've got a bead on my position."

"The multioptic band is showing me that they are passing you, but they don't seem to have noticed you," Brigid confirmed.

"Hold your spot, Grant," Kane said. "I've got a small patrol coming up on your right."

Grant scanned the forest, spotting the group that Kane had mentioned. They were being lead by a squat, compact man in the gray coveralls of the consortium. He wielded a Calico submachine pistol, and from his position in the group and the hand signals he communicated with, he was the leader of the hunt for the Cerberus trio. "Got him. Once this bunch passes, I'm going to take them from behind."

"The rest of the group isn't coming toward us—you don't have to risk it," Kane offered.

"You want to leave a bunch of thugs willing to work for

the millennialists running around India?" Grant inquired. "Besides, I've got a couple hundred rounds of artillery ammunition to blow the hell up."

"I'm so glad he's on our side," Brigid said aloud.

Grant smiled, slipping through the waist-high foliage to flank Devon Lan and his cadre of hired guns. "I'd say I aim to please, but I don't. I just shoot to kill."

DEVON LAN GRIMACED at the thought of the three Cerberus interlopers, Kane, Grant and Brigid Baptiste, interfering with his plans. He tried to dismiss the knowledge that he was here at the whim of the Millennial Consortium, and that he was subordinate to Christian, the ex-Magistrate turned mercenary, but he couldn't.

The war to cripple the Nagah and to steal their secrets was his. He was the one who was taking the risks, he was the one who recruited most of these thugs and he had literally organized this entire operation based on the information leaked to them by their Annunaki benefactor. Lan was the man who set this up, no matter who pitched in to do the grunt work.

"My freaking war," Lan whispered. "Where the heck is Nguyen?"

"We lost track of him, sir," Guapo answered. He was a South American pirate who had been picked up on the Vietnamese coast. The hired gun shook his head, unable to believe that a warrior was so insecure in his own appearance that he had to censor himself with weak, half-baked versions of curse words, even at his most angry. It bespoke an intellectual dishonesty with his own emotional state, and smacked of childishness.

"Darn it!" Lan snarled. "Find that idiot!"

Guapo couldn't help but chuckle at the frustrated millennial commander.

The chuckle caught in his throat, however, as a shadow suddenly loomed over Lan. Guapo swung up his SIG AMT rifle, but Grant threw a rock with devastating accuracy. The sharp stone struck the gunman in the center of his face. The fragile nasal-cranial opening collapsed under the force of the impact, splinters of skull spearing into his brain and effectively performing a deadly lobotomy on the mercenary.

Lan froze in horror as he watched the center of his minion's face cave in under the force of the hurled missile. He tried to turn, but big, powerful arms wrapped around Lan, heaving him into the air. It felt as if a pair of anacondas were squeezing the breath from his chest when Grant whispered in his ear.

"You want to live, asshole, you better stay quiet," Grant told him.

"Buzz off," Lan whimpered.

Grant's sinewy arms squeezed, and Lan could feel a rib crack under the strain. "Did you want me to fuck off?"

Lan's face was beet-red from pain and inability to suck in a breath. "What...do you...want?"

"A shield for now," Grant answered.

The rest of Lan's unit wondered why two of their number had fallen behind. When they saw their commander dangling like a rag doll in the embrace of the giant ex-Magistrate, the remaining gunmen shouted in dismay.

"Kill...this freaker!" Lan croaked to his men as Grant dragged him, legs kicking wildly, back toward the artillery nest.

It felt like a thunderstorm was blowing through his ears, the blood pressure in his skull rising to where he thought his head would pop off his neck. Suddenly, the pressure on his ribs disappeared and he was sailing through the air, landing face-first in a stack of sandbags. Lan struggled to get to his hands and feet, but a boot to the kidney folded him over, laying him out on his side. He wondered where his weapons went. He knew that he dropped the Calico when Grant snatched him up like a toy. Unfortunately, when his numbed, oxygen-starved hand slapped at his holster, he found that his handgun was gone. Lan desperately wanted to vomit, nausea seizing his gut.

Grant moved swiftly, turning the sole remaining mortar tube and aiming it at a ninety-degree angle to its original arc of fire. Somewhere in Lan's mind, he realized that the big Cerberus fighter was turning the heavy weapon toward the consortium forces. Grant worked with a speed and efficiency that made Lan wonder if it was the result of his asphyxiation-starved brain.

The mortar tube belched out the first of its rounds, and Grant adjusted the base, popping in a second shell in rapid succession. A third mortar bomb was dropped into the muzzle and fired instantly without a change of angle. Lan blinked, trying to recover his senses. As the millennialist sat up groggily, unable to concentrate on any one physical task, his eyes wandered to the field beyond the sandbags.

There, a tall, wolflike man and a woman with hair the color of flame tore through the remains of his patrol unit, their automatic weapons seeming to spit fire in the night. Lan croaked incoherently at the sight of a dozen bodies laid out by the two people who could only be Kane and Brigid Baptiste. Gulping down air, but recovering his senses too slowly for his taste, Lan cast about, looking for a weapon of some kind. He spotted a crowbar that had been used for popping the tops off ammunition crates and grabbed it.

Lan turned in time to see the waffle tread of Grant's boot fill his vision. He slumped into unconsciousness, realizing that he had failed his masters.

KANE AND BRIGID VAULTED over the row of sandbags surrounding the wrecked mortars. Grant stepped back from kicking an Asian consortium member in the face. The man was obviously a full recruit as he wore the classic uniform of the millennialists and had a badge with the emblem of the organization.

"Who was that?" Kane asked.

Grant shrugged. "Some fused-out moron with delusions of adequacy. He's out cold."

"Merciful of you," Brigid noted.

Grant had struck three of the projected camps, thanks to the coordinates given to him by Bry.

"Merciful, my ass," Kane said. "You just want him to tell the consortium who crippled their army. And they're not known for being nice enough to *only* shoot the messenger."

"I take immense satisfaction knowing that the right people hate me," Grant replied with a grin. "Looks like we've got the attention of the mercenaries at least."

"The salvo didn't bring in the skimmers," Kane added. "But Lakesh might be able to take them out."

"I'd rather he land and pick me up," Grant returned. "Sure, those things might be operated by a telepathic interface, but my brain's wired for combat piloting. I'm not even sure Lakesh has done anything on a computer flight simulator in fun."

"We'll know soon enough," Brigid said. "Look!"

A silver bolt speared through the sky from the direction of the Nagah's underground base. The three Cerberus warriors dialed in their multioptic visors, but tracking the speeding spacecraft as it sliced the air was difficult.

"Lakesh!" Kane said. "Slow down! You'll never be able to hit anything!"

"Slow down?" Lakesh asked over the Commtact.

"You got your comm working?" Grant asked.

"Domi let me use hers," Lakesh replied. "She's back at the hangar helping out Manticor."

"Well, ease up on the throttle!" Grant commanded.

"What are you talking about?" Lakesh asked.

Above them, lances of silvery fire emitted from the skimmer, causing two objects in the night sky to blossom into flowers of orange flame and greasy smoke. Kane watched as the silvery skimmer hovered for a moment, as if to gloat triumphantly over the blazing wreckage that spiraled toward the earth below.

"Shit," Kane whispered. "It's undamaged!"

"Enlil?" Brigid asked. "But…"

The skimmer dropped rapidly, like a silver coin after a gentle toss. Shimmering beams of silvery light pulsed from the craft, punching into the ground with rapid, brutal efficiency. Kane grabbed Brigid.

"Time to go!" Kane bellowed. The two people raced frantically out of the exposed artillery pit. Once Enlil was finished carving up the consortium forces, there was no doubt that the overlord would want to take a few shots at his mortal enemies.

Grant took a moment to heave the unconscious Lan out of the mortar pit. The stunned millennialist rolled down a slope, hopefully to a safe distance from the explosion he'd planned.

Grant set the radio-controlled explosive charge in a full crate of 120 mm warheads, then leaped away, hot on Kane's and Brigid's heels.

"There's another skimmer?" Lakesh asked over the Commtacts. "Dear God!"

Grant spotted Lakesh's ship in the distance, then looked back to see the Annunaki-controlled craft hovering above the stockpile of ammunition they'd just evacuated.

Enlil's voice reverberated from a speaker. "If you want something done right, you have to do it yourself. It's time to die, humans."

"Right time, wrong target," Grant responded, thumbing the remote on his charge.

A column of thunder and flame erupted beneath the hovering ship, the combined force of scores of warheads releasing a concussion wave that made the hillside beneath Grant's feet seem to heave with a life of its own. The blazing gout of force that shot skyward had been meant to pound the responding consortium forces into uselessness. Enlil's ship had taken care of the human army, but Grant's detonation still bought some time.

The skimmer toppled end over end through the sky, its silvery sheen blackened by the touch of superheated flames. The crack of snapping trees sounded as the spacecraft slammed into the forest.

Kane and Brigid caught up with Grant, who pocketed his remote detonator.

"The ship just looked knocked around," Kane mentioned.

"Still knocked that asshole out of the air," Grant said. "If he wants to pay me back, he's going to have to cut through some angry Nagah to get to me."

"Right. Lakesh, you still there?" Kane asked.

"I'll be over you in a few moments, friend Kane," Lakesh responded. "Any time friend Grant wants to take over flying this consternating contraption, he's fully welcome."

Grant smirked. "Crippled an army, knocked down a god and get to try out a new ride. I guess the squeaky wheel does get the oil."

Kane took a breath, then thought the better of it. It was rare enough that Grant had a display of a jovial mood. There was still work to do, and as Kane looked toward the skies, he knew that a mere explosion, no matter how many bombs were in it, was never going to be enough to bring down Enlil.

Chapter 20

The emergency first-aid station in the hangar was well equipped as Domi tended to Manticor. She was able to set up an intravenous bag for the serpent man. Domi was thankful that the blood of the Nagah was not drastically different from human and that a simple saline solution could be used to restore blood pressure. Over her shoulder, Hannah watched, nervously as Domi administered a shot of morphine.

"Will he be all right?" Hannah asked.

Domi's lips were a pale gash in her face as she took Manticor's pulse again. "His heartbeat's returning to normal. The IV I gave him is already working."

Hannah took a deep breath. "No one else cared about me as much as he did…."

Domi nodded. Now that she was done, she took Hannah's hand into hers, giving it a gentle squeeze. "He'll pull through."

"He'll never walk again," Hannah said softly.

Domi squeezed Hannah's hand. "It doesn't matter."

Hannah frowned. "It will to him. He was born to be a warrior."

"One of the bravest warriors I ever knew was a champion even after his legs were cut off," Domi said. "He battled a terrible monster and gave his life."

"Who was he?" Hannah asked.

Domi thought wistfully back to ZOOs, the leader of the pantheon of robot pilots in New Olympus. "A good man who called himself Zoo. He fought inside a suit of mechanical battle armor. And he was only one of many brave people who had lost their legs or suffered other horrible injuries. Their loss enabled them to pilot the machines they had found, however. They were able to fit into the war bots so that they could protect others."

"An army of cripples," Hannah repeated. She gave Manticor's thigh a caress.

"He doesn't need a robot," Domi said. "He's earned a peaceful life."

Hannah nodded. "But he'll condemn himself."

"If he loves you, he'll hang on," Domi countered. "He'll adapt. He'll change. He'll overcome. That's what Moe did."

"Lakesh was rejuvenated by the power of Enlil," Hannah said.

Domi nodded. "And Brigid can figure out the cobra baths, if it's really that important."

"I don't care," Hannah said. "He's alive. And I'm not going to keep quiet about my love for him anymore. All this denial shit…"

Domi smiled. "That is going to be the thing that really keeps him alive."

Hannah hugged the albino woman. "Thank you."

A skimmer hovered in the hangar doors, and Domi pulled away from Hannah, hand dropping to her pistol. When she saw the falsified scarring on its hull, she relaxed. She hadn't been able to hear the others because she had lent her undamaged Commtact to Lakesh as he flew the ship out to assist Kane. Now, they were back.

The skimmer's landing was much better than the sloppy bounce and jump of its departure. Either Lakesh had gotten better at flying, or someone else was at the controls. When the boarding ramp touched the ground, Lakesh, Kane and Brigid were the first ones off, running over to check on Hannah and Manticor. Grant strode down the ramp, ducking his head so as not to bark it against the bottom of the skimmer.

Domi rushed over to him, throwing her arms around his waist.

"You're covered in blood," Grant said, looking down at her.

Domi shrugged. "I've been making myself useful."

"Lakesh told me," Grant replied. "Scared all the citizens, I hear."

Domi frowned. "Yeah. But sometimes you just have to kill a bunch of fused-out slaggers, right? 'Sides, I helped Manticor, and gave Hannah a little pep talk."

"He doing any better?" Grant asked, walking with her toward the others.

"I've got an IV in his arm, and painkillers. He's resting," Domi said. "Pulse is normal, for a human. I had to check Hannah's pulse to see if their hearts beat the same."

"Smart girl," Grant said.

"Learning," Domi replied with a weak grin. She was feeling the exhaustion of the past few hours. Her adrenaline surge had faded, and aches from strained muscles and battered knuckles started to eat through the painkilling endorphins released during her rampage.

It was a good pain, though, she thought. The people she cared about were alive because of it.

ENLIL STRODE OUT OF THE SKIMMER, flanked by a half-dozen Nephilim soldiers. His gaze scanned the horizon beyond the hammered section of forest that had been smashed by his toppling ship. Beyond the swathe of destruction, flaming sections of forest blazed, smearing the night's starry blue with choking black. Looking up, he could imagine that the clouds were eating the stars, blanking them out as entropy swallowed the universe.

The stench of roasted human flesh wafted through the air, mixed with the undercurrent of burning wood. Bodies had been blown to shreds by Kane and his allies in their effort to rout the Millennial Consortium's desperate bid to take over the war materials of the Nagah. Enlil had engaged them, as well, his brilliant mind commanding the skimmer's gunnery computers to engage any human that his ship's sensors could pick up. In a way, it was more satisfying than using the power he lost when *Tiamat* was destroyed. Down here, close to the battle, he could enjoy the carnage he wrought with satisfaction.

There were times when Enlil felt as if he were taking matches to ant mounds, eliminating the rebellious apes who wouldn't have developed without his guiding hand.

The Nagah, however, were an insult created by Enki. Enlil had crafted his Nephilim warriors before his brother crafted the serpent people. But Enki, ever the soft heart, gave his creations autonomy. With the addition of free will, Enki's warriors were a fierce people, choosing their paths and able to adapt to unexpected situations. When Nephilim and Nagah clashed, Enlil's warrior drones were exterminated.

The thought of having an army of venom-fanged, highly trained warriors was attractive to Enlil. If he could convince them that he was their benefactor, then he could take the subterranean realm's forces and reestablish his unopposed mastery of the Earth. Without the Tuatha de Danaan to interfere, and with his brethren scattered across the globe, scrounging for their feeble stores of ancient treasure, Enlil would be a supreme force on the planet.

He walked through the grass and stopped. A man lay in the mud before him, dressed in the clothing and wearing the symbol of the consortium. Enlil reached down and hauled Devon Lan to his feet like a rag doll.

"It was my attack," Lan whispered.

Enlil tilted his head at the pathetic, delirious victim of Kane and his allies. "I thought the commander of this operation was a Magistrate named Christian."

"He's a blowhard...a gun-obsessed, foul-mouthed fool," Lan answered. "I did all the work. This was mine! I deserve all the credit."

"Instead, you will receive all the blame, as the army you worked so hard to assemble has been crushed by three people," Enlil told him, his voice soothing and seductive.

Tears formed in Lan's eyes. "Of course. I do the work, but someone undeserving gets the credit for victory. I exist only in failure, and then I earn only derision."

Enlil nodded. "No one respects a creative vision." His hands rested on Lan's shoulders. "No one, except me."

Lan swallowed. "My lord, give me a chance. I will storm the gates of hell, unarmed if necessary."

Enlil smiled at him. He turned Lan gently around and accepted a nodule from one of his Nephilim. He inserted the node into the base of the human's neck, cybernetic smart metal tendrils piercing his skin and connecting with his central nervous system. The initial connection to his spinal column released ferocious waves of agony through his back and neck, but after a few moments, the man-machine interface node released painkilling endorphins, soothing the former millennialist. Ribbons of living alloy wrapped around Lan's limbs and torso, sealing him in flexible, bullet-resistant armor. Around his right forearm, three snakelike heads grew, their bulbous tips glowing with inner fire.

Lan turned back, clad in his armor, then knelt before his lord.

"What is your name, son?" Enlil asked.

"Devon Lan, servant of Enlil," Lan answered.

"Rise, Lan," Enlil summoned. "We have places to go."

Lan nodded. "Where, sir?"

"To retrieve my brother's nanomachine vat," Enlil said. "I have an army that needs rebuilding, and hopefully, I will add the Nagah to that force. If not, perhaps you could recruit a new force. One which will be guided by your brilliant vision."

Lan's chest puffed out. "Yes, sir."

Enlil grinned, and led the way through the forest toward the Nagah's underworld lair.

His army had already grown by one. Soon, it would become even greater.

MANTICOR LAY BACK IN THE DOLLY, boxes raising him to eye level as Grant wheeled him through the hallways. The morphine's slumber had not lasted long, his magnificent physical conditioning returning him to wakefulness. His mouth felt like cotton inside, and the chuckle that took him over at that thought alerted him that while he was awake, his faculties hadn't quite returned.

"What's funny?" Grant asked.

Manticor rolled his head back, looking at Grant out of the corner of his eye. "I'm a cottonmouth snake."

Grant smiled. "Need something to drink, or just keeping your spirits up?"

"Both," Manticor said, sighing.

Grant dug into his war bag. He had a canteen inside, and he pulled it out. "Drink up."

Manticor fumbled with the canteen, his perceptions numbed. He couldn't quite feel the stopper with fingers that felt like wood, but finally he unscrewed it. With a tip of the bottle, he drank deeply, swallowing cool, clear water. The canteen was empty in six long swallows, and he pulled his lips from the mouth of the bottle, gulping down air.

"Sorry, Grant," Manticor said.

"No worries," Grant replied. "Hang on to the canteen, would you?"

Manticor nodded. "That'll work."

Grant gave the serpent man's shoulder a squeeze. "You'll be back in action soon enough."

"That's what Domi told Hannah," Manticor replied. "At least in my dream."

"Nah, she really said that," Grant told him. "Just hang in there."

Manticor's eyes clenched shut. "For what? I'm being rolled around like a delivery package. It's not like I'll ever walk again."

"So what?" Grant asked.

"So what? I have a duty," Manticor answered. "I'm her protector. What am I going to do? Run someone over with my wheelchair?"

"Some of the toughest people I ever met were wheelchair bound," Grant told him.

Manticor looked back at him. "What, those Greeks with the robots?"

"Some of them," Grant answered. "And for a while, Erica van Sloan was in a chair. Didn't stop her from being a menace to us."

Manticor frowned. "I dunno if it'll be the same."

"Who cares?" Grant asked. "So you're not kicking people in the face. What matters is that Hannah isn't giving up on you. Did you get your dick shot off?"

Manticor chuckled. He cursed how giddy the morphine made him, and tried to regain his composure. "No."

"Then I don't see a thing keeping you from her, especially now that we're going to hunt down Durga and kick his ass all the way to Calcutta," Grant said.

"I'm not royal blood," Manticor replied.

"You're a Nagah. And what's more, you're a Nagah with a sense of duty," Grant said. "What the hell is more worthy than that?"

Manticor lifted his closed fist. Grant recognized the gesture, and he brought his own fist around for a knuckle bump. "Point made, Grant. Point made."

Another thought crossed the wounded bodyguard's mind to make him laugh.

Behind him, Grant leaned in. "Thinking about how you can't break a foot off in Durga's ass anymore?"

"Nah. I was thinking about heading back to the council chamber to get what's left of them," Manticor said. "Thrown 'em at him. Kick in the face at thirty feet."

"That's some strong kung fu, Manticor," Grant said with a chuckle.

The pair bumped knuckles again. Slowly but surely, the cobra warrior's spirits were crawling up from the wreckage. Durga wasn't down for the count yet, but that wasn't what mattered right now. Manticor's depression had been chased away by Grant's compassion and humor.

As far as battles go, Grant thought, that's my favorite kind to win.

DURGA AND FARGO WERE surrounded by a cordon of the prince's loyal guards, thirty strong, all of them armed with black assault rifles and strapped into Kevlar body armor that Durga had set aside for his warrior elite. It wouldn't protect the snake men from head shots, but as the battle in the council chambers had proved, scoring head shots in the midst of a blazing firefight was not going to be easy. The American-made M-16s that Durga's personal elite carried were equipped with 40 mm grenade launchers.

For now, the cobra bodyguards had tear gas, flash-bang and rubber baton rounds in the grenade launchers. The weaponry was for crowd control, the less than lethal options in the launchers meant to preserve as much of Durga's future constituency as possible. Durga needed new bodies in order to maintain his bid for power.

Another of Durga's followers was back in the office, repeating a page of script that the prince had prepared for him. The voice-alteration module in his computer rendered the new speaker indecipherable from the original word of Enki.

"I particularly enjoy the touch where Enki has been in telepathic contact with you," Fargo mentioned as the group journeyed toward the cobra baths.

Durga nodded, smiling. "I wouldn't have been able to come up with that had I not been playing Enlil like a fiddle."

"You've been in contact with Enlil?" Fargo asked. "And been manipulating him?"

Durga shrugged. "How do you think I captured a skimmer?"

"So, you've got the consortium and Enlil working to take

over the Nagah," Fargo mused. "And did you intend to bring the Cerberus folk into this?"

"It was inevitable that they were going to be involved in our conflict, just by the very nature of their opposition to both sides I've been toying with," Durga replied. "Letting you live and escape wasn't part of some overarching plan. I figured you had a few options open to you to get back into our city. One was sucking up to the consortium, and the other was seeking refuge with the most powerful enemy of the consortium. Either way, Kane and his companions were on the way."

"You set up all of this based on a lot of unstable premises," Fargo noted.

"I've been plotting for thirty years to take control. It was getting to the point where I was going to set up my own variation of the consortium to make its attack, which is why I ran so many expeditions into the human territories. Not all of my Nagah warriors have bathed in the nanomachines," Durga said. "Many are cobra at heart, and they have scoured the planet, keeping me informed of all that was necessary for me to advance my cause of forming a Nagah crusade."

"So when the stories of Kane and his outlanders rose, you began factoring him in," Fargo said. "And when the Millennial Consortium made its presence known…"

"Precisely," Durga said. "Suddenly I had an embarrassment of scapegoats to launch my crusade. I paused my plotting, and observed. When the Annunaki awoke a while back, I was afraid that I wouldn't be able to conduct my plan. Instead, Lilitu's greed handed me another faction on a silver platter, destroying their central power base and scattering the overlords to the four winds."

"Thirty years," Fargo mused. "Even longer. Garuda was said to have been killed by a helicopter's machine gun, but the weapon you manned on your jeep, it was in the same caliber, wasn't it?"

"Yes," Durga answered. He smiled. "Astute observation."

"Shit, you killed your own mother," Fargo replied. "Now it should be obvious that you gunned down your dad if you were ruthless enough to pull that off."

The group entered the hall of the cobra baths. Ancient mechanized pumps and glowing green liquid in transparent tanks lined the walls. In the center of the great chamber sat a coppery bowl three feet deep. Golden-colored pipes snaked off the tanks to the deep pool.

"Would you like to take a dip?" Durga invited.

Fargo looked over the edge of the burnished, shiny pool bed. "You mean, cast off this human coil and become a snake man?"

Durga nodded. "Or you could maintain your current visage, and be able to pass among the humans as my agent."

Fargo scratched his chin, looking at the bowl. Durga tilted his head, noticing an unnatural focus in the man's eye. The archaeologist doffed his hat and crouched near the edge of the bowl. "Baptiste said that there would be some form of control interface."

"Correct," Durga answered. "You see something?"

"It's what I don't see," Fargo replied. "No drain."

"The nanite solution sucks back up through the pipes," Durga replied. "Actually, the changing waters have always been observed to flow back into their tanks after they have initiated the change. I guess the miniature robots literally carry the suspension solution back with them as they climb out of the bowl. A matter of programming, perhaps?"

"Shovels and crowbars," Fargo requested. "Someone get the pipes off so we don't damage them."

Durga directed his snake soldiers. "A chamber beneath this one. We'd always considered this to be the lowest portion of the Nagah city."

"Right, but this place has been through a flood that killed thousands, and destroyed or cut off sections of the city," Fargo replied. "The quakes caused by nuclear missile strikes on the mountain range above would have further isolated the sections beneath."

"Though, we have the nuclear reactor packed a full mile beneath the city," Durga replied. "That was set up in the second half of the twentieth century."

"The Indian government did all this digging and didn't discover you?" Fargo asked.

"It was a mutual effort," Durga said. "Back in the time before skydark, the Nagah were still interacting with humanity, just on a clandestine level. We combined efforts to fortify a warbase in this region in case Pakistan made an attempt to take back the Kashmir."

"So India kept you quiet as their ace in the hole," Fargo noted as the soldiers dismantled the pipes around the bowl.

"You noticed the disparity in architecture on the hangar levels," Durga pointed out. "We simply pulled back to allow the humans to make use of those sections of our city. No unauthorized human ever saw a Nagah, just the evidence of an abandoned, damaged, underground city."

"It was never a matter of hating humans," Fargo stated.

Durga laughed. "Without humans, I wouldn't be the king

apparent now. Sure, I called you hairless apes before, but the thing is, it was an act. Some of my most loyal and capable followers are mammals."

The bowl cracked free under the efforts of a dozen strong cobra men. It clattered as the soldiers hefted it out of its slot in the floor. The depression in the floor had a hatch in the center, where a drain would have been, had it been a standard pool. Fargo leaped down and looked at the locks holding it in place. "Durga, how knowledgeable are you about the pictogram language?"

"I've been studying it all of my life," Durga said, crawling in.

"Good, you're more familiar with this, then," Fargo told him. "These locks look as if they have to be released in a certain pattern. If we get it wrong, then a booby trap will go off."

"How bad would it be if we failed?" Durga inquired.

"Nanites programmed to turn our flesh into viscous paste," Fargo mused. "Or just poisonous gas. Either way, it wouldn't be the prettiest, or most comforting of deaths."

Durga studied the latches. "High explosives wouldn't clear the way, would they?"

"Normally with ancient societies, I would have said yes," Fargo answered. "But this was supposedly installed by Enki, and his enemies were his brother and the Tuatha de Danaan. Seeing what the Nephilim's ASP blasters can do, we have to open this the right way, or else we're going to be the most fucked humanoids on this planet."

Durga looked down at the locks. "Charming."

"Of course, we could always do this the safe way," Fargo mentioned.

Durga pressed the earbud communicator he wore. "All units, report in. What is the progress of the Cerberus expedition?"

"They open it up, fine," Fargo mused. "They open it and set off the trap, no skin off us."

Durga winked. "I think this is the start of a beautiful friendship."

Chapter 21

Lakesh leaned against the wall, and Domi took a moment to wipe his sweaty brow with a rag. He smiled at her and stood back up, but she pushed him back to a leaning position.

"You lost a lot of blood," Domi said.

Lakesh shook his head. "I'll be fine. Just some flesh wounds, really. No vital blood vessels were hit."

"You got shot up enough to put your arm in a damned sling," Grant complained, settling Manticor's improvised dolly-wheelchair. "What the hell did you expect us to do when you flopped over unconscious?"

Lakesh bristled at the attention. "We have neither the time nor the materials to deal with this right now. Yes, I'm light-headed, and my arm has been left incapacitated. However, I'd prefer to keep moving."

Grant slid Lakesh's arm out of the sling. Stripes of red showed through the bandages where rifle rounds had gouged his skin.

"Grant, could you get the two of them back to our quarters?" Kane inquired. "The rest of us will continue on."

Grant nodded. "That sounds like a good plan."

"Why shouldn't I do it?" Domi asked.

"Because he could carry both of them at the same time if the shit hits the fan," Brigid replied. "You're strong, but you just don't have the acreage to run around with two fully grown men in your arms."

"And we'll need the extra firepower if we come across Durga's people," Kane replied.

Domi nodded. "All right."

Lakesh grimaced. "I'm sorry, friend Kane."

Kane regarded the scientist for a moment, then rested a consoling hand on his shoulder. "You damn near lost a limb trying to protect the queen. And according to Manticor, you blew the head off one of the assassins, who outnumbered you twenty to one."

Lakesh's agonized features relaxed a little. "I still failed."

"Everyone does," Kane told him. "Now stop beating yourself up. That's my job."

"Let's go!" Grant said, wheeling Manticor's dolly once more.

"Good luck," Kane said. "Get a spare Commtact plate out of our gear. We'll need your brains, if we can't rely on your gun."

"That's another spare I'll have to dig out back at the quarters," Lakesh admitted.

"A little saline solution to bring your blood pressure up to speed, and you'll be able to hold your own keeping the room secure," Kane told him. "And just remember, you've been staying on your feet without painkillers."

Lakesh winced. "I am in no need of that reminder, friend Kane."

Grant blew a sharp whistle down the hall, and Lakesh trotted off to catch up with the big ex-Magistrate.

He turned back to catch Brigid smiling coyly at him.

"You two have come a long way," she mentioned.

"If Domi vouches for him, he can't be all bad," Kane answered.

Domi punched Kane in the bicep. "Lay off him. Come, on, I caught a whiff of tear gas up ahead. That's where Hannah says the baths are."

"Tear gas. Durga must be trying to minimize collateral damage among his people," Kane noted. "That explains why the hallways are so empty."

"He's inadvertently doing us a favor," Brigid said. "Whoever is portraying the voice of Enki is warning about human interference in the affairs of his children."

Kane sighed. "Well, it wouldn't be a day at the office without someone trying to kill us."

Kane took the lead, the others falling in step behind him. All four people took out handkerchiefs to cover their noses and mouths as the chemical sting of tear gas grew stronger. They pulled down their multioptics to protect their eyes. As it was, Kane could feel the burn in the back of his throat and nose as wisps of the chemical cloud made it through his scarf around the corners of his mouth.

It was a hard walk through the terrain, and through the lenses of the multioptic visor, he could see Nagah curled up, clutching chests or heads. Strewed between the stunned cobra folk were neoprene rubber slugs, another less-than-deadly weapon launched from a grenade tube. The ones shot were near clubs and handguns, which they'd dropped when they were struck by the soft-bodied slugs. With the rib-breaking force of the baton rounds and the lung-burning agony of the tear gas, the Nagah were suffering.

Kane had to fight the urge to stop and drag the serpent men and women to safety. They were in pain, but if Kane and the others didn't stop Durga, things would become far worse. The tear gas would dissipate, and broken bones would mend.

Kane didn't like having to triage the needs of the suffering against the safety of the entire city, and perhaps the world, but he did it.

Stay strong, he silently urged them.

Hannah stepped ahead of him, pointing to an archway. Through the muffling of the scarf, she explained herself. "These are the cobra baths. There are usually guards here."

Kane let the Sin Eater snap into his hand. "Keep to cover."

"You'll be outnumbered in there," Hannah replied.

Kane grunted in affirmation of her statement. "I'm not going to walk into an ambush. Just the same, keep something solid between you and the enemy guns."

Hannah nodded. "Be careful."

The Nagah princess went to the back of the group, and Brigid guided her into an arched doorway with a thick lip. The thick stone would provide her with more than adequate protection from enemy gunfire. Kane pressed his ear to the chamber door. Though he was tempted to roll in a few nondeadly grenades from his war bag, he held off, cracking the door just enough to see inside.

The cobra baths were empty, though it was obvious that someone had been in there. Pipes were scattered along the floor, and the coppery dome of an overturned tub was propped in a corner. Kane slid through the opening, the Sin Eater's muzzle leading the way. He spoke low, so only Brigid could hear him over her Commtact.

"It's empty, as far as I can tell," Kane said.

"Utility tunnel access?" Brigid inquired.

Kane's sharp eyes were already searching the corners, the ceiling and the floor for signs of the hatches. None was apparent, but the bath chamber's equipment was in disarray.

As it was, he doubted that an army of Nagah could stuff themselves into the utility tunnels. His point man instinct gave the room a clean pass. "Come on in. This place is secure."

Brigid, Domi and Hannah entered, guns drawn. They shut the door and took their scarves from their noses and mouths, breathing in the relatively fresh air, coughing off the irritant effects of the tear gas that had seeped through their rags. Brigid looked at the pit in the center of the floor, walking closer to it. Kane checked the perimeter of the vaulted room, then glanced at Hannah.

"Large place for such a little tub," Kane said, pointing to the overturned bowl.

Hannah nodded. "The room is sized to accommodate even the largest of families for the transformation from man to cobra, both for pilgrims making the change, and for observers, especially from the royal family."

"They tore it up," Domi noted.

"It was to get to this hatch in the middle of the floor, but there appears to be a puzzle-style lock on it," Brigid said.

Kane and Hannah joined her as Domi took over watching the door. The three people looked at the latches. Pictograms adorned the seven locks that secured the hatch to the floor.

"These haven't been touched, so Durga didn't go down there," Kane noted. "Think you can figure this out?"

Brigid knelt, looking at the symbols. "I would presume their reluctance to open the control chamber stemmed from the potential for springing a trap. One misstep and we could unleash doom upon the whole underbelly of this city, or worse."

"The patterns look familiar," Hannah spoke up. "Perhaps it's one of the passages repeated on the columns."

Brigid nodded. "Absolutely, but which passage? I don't want to misspell the unlocking code, given some of the security measures we've seen in other ancient treasure troves."

Kane grimaced. "The longer we take here, the more likely this area is going to get crowded. We don't just have Durga to worry about, remember."

As if to confirm the Cerberus warrior's concerns, his Commtact buzzed to life. It was Grant.

"We've got company. A pair of Nephilim just chased Lakesh and me out of our suite," Grant reported.

"Manticor?" Kane asked.

"Still with us. I wheeled him along," Grant answered.

Kane shook his head. "It'll be difficult getting to the cobra baths. Durga's troops have laid down a lot of tear gas and it's lingering."

"I can handle a little cry juice," Grant replied. "Though Lakesh will end up useless after that. Plus, it wouldn't deter the Nephilim."

"It's your prerogative," Kane told him. "Personally, I'd rather have Enlil's forces hampered."

Gunfire crackled, the racket audible through the Commtact.

"What was that?" Kane asked.

Grant's chuckle answered that question. "Looks like when Enlil opened fire on the consortium, he made a few enemies."

"Their troops made it in?" Kane asked.

"The Nephilim and the millennial shits are exchanging fire. For once, I'm torn as to whose ass to kick first," Grant explained.

"Whoever's doing better," Kane said. "Baptiste and I are going to try and find our way to the hidden tunnels beneath the cobra baths."

"Good luck," Grant told him.

Kane turned back toward the pit and looked at Brigid.

"You're going to help?" Brigid asked.

"Call it a belt-and-suspenders approach," Kane said. "I get a bad feeling, it'll be my intuition picking up an error in your spelling."

Brigid looked down at the hatch. "I know that your so-called instinct has a latent psychic aspect, though it's primarily based on your normal, if highly acute senses. We'd be pushing your limits."

"I seem to be picking up strong flashes," Kane said to her. "Remember that bit before Grant called in."

"As much as the skeptic in me wants to say that it was purely coincidence, your intuition has not steered us wrong in the past," Brigid noted. "However, I will do my best not to get the pattern wrong."

"You have an idea?" Kane asked.

"I'm recalling one of several passages about how Enki crafted the Nagah from a sense of love," Brigid told him. "Correlating that pattern of pictograms with the symbols available for these locks, I might have the code."

"Wouldn't that be too obvious?" Hannah inquired.

"It might, but given the sequences of pictograms utilizing similar symbology, the same glyphs could construct at least a half a dozen different sentences in the writings on your walls," Brigid noted. "However, putting it into the context of this particular chamber, which creates all new Nagah, I can easily see it being the actual disarmament sequence for the lock."

Hannah looked to Kane for a translation.

"The more nervous she gets, the wordier she gets," Kane answered. "The opposite of Domi, actually."

"She's got brains, I've got brawn," Domi agreed. "Kane has looks."

Kane wrinkled his nose at her comment. "Let's hope your talent for minutiae will carry us through this."

Brigid took a deep breath. "If not, it's been nice working with you."

GRANT HANDED LAKESH A SPARE Sin Eater and a trio of 20-round magazines. "Use this to protect yourself and Manticor. I know it'll be hard with one hand, but it's big and heavy enough to control the recoil, and I've seen you shoot this much better than that midget .45 Domi gave you."

"Thank you, friend Grant," Lakesh said. He looked at the heavy cannon in his palm. "I only hope that it won't come to that." He stuffed the extra magazines into his sling where he could reach them easily. By stuffing the barrel into his belt, he'd be able to secure the Sin Eater to reload it. Grant stalked off with a grace and stealth that belied his enormous size.

The surviving Nephilim drone stood astride the corpse of his partner, his ASP spearing yellow-white lightning at the attacking consortium gunmen. The reek of roasted human flesh filled the corridor, bullets pinging off the armored Annunaki servant's smart-metal sheath. A round creased the humanoid's reptilian head, and he staggered.

Grant took that as his opportunity to even the odds. Copperhead in one fist, Sin Eater in the other, he poked out from behind a column and triggered both firearms in full-auto. His powerful, sinewy arms held the two weapons locked on target despite their effort to buck and recoil. Veins stood out under the skintight shadow suit, muscles rippling as he ripped the millennialists with both weapons.

A dozen human soldiers had survived their ambush on the two Nephilim warriors. By the time Grant was done, he'd reduced their numbers to three, nine corpses joining the five charred lumps of smoking flesh on the ground. It was a wave of slaughter, and the surprise Grant had sprung on them was ruthless. He wasn't proud of himself for gunning them down from behind. The three survivors broke and ran for their lives, lobbing a grenade toward Grant.

The big man leaped, diving away from the landing spot of the thrown minibomb, but an ASP bolt lanced into the explosive canister, the energy blast tearing through the grenade's detonation core. Instead of a lethal radius of ten yards, the grenade produced a meek pop as what was left of its explosive charge cooked off in the ASP's heat. The rest of the munition had been reduced to carbonized slag.

Grant scurried to his knees and looked at the Nephilim as it staggered against a wall, clutching its bleeding head, too dazed to be a threat. Grant wondered if the drone's self-preservation initiative had been inadvertently responsible for his rescue. Maybe the head blow had shaken the humanoid's brain enough to give it a sense of gratitude for Grant saving its life. Ultimately, Grant didn't care about the whys, just that for a moment, the creature had reacted with life-saving mercy rather than as a mindless killing machine. The wounded reptilian warrior staggered away, blood pouring into its eyes.

Grant took a moment to reload his weapons, then glanced at Lakesh, who was still dutifully guarding Manticor. Grant keyed his Commtact. "Better pull back a little bit out of sight."

"Manticor is out of the line of fire," Lakesh said. "But from this vantage point, I observe some activity farther down the corridor."

Grant padded to a corner across from Lakesh and peered around it. Sure enough, the three consortium mercenaries had retreated and met up with another platoon of gunmen. A quick count put at least twenty downrange. Grant positioned his Sin Eater in its forearm holster, freeing his hand to root through his war bag for a pair of grenades that he hooked on to his belt.

"Lakesh, draw their attention down that hallway," Grant whispered. "Just a few shots—don't stand and fight. I need to get close enough to drop these in their blind spot."

"Absolutely, friend Grant," Lakesh responded.

The scientist was still rubbery on his feet, but he soldiered on, despite his wounds and exhaustion. Grant slipped along the wall, keeping to the shadows, grenade in one hand, thumb through its cotter pin ring, Copperhead locked in his other hand. He paused, seeing a massive form with a blunt, close-shaved head.

Grant recognized the man as one of the Cobaltville Magistrates, Christian. The bulky man was not much more than a thug who got off on bullying others. With the implode grenade, Grant would remove another overtrained hired gun from the planet.

Something scraped the floor behind Grant and he froze, looking back. There were more armored figures, one an Asian human wearing smart metal and another Nephilim. The two heard the sound of the consortium platoon and looked down the hall. Grant recognized the human as the ranting maniac who had claimed he had been the mastermind of the millennialists' attack on the Nagah catacombs.

"Christian!" Devon Lan bellowed. "You ignorant, gunobsessed thug!"

Grant grimaced. Even though he was in the shadows and out of sight, he was caught in the cross fire.

Consortium gunmen and ASP-armed servants of Enlil opened fire, their weapons filling the air inches in front of Grant with sheets of flying death.

LAKESH HEARD GRANT'S WHISPERED curse and realized that his ally was in trouble. Suddenly, a whole new chorus of battle arose, energy weapons and rifles yammering fiercely. Lakesh grimaced, the borrowed Sin Eater perched in his hand.

"Friend Grant?" Lakesh whispered. "Are you hit?"

"Give these fuckers a few moments," Grant grumbled. "I'm pinned down, left and right. If you can, work back around and pick up Manticor."

"You're surrounded," Lakesh admonished.

"Just protect Manticor," Grant hissed. "If I can get out…"

Lakesh saw that the consortium gunmen were focused on the direction that vomited lances of energy toward them. Assault weapons roared incessantly, and they wouldn't notice a stampede of elephants charging at them until it was too late. Lakesh gritted his teeth, then thumbed the Sin Eater's selector to full-auto. "I'll cut you an escape route."

"Lakesh!" Grant growled.

The scientist swung around the corner, bracing his arm on a raised lip, tilting the machine pistol so that if it rose, the stone against his forearm would keep the weapon locked on target. Braced, he triggered the Sin Eater. The weapon snarled out its lethal message, brass flying from its breech as heavy-weight slugs poured toward the backs of the consortium gunmen. Two mercenaries were torn from the wall, bullets shredding their backs and pitching them into the open.

An ASP bolt struck one of the dying thugs, the beam slicing him in two. The other flopped to the floor, the back of his khaki shirt drenched in blood. The sudden demise of two of their own from an unknown source caused three more gunmen to stop shooting. One craned his neck to see where the gunfire came from, and a second spear of yellowish fire vaporized his head, leaving a blackened stump atop his neck.

Lakesh milked the trigger again, the Sin Eater bucking at the end of his good arm.

Christian, a former Magistrate, howled orders for his men to alter their stance. Consortium killers scrambled, moving to where they would be protected from both the Nephilim intruders and Lakesh's fire.

With a surge of speed, Grant burst into the open, his Copperhead chattering. The consortium gunmen recoiled, taking cover from the big ex-Magistrate's assault. The hallway that Grant had just exited vomited a cloud of smoke and debris, indicative of a grenade's detonation. Covered from behind by the rolling minibomb, Grant had enough breathing room to race toward Lakesh. The scientist winced as he tucked the hot barrel into his belt and fed it a fresh magazine. By the time Grant reached him, Lakesh had finished reloading and fired single shots, powerful rounds stabbing into the shadows that Christian's consortium thugs had retreated toward.

Grant skidded to a halt, hurling himself behind a corner as the enemy opened fire. Lakesh ducked back before a rain of bullets peppered the wall he'd been braced against. He looked at Grant.

"That was the stupidest thing you've ever done," Grant grunted.

Lakesh swallowed hard. "You're telling me?"

Grant's dour mood cracked, a smile shining through. "Stick with us, man. You're learning well."

That elicited a laugh from the scientist. "It was viscerally satisfying."

"Thanks," Grant finally admitted. He took the second grenade off his belt. "Got a few more distraction shots in you?"

Lakesh rattled the magazines in his sling. "Two mags left."

"That's my boy," Grant replied. "Fire at will."

Lakesh swung around, blazing off fast single shots toward the encamped consortium gunmen. Christian's force returned fire, their shadowy corridor lit as if by lightning. Grant whipped the grenade around the corner, his brawny arm launching the miniature bomb with such force, it seemed to be rocket-powered. The grenade bounced once, twice, then thudded in the midst of the millennialists' position. There was an inarticulate cry of dismay, then a thunderous flash as the weapon detonated. The clap of doom that resounded was followed by a secondary one as the implode grenade had vaporized the atmosphere in a large diameter through thermobaric principles. The rush of air pulverized anything that wasn't incinerated by the superheated fireball put off by the grenade.

Lakesh slid down the wall, shaking from adrenaline overload. Grant padded over to him and gave him a clap on the shoulder. "Not bad for a two-hundred-and-fifty-year-old whitecoat."

Lakesh chuckled. "I'm only two hundred and fifty? Right now I feel five hundred."

Grant helped Lakesh up. "Come on, we've got to get back to Manticor."

"Yes. Time enough for sleep when I'm dead," Lakesh

agreed. Putting one leaden foot in front of the other, he followed Grant down the hall to get back to Manticor.

An ASP bolt seared the air just over Grant's shoulder, and the big Cerberus warrior slapped his palm into Lakesh's chest, shoving him back behind cover. A wild leap took Grant to the cover of another corner as an energy bolt seared the floor where his feet had been a moment ago.

"Grant! You accused me of having delusions of adequacy!" Lan shouted. "Now we're going to see who the real failure is!"

Chapter 22

Brigid and Kane looked at the last of the latches. None of the combinations that the former archivist's eidetic memory told her was right felt good to Kane, and he kept her from completing the handle's sequence.

"This is exactly as the pictograms were carved," Brigid replied. "There's no other way it makes sense, unless…"

The flame-haired woman looked up at Hannah. "Hannah, does this make sense? I'm just going through the images, not the actual context."

Hannah dropped down into the pit with them. "No. The syntax is all wrong. Let me get a look at all of the options."

The Nagah princess twisted the puzzle-box handle around, looking at the symbols. "What in the hell?"

"Nothing seems right?" Kane asked.

"Completely confusing. According to this, the saying that Brigid has put together is 'And Enlil did so love his children that he entrusted them his secrets,'" Hannah explained. "But the only viable option that fits into the sentence structure reads 'cut them off from his secrets.'"

"Which comes out completely wrong in terms of the translations you've put all over your city," Brigid noted. "But it does make sense thematically, and in the context of the security mechanism."

"He kept his secrets away from the Nagah to protect them from others who'd want to get in here," Kane said. "If the Nagah had control of the nanites, they'd have immortality, complete recovery from all but the most heinous injuries—"

"And the ability to infuse our bodies with power like you wouldn't imagine," a voice boomed through the room. It sounded like Durga.

Domi backed to the edge of the pit. "Loudspeaker. We're still alone in here."

Reflex urged Kane to grab Domi around the waist and yank her into the hole. As he collapsed to the bottom, Brigid and Hannah followed suit, though Kane was moving too swiftly, too automatically on reflex to know if he'd shouted for them to get down.

The bellow of an explosion increased the pressure in the chamber, and as Kane pushed Domi to the bottom, shielding her with his back, he felt the rush of air as a propelled steel door whooshed past, its bottom edge missing his spine by mere millimeters. A clatter of colliding metal resounded in the wake of the bull rush of air from the detonation, steel bouncing off the copper pipes.

Kane looked over the lip of the pit, the smoke swirling and clearing back out into the hall. As the mist dissipated, he could see Durga and Fargo standing side by side, flanked by dozens of serpent men.

"Knock, knock," Durga said with a chuckle.

Kane's Sin Eater was out, aimed over the edge of the pit. He stayed low, but none of Durga's followers had entered.

"Finally see you picked a side that can win, Fargo," Kane commented. "But from where I sit, the two of you will end up with a couple more holes in you before the minute's through."

"You wouldn't want to do that, Kane," Fargo prodded. "Sure, shooting us might help you, but Durga tosses his grenade in there with you, well, we're not exactly sure just how many Nagah in this city will be killed."

Kane glanced down at Brigid. She nodded in confirmation. "Depending on Enki's proficiency with nanites, improperly opening this hatch could unleash a plague of eaters that could devour every living organism for hundreds of square miles."

"The grenade wouldn't affect them?" Kane asked.

"They're too small. Overpressure wouldn't disturb their mechanisms," Brigid replied. "The force of the detonation would only increase their dispersion. The only thing that might stop them is an implode grenade, but even then, the fire blast wouldn't get through the hatch—only the concussion wave created by the atmosphere rushing back into the void created would break the hatch. Then the nanomachines would come out."

"Be reasonable, Kane," Durga said. "I'm not going to have your people tortured or killed. I'll actually be able to arrange for some clemency for you."

"Sorry, Durga. I was born at night, but not last night," Kane answered. "Especially with your bit back in the hangar, planting the seed in others that I might be jealous of you."

Durga raised a scaled eyebrow. "That was before all my plans got pushed forward. But yes, I would have had one of my untransformed boys take a potshot at me with an old Sin Eater. Really too bad we didn't get that far, did we?"

Durga drew his sidearm from his hip holster. Kane recognized it as a Sin Eater. "This is the weapon I killed my driver with after I gunned down Garuda. This way, poor little lost Durga was the sole survivor of the group that the king led. So many lost…"

"Yeah, yeah, we get the point," Kane snapped. "You shot daddy. Your mommy got sprayed all over a wall an hour ago. And to pay back the world for not understanding your dreams…"

A bullet pinged off the floor near Kane's elbow, whizzing past his ear.

"Talk about my mother some more," Durga growled. "Please."

"Touchy, touchy," Kane said, clucking his tongue. "You can kill her, or rather, have her killed…"

Durga leveled the machine pistol at Kane's face. Kane aimed at the hatch.

"Shoot me, maybe I won't pull the trigger and kill you and your boys," Kane warned.

"Risking thousands of lives?" Durga asked. "Interesting bluff."

"Die quick, or die slow under your rule?" Kane asked. "I'd go for quick."

"So we're both threatening each other with the same oblivion," Durga said, chuckling.

Kane shrugged. "You really aren't giving me many options. I shoot you, you end up killing everyone in the city. You shoot me, you kill yourself. I'm counting on your will to live winning out here."

"Well played," Durga said. He clipped the grenade to his belt.

Kane motioned for the three women to get out of the pit with him. Brigid, Domi and Hannah took cover behind the wreckage of the steel door. Kane sat on the edge of the pit, gun still aimed at the lock. "We're at an impasse now. Because there's no way in hell that I'm going to let you get through this hatch."

"And there's no way I'm going to surrender the power of the Annunaki to an ape like you," Durga responded. "So, we'll have to think of something."

"I'm all for anything involving you fucking off, eating shit and dying, in no particular order," Kane growled. "Throw me your compromise on that."

Fargo and the prince's minions swarmed into the chamber. Out of his peripheral vision, Kane could see that his three companions were behind solid cover, and their weapons were ready. Secured behind steel, copper and stone, the Durga's cobra warriors would have the toughest time getting through to the women.

It would be a rout the moment a trigger was pulled. Durga realized that as he stood across from Kane in the depression the gold-colored tub used to inhabit. He looked down at the hatch.

"So close, yet so far," Kane said. "What's your suggestion, Prince?"

"That's 'King,'" Durga answered, irritated.

"That would require the emergency council's approval, Durga," Hannah called out from her position. "And since a good number of them are dead thanks to your cultists..."

Durga glared at his former bride-to-be. "You've got courage, Hannah. Show some brains, too, and you can survive this."

Hannah laughed. "And I had thought I'd lost my mind when Manticor was shot."

"The two of us, strong-willed, brave, brilliant," Durga said. "We could mold this city. Don't want me for a lover, fine. I'll grow Manticor some brand-new legs."

Kane's eyes flickered until he caught a glimpse of Hannah in his peripheral vision. It was a tempting offer, and he didn't relish catching a bullet in the back of his head.

Of course, at that moment, Grant's voice cut in over his Commtact. "Kane, we've got some serious shit going on."

Kane kept his jaw locked, but he managed an interrogative grunt that escaped Durga's notice.

"Can't talk?" Grant asked. "Well, this is just informative right now. Looks as if Enlil's been recruiting and he's got one of the consortium commanders on his side. Luckily, with all the panic, people have hidden in their quarters, because this just turned into a three-way dance."

"Four," Kane subvocalized.

Fargo pointed casually to Kane, drawing Durga's attention. "Sounds like there's more trouble afoot. What's Grant telling you?"

"Enlil and the consortium just stopped by for a cup of sugar," Kane quipped. "Didn't Enlil tell us he wasn't within one thousand miles of here?"

Durga shrugged. "I wouldn't trust that scaly bastard farther than I could spit."

The hairs on the back of Kane's neck rose and the Cerberus leader lunged aside, two streams of poison jetting from Durga's fangs. The misty venom caught Kane in his left eye and burned on contact, causing the normally sure-footed fighting man to trip and stumble. The entire left side of Kane's face felt as if it had been struck by a spiked maul, and he could feel the skin around the eye go numb instantly. Kane's tear ducts kicked into overdrive, trying to flush the foul irritant from his agonized tissues.

Had Kane been hit head-on, he would have been blinded. As it was, the pain was a distraction, allowing the renegade cobra prince to swing the frame of his Sin Eater across Kane's jaw. The blow was a jarring one, making Kane reel back against the side of the pit. His gun clattered onto the hatch, rocked loose by a hard knee against his wrist. Durga had lunged in quickly, and his intent was to take the Cerberus warrior as a hostage.

Gunfire crackled all around the two combatants. Kane could pinpoint Domi and Brigid by the sounds of their handguns amid the din of Durga's allies. Bullets struck their steel barricades and ricocheted. Spent slugs rebounded, hammering into Kane's back and shoulders, one bullet clipping his ear before it popped into Durga's hood.

"Idiots!" Durga spit, spinning away from Kane and clutching at the perforated sheet of muscle between his head and shoulder. "Pull back! They're dug in too well!"

Kane took advantage of Durga's momentary distraction and skidded to the floor, his legs scissoring between the snake man's. Lower extremities suddenly seized, Durga found himself off balance. With a powerful tug, Kane yanked Durga's feet from under him, toppling him into the pit.

The gunfight still blazed around them, and Kane knew that Durga had enough information to open the hatch to Enki's control chamber. With a lunge, he dived into Durga's back, bringing down all of his weight and muscle on the cobra prince. Their bodies crunched against the bottom of the depression. With some satisfaction, Kane listened to what could have been the snapping of a bone. Still half-blind, the ex-Magistrate speared a hard-knuckled punch into Durga's kidney. The blow would have paralyzed a normal man, but the tough scales of Durga's hide blunted the force of Kane's strike. For his trouble, the ex-Magistrate caught an elbow in the mouth, upper lip splitting against his teeth. Blood sprayed from the impact, and Durga twisted, reaching for the human's throat.

Kane figured two could play at the spraying game, and he blew a crimson cloud of mixed spit and blood into Durga's eyes. The torrent caught him off guard, and the cobra man blinked, trying to wipe the bloody saliva off his face. Kane brought the hard edge of his hand down on Durga's clavicle. The impact sounded like breaking wood, and Durga howled in pain.

There was the crack of leather, a tough coil suddenly snaking around Kane's throat like a noose. With a hard yank, Fargo had trapped Kane in an asphyxiating grasp with his whip.

"Stop shooting, or I break Kane's neck!" Fargo bellowed.

Durga squirmed out from under Kane, then lunged, sinking his fangs into Kane's neck above the collar of the shadow suit.

"Kane!" Brigid screamed. Durga winced as rounds tore into the floor near him, but as long as Kane was between Brigid and Durga, she couldn't put a bullet into his skull.

"Bitch," Durga spit.

"What the hell are you doing?" Fargo asked. "You killed him!"

If agony and the leather of Fargo's whip hadn't combined to constrict Kane's throat, the ex-Magistrate would have disagreed. Certainly, the venom seared through Kane's neck muscles, but fortunately, Durga hadn't struck a major blood vessel. Every nerve in the man's body felt as if it were being seared by an open flame, but he could still breathe.

Durga gave Kane's cheek a light slap. "Hurts like hell, doesn't it?"

"Fuck...off," Kane sputtered.

"He won't die from the bite. A Nagah's venom is dilute after a spray," Hannah called out to Brigid. "Kane will just wish he was dead for a week."

Durga licked his front teeth. "Give me a little while to build up some more venom."

"Or better yet, throw down your guns, or I pull pretty-boy's head off," Fargo threatened.

Kane's left arm lay limply at his side, but he had enough strength to grasp the cord of Fargo's whip. He couldn't pull any slack around his throat, but at least the threat of a broken neck would be averted, should the archaeologist yank on the whip again. Kane could only blink his right eye, the left one swollen almost shut from its exposure to Durga's venom. At least that side of his face had gone numb, something he was thankful for.

Of course, it was a small favor. He heard a handgun clatter on the tile.

"Good, Baptiste," Durga called. "What about you, Domi?"

Kane grimaced. Brigid had surrendered her weapon, which meant that the others were that much closer to being killed. Disarmed, there'd be nothing holding back Durga's warriors. "Baptiste…pick up your gun…"

"I'm not going to risk your life, Kane," Brigid said. "You want the hatch opened, you tell your new toady to let him go."

"I already know the code," Durga said. "I was listening at the door."

Kane craned his neck, trying to see Brigid, but as she was approaching around his left side, he was practically blind. He did, however, hear her cluck her tongue against the roof of her mouth over his Commtact. Three clicks. Two clicks.

Kane clenched Fargo's whip tightly, then folded his legs, getting all the traction he could against the side of the depression in the floor. Fargo tried to snap Kane's neck by jerking on his end of the whip, but once Kane extended his legs, the archaeologist tumbled to the ground. Durga fared no better, as Kane's body rammed into his chest like a charging bull.

Brigid hadn't needed to finish her countdown as the doorway filled with the blossoming cloud of a stun grenade. Cobra men wailed as their eardrums ruptured at the bellow of the minibomb's deafening bang.

The Cerberus warriors had regained their advantage, but right now venom slowed Kane too much to do more than crawl out of the hatch. It would be a handful of seconds before Durga's soldiers recovered their senses, but once they could see straight, the chamber of the cobra baths would fill with the rattle of automatic weapons once again.

DEVON LAN LOVED WIELDING THE POWER of the ASP blaster on his forearm. He felt like a god, able to summon lightning with just a gesture. The smart-metal armor had saved him from serious injury, glancing bullets leaving only discolored smears where they had been deflected by the Annunaki alloy. The enhancing effects of Enlil's gift to him felt like a drug. He stalked closer to where Grant and Lakesh had taken cover.

Simply by holding his forearm in front of his face, Lan was able to protect his head from the Cerberus interlopers' gunfire. Each time they took a shot at him, it was wasted ammunition, and he replied with a gleaming yellow lance of energy that carved through stone, getting closer and closer to his targets.

"Now you see the power of a man with a vision," Lan called out. "Enlil has granted me a portion of his godlike power! I can create! And I can destroy!"

"You can also bore the fuck out of us with your stupid chatter!" Grant answered.

"Your self-aggrandizement speaks to serious psychological issues," Lakesh shouted around the corner. "Perhaps if you sublimated your belligerence, you'd have people respect your contributions more."

Lan bellowed in blind rage, spearing another bolt through the corner Lakesh hid behind. "I'm belligerent? I am right! I don't have to be nice. I'm sick of idiots walking around and going 'Uh-uh' to valid criticisms of their stupidity!"

"Correctness is no substitute for courtesy," Lakesh countered.

"That's what they said, too!" Lan's next shot elicited a yelp from the scientist.

Grant fired at Lan, Copperhead chattering. Lan shielded his head against the swarm of tiny 4.85 mm bullets. "The whole world is afraid of someone with an opinion. They try to snuff you out, silence you."

Lan punctuated his declaration with an ASP bolt that shredded the ceiling near Grant.

"See, Enlil? I've orchestrated the destruction of two of your greatest enemies!" Lan cried out with heady glee. "They can't hurt me!"

He advanced toward the trapped Cerberus adventurers.

GRANT COULDN'T BELIEVE that Devon Lan was so stupid as to waste his breath on declarations of his own power and smarmy comments about those who denigrated his prior contributions. He winked to Lakesh.

The scientist wasn't in the best of moods, especially since a tendril of ASP bolt that penetrated a section of wall near his thigh had charred his pant leg slightly. Still, Lakesh was riding an adrenaline rush again, so his pain dissipated. Grant winked at him, and Lakesh nodded in response.

Both men understood that it was vital to get Lan as far from Manticor as possible so when they gunned down the armored man, they wouldn't hurt their crippled ally. Grant flicked his Sin Eater to full-auto, then held out his fingers, counting down to their combined attack.

Lan paused in the hallway as a bullet cracked in the distance. Was the loudmouthed fool actually aware that he was walking into a trap? Grant took a quick look, then watched as Lan collapsed. As the former millennialist flopped onto the floor, Grant saw a gory wound in the back of his skull. Glancing up, he saw Manticor, lying on his belly, a smoking pistol in his grasp.

Grant motioned for Lakesh to follow him and the two men rushed to their friend.

"We almost had him," Grant said.

Manticor shrugged. "I'm not feeling doped on morphine anymore. Besides, that little rat was getting on my nerves."

Grant chuckled and scooped up Manticor. "Good enough reason. Feel like you have your groove back?"

Manticor rolled his eyes. "I'd rather have my feet and some aspirin, but—"

"Bastards!" a voice bellowed.

Grant and Manticor looked to see Christian, a bloody mess from the grenade, limping into the open, trying to level a shaky gun at them. The blast had ruined the big millennialist's coordination, but at this range, and on full-auto, the Sin Eater would rip the two apart.

Lakesh stepped from behind Grant, his borrowed machine pistol barking out single shots that marched a line of gory craters up the middle of the gunman's chest.

Grant chuckled.

"You left your hands full, when there are still consortium malcontents about," Lakesh admonished.

"So?" Grant asked.

Manticor nodded. "He had you for backup."

Lakesh cleared his throat. He felt a twinge in his heart. "Thank you, gentlemen. It won't make up for the queen's demise…"

"But at least you feel useful again," Grant concluded.

"Hannah and the others," Manticor said, still a little groggy. "How are they doing?"

"They're behind cover, and Durga bit Kane," Grant answered.

"Then leave us two useful bastards behind and go help them," Manticor told the big man. "We can hold the fort."

Grant laid Manticor against a wall, retrieved his war bag and took off to catch up with Kane.

He hoped it wasn't too late for the rest of his compatriots.

ENLIL WALKED THROUGH the hangar. All but one of his Nephilim warriors were gone now, their bullet-torn bodies strewed about the entrance to the Nagah's underground city. The overlord looked around in disgust, trying to block out the reek of cooked flesh. Disdainfully, he kicked aside one blackened corpse, pieces of ashen limbs crumbling as it flipped over on the floor.

His Nephilim minion followed, as silent as always, awaiting the Annunaki god's command.

"Return to our skimmer and pilot it back home," Enlil told the mindless drone.

The Nephilim nodded, absently brushing its bloodied forehead. The dazed and crimson-streaked minion turned and left through the hangar doors. Enlil sensed something was different about the creature who'd just walked away, but dismissed the anomaly as related to its minor head injury.

Once the Nephilim healed, all would be well again.

Enlil looked at the skimmer he had given to Durga. False scarring marred its perfect skin, and the overlord could see where a curious examiner had chipped off the charred, bubbled hide, exposing the perfect, seamless metal beneath.

"A waste of energy," Enlil mused. "Knowing Kane, he'll cause irreparable damage to the cobra baths."

He sighed. He rubbed the skimmer's hull, feeling its warm, living metal beneath his fingers. Enlil considered Durga. Though the overlord would be denied the treasure of Enki's genetic manipulation so, too, would the Nagah prince. Given the carnage and destruction in the hangar, both the consortium and the cobra folk had lost significant resources. The millennialists had wasted manpower and good faith in the Kashmir region, and the war between the Nephilim and the human soldiers had destroyed a dozen helicopters.

Enlil had sacrificed a mere seven Nephilim, and a smart-armor module.

He smiled. It was a fair trade.

He climbed aboard the scar-covered skimmer, then slid into its pilot chair. He rested his hands on the controls and willed the craft to rise. It responded to its master instantly, with the certainty and grace of a dancer. Engines powered up, and the silver craft exited through the hangar doors, picking up enough velocity to escape Earth's pull.

The Kashmir faded into the distance behind him, a failed plot but still one that provided the Annunaki with some small victories. Whether Kane or Durga survived to see the sun was no matter.

The winner of this conflict was merely a mortal.

Their time would end soon enough.

Chapter 23

Kane started to regain feeling in his left arm as soon as Hannah withdrew the syringe from it. He looked at her, feeling the antivenin course through his veins. "Why do you have a needle full of antivenin?"

Hannah smiled weakly. "In case that bastard Durga ever bit Manticor. I wanted to be able to save his life."

"So Durga's venom wasn't diluted?" Kane asked, the pounding in his head beginning to fade.

"I was trying to keep you from panicking, though honestly, the survival rate of humans against our natural poison is ninety percent," Hannah replied. "However, we need you at full strength, or as close to it as we can get."

"Aren't Nagah immune to their own species' venom?" Brigid asked.

"Manticor is a second-generation descendant of a human. Durga and I are natural Nagah, or at least our bloodline goes back to Enki's original manipulation of our ancestors' genes," Hannah answered. "Royal bloodline venom is slightly different, requiring a different antivenin."

Kane flexed his arm. He could feel the swelling start to fade over his left eye, but he was still half-blind. His self-diagnosis was interrupted when he heard the crack of Domi's .45.

Bullets clanged on steel, and Kane crawled over, looking at whom she was targeting.

Durga's soldiers had advanced into the chamber with steel plates, and used them to create a barricade between the Cerberus rebels' position and the pit. Kane grimaced.

"They kept their legs covered on the advance," Domi grumbled. "I couldn't take them down."

Kane clapped Domi on the shoulder, then crawled back to the others. "Durga and Fargo have unimpeded access to the control room."

"Provided there aren't further security measures barring the way," Brigid mentioned.

"Either way, the Nagah have a moving barricade and could flank this little foxhole we've found ourselves in," Kane said. "Any suggestions?"

"Yeah," Grant interjected over the Commtact. "Try not to get bit by the six-foot-tall snake man next time."

"How about you bite me, Grant?" Kane said, frustrated. "Where the hell are you?"

Grant chuckled. "I'm down the hall from the cobra baths. It looks like a busy day there."

"Oh, it's all manner of fun here," Kane answered. He took a cleansing breath to get rid of his frustration. "We're pinned down by at least fifteen snake men. Got something to help out?"

"My war bag," Grant said. "But I don't want to use up my grenades in case Enlil makes another move."

"That's not going to happen," Lakesh interjected on the Commtact. "Bry spotted a skimmer taking off from the hangar."

"Shit, and I liked that ship," Grant snarled. "She handled smoother than glass."

"Get us out of here and I'll go punch Enlil in the kidneys for you," Kane said.

"Friend Kane, you sound in poor health," Lakesh noted.

"Durga gave him a love bite," Grant chided.

Kane growled. "The more you two joke, the closer Durga gets to whatever powerhouse technology was left behind by Enki."

The entrance to the cobra baths suddenly shuddered under the tremendous power of an exploding grenade. A torrent of concussive force swelled through the archway, shredding Nagah warriors standing just outside the doors and bowling over the shield-carrying snake men trying to flank Kane and his allies. A splintered bone stuck through the neck of a rifle-carrying follower of Durga. Its jagged broken shaft entered through the back, and the exit hole in his throat poured blood in a waterfall down his chest. Entering a death seizure, the mortally wounded serpent triggered his assault rifle, bullets spraying the twisted steel wreckage that the Cerberus contingent and Hannah had hidden behind. Ricocheting bullets rang on the bent, deformed heavy doors, bouncing all around the chamber.

A second gun-wielding snake man whirled, triggering his weapon into his dying comrade in hopes of ending the wild storm of deadly bullets. His burst cored the Nagah, but Kane triggered his Copperhead, scything down the armed Durga minion. Grant's Sin Eater roared through the doorway as the big warrior mopped up the last of the resistance still kicking in the wake of his grenade attack. Kane lurched from his hiding spot, looking around at the strewed bodies of the snake men. Some were alive, but their injuries would keep them from engaging in further hostility.

One Nagah reached up, clutching at Kane's leg, eyes soft as he clasped his other hand over a wound in his upper chest. "Mercy…"

The flash and bark of a handgun behind him forced Kane to spin, but Hannah had shifted her aim, firing into another writhing, wounded serpent man. Kane looked down at the pitiful, wounded creature who had begged him for mercy. Hannah's gunshot had cored through the center of its forehead, the first shot that had been fired.

"Stop it," Kane snarled.

Hannah glared at Kane. "They are followers of a maniac, killers who found justification in Durga's war for supremacy. You'd show them compassion?"

"They're wounded, no longer threats," Kane said.

Hannah snorted in derision. "They'd bide their time and come back, worse than ever."

Kane took a deep breath, trying to control his anger. "He didn't have a weapon, Hannah."

Hannah opened her mouth, her dripping fangs folding down. "No Nagah is ever unarmed!"

It would be worthless to continue this debate while the menace of Durga and Fargo still threatened. He turned his attention away from the ruthless princess. Kane looked at the hole, the hatch pulled open. There was a ladder made of D-shaped iron rungs leading into the depths, an unholy red glow emanating from below. Stepping closer, he could see three pulsing, glowing lines etched into the wall.

"What the hell is that?" Kane asked as Grant joined the group.

Brigid knelt and touched the illuminating strip carved parallel to the ladder. The air above it was warm, but when she pressed the line, it was icy cold, a chill crawling up her finger as heat seemingly leached from the contact. The material was solid, and where Brigid had touched it had suddenly become brighter. "I'd say it was bioluminescent, but this is some form of metal. We know that the Tuatha de Danaan were aware of deposits of orichalcum, and that the Annunaki were able to create alloys of the metal for other purposes."

"An energized, never-dimming light source," Kane said. "Just enough chemical reaction in the metal to keep it lit for…what, thousands of years?"

"Activated by ambient heat, most likely," Brigid answered, rubbing her numb finger. "It absorbed thermal energy from my touch."

Kane frowned. He crawled onto the ladder and began his trek into the depths of the city. Loud rumbles shook, their vibrations running through the rungs of the ladder. "Something's going on."

Static hissed in Kane's ear over his Commtact. He could barely make out Lakesh's voice over the crackle of white noise. "Kane, we're starting to pick up severe electronic interference. Bry pinpointed a massive—"

The harsh rustle of the jammed communication signal gave way to a monotone howl that made Kane's teeth ache. He deactivated the Commtact, then bent to retrieve the Sin Eater that Durga had taken from him. "We're on our own, gang. Durga turned something on down there."

"That pretty much screws our day," Domi noted, taking her Commtact from behind her ear and pocketing it. She followed Kane into the ladder pit.

The Cerberus exiles were no strangers to entering the dark underside of a hidden culture. That there was a mad being with aspirations to godhood present was not new to them, either. However, the lack of novelty about the threat they faced was no comfort.

They were going to face a battle for their lives, as well as for those of the thousands in the Nagah city.

FARGO LOOKED ASKANCE toward Durga as his fingers ran over the glassy smooth console jutting from the wall. A monitor above the console flashed with golden symbols, pictograms blinking into existence as he operated the interface. The chamber they were in was lit by the metallic indentations along the domed, high ceiling. The console was one of many dotting the circular wall, but it was the only one with a glassy smooth surface. The rest had conventional tile keyboards and more conventional looking monitors. Eight hallways entered into the junction, including the one they had just passed through.

Fargo was dismayed at a lack of tanks similar to the ones above. What good was having a control panel without anything to give commands to?

"We shouldn't have unplugged the pumps," Fargo said as the chamber around them thrummed loudly, hidden machinery grinding and pulsing. "I mean, you are talking to the nanites, right?"

"I am," Durga said. "And they are speaking back to me."

"In English? Because all I'm seeing is chicken scratches on that monitor," Fargo said.

Durga frowned, then stepped over, grabbing Fargo's wrist. He pressed the human's hand against the glassy console, and Fargo felt a surge of electricity pour up his arm, wrapping around his heart. Fargo wanted to pull away for a moment, grimacing against the prickling that stabbed at his chest. The initial pain suddenly faded, dissolving to a subtle warmth that made him feel as if he were floating in a placid, sun-drenched pool.

Fargo stopped struggling against Durga as whispers began to rise in his hearing.

"You tell me what language they are speaking to you, Fargo," Durga said.

The archaeologist blinked, trying to focus on the multiple voices, each saying something different. "Stop it."

"Wait," Durga warned. "Wait for them to coordinate. It will take a few moments."

Fargo's throat tightened. The quantity of messages thrown into his brain seemed to decrease, but not the number of different speakers.

"Austin Fargo, we welcome you to the interface."

"Who are you?" Fargo asked.

"We are the interface," the chorus answered. "What is your request?"

"What are my options?" Fargo inquired.

There was a rustle in his mind, then images began flashing on his retinas. He saw dozens of iterations of himself, each of some different form, but hewn from different substances. Some looked like crystalline glass, others looked like carved marble, while yet others had animal-like hides, visions of himself as a Nagah or with the heavy armor of a rhinocerous. Other images showed on his mind's eye, views of the world through various spectrums. The strangest images were flame and electricity, cast in his shape.

"Pick one?" Fargo asked. "And never become normal again?"

His hand radiated intense heat, and Fargo's "options screen" vanished, leaving him looking at his hand, engulfed in flickering orange plasma. He swallowed, but the chorus spoke up, soothing him. "This transformation lasts as long as you wish, and can be altered at any time. We are the interface to the nanomachines that entered your body when you touched the true pool."

Fargo's lips parted, the flame around his hand snuffing out as he wished for it to be extinguished. He turned his hand over, and as he did so, his skin shimmered like polished metal. Then he flexed his fingers, realizing that they were composed of fine, seamless metal. His lips parted in awe. "The true pool?"

Again an image flashed in his mind's eye. It was an Annunaki lord, standing at the console and operating it. The being turned and looked Fargo in the eye. "The true pool. The nanomachinery that have been mentioned of late are secondary constructs, developed by Enlil, or degraded from constant use across four centuries."

"Degraded," Fargo repeated. "They have settled into one particular program. The creation of Enki's Nagah."

The Annunaki visual representation smiled, obviously pleased with Fargo's interpretation of the data it had provided. "Exactly. The true pool, left inert for millennia, has far greater capability due to the fact that it has not had the same data burned into its operating system."

Fargo lowered his hand as it returned to normal, supple human flesh. "If Enki had this power, how come he didn't defeat Enlil?"

"The changes do not allow for unlimited power, just unlimited opportunity to adapt," the interface chorus responded. "As well, the creator Enki knew there was cause for restraint, even of the greatest of powers. He was not like Enlil, who would burn the heavens with the guns of *Tiamat*."

"The power to be invincible," Durga spoke up, cutting into Fargo's conversation with the interface. The cobra man threw his head back in laughter. "To think I was working with so pedestrian a concept."

"*Tiamat,* your original goal, by use of the captured skimmer," Fargo mused.

Durga stepped away from the console. "Toys, compared to the brilliance of Enki."

"Brilliance?" Fargo asked. "Just because I can mimic the periodic table of elements, or see in spectra beyond normal vision? Simple parlor tricks aren't going to change the world."

Durga circled Fargo. "Your lack of imagination disappoints me. I am now immortal. Who can stop me now?"

The answer came in the form of a handgun that boomed in the darkness. Durga clutched his heart. He collapsed to his knees, blood pouring over his fingers. The cobra prince sputtered, blood frothing on his scaled lips. Thick crimson trailed down, soaking his pants, creating a circle of red around the kneeling figure.

Fargo's eyes widened in surprise, but he walked closer to Durga. "I hate to say it, but I told you so. A man with a gun trumps your magic act."

Durga's face looked pained as Kane stepped into the open, his Sin Eater smoking. "You…"

Kane lowered the handgun. "Give up, and we'll do our best to stabilize you. Just surrender."

Durga's eyes glared angrily at the Cerberus leader as Domi, Brigid, Grant and Hannah followed him into the interface control room. "I'll die before I kneel before—"

Durga looked down at his position, then coughed. "Fuck!"

With a ragged wheeze, Durga slumped on the ground. He twitched, struggling for breath.

"Fargo, whatever you've taken, you best put it back," Kane ordered, looking at Durga as his blood pooled on the floor around his feet. The puddle extended, undulated as it flowed along the uneven floor, looking as if it were the shadow of a serpent's tail where Durga had lost the vital fluids.

"I don't know," Fargo began. "Let me ask."

The archaeologist felt separated from reality again, faced with the image of the Annunaki Enki standing before him.

"The interface and the nanomachines may be expelled from your body with a simple wish," the chorus said. "All you need do is ask."

"Then I ask," Fargo said. "I only wish that I had the knowledge that I had been searching for all my life."

"You asked, and the interface shall honor your wishes, but not in the order you requested," the chorus whispered to him.

Fargo reached out to the console, his arm rising unbidden. A jolt ran down the length of Fargo's arm, the warmth that filled him before cooling, fading. A knot remained, a pain behind his eyes that hummed with a tantalizing song.

"Goodbye, Austin Fargo. Relish the gift we have left you," the interface told him.

Fargo's arm dropped against his side, numbed.

"It has been relinquished," Fargo whispered. "The gift has been returned."

"Gift?" Kane asked. He waved Fargo away from the console with the Sin Eater.

Brigid looked at the smooth, glassy surface. She stalked closer to it.

"No," Fargo and Kane said in unison. Brigid held back from the interface, looking at the two men.

"Why?" Brigid asked.

"Bad feeling about it," Kane said.

Fargo's response was more heartfelt. "It is not a gift that is meant to be used by humankind, not yet. Enki intended it for the world when it was needed most."

Brigid looked down at the mirrored console. "Wouldn't now, with the planet filled with patches of radioactive wasteland, and technology as sparse as desert scrub, be the 'when the world needed it most'?"

Fargo took a deep breath. "I cannot believe what I am seeing now."

"Seeing?" Grant interjected. "I thought you gave those things back."

"Please, just believe me," Fargo said, an urgency in his voice that added a credence that hadn't existed before. "There are travails that you cannot imagine."

"We can imagine a hell of a lot," Kane replied. He returned the Sin Eater to its forearm holster.

Hannah toed Durga's shoulder, watching his breath seizing up, his eyes widening with horror. "Good riddance."

"Hannah!" Kane snapped.

Hannah sneered at Kane. "This sick cretin was a rapist and a murderer. His prospective brides before me either died or retired into obscurity to escape spending their lives with him."

"So, you stuck around for it?" Brigid inquired.

"Manticor was the leash he had around my neck," Hannah told them. "You know, as the highest-ranking, living member of the royal family, I could make certain that you will not be welcome here in our lands ever again."

Kane looked down at Durga, who lay still on the ground. Something was different, and it was more than just the dullness that came with death. It sounded a mental alarm that he tried to interpret as he examined the corpse. "Hannah, what makes you think that we would want an ally who'd relish the suffering of an enemy?"

Hannah strode up to Kane until they were face-to-face. The Nagah regent was an undeniably beautiful creature, but anger had twisted her expression. Her sensual appeal had faded as her rage waxed. "You're welcome to leave."

That's when the anomaly of Durga's death mask struck.

The prince had died with his eyes open, but they were both clear. The baleful red lamp that blazed in a rage from his right eye socket had been doused, returning to a normal golden iris on a white sclera.

Kane grabbed Hannah by the shoulders, dragging her away from Durga's corpse. "Everybody! Get the hell out of—"

A thick, muscular trunk lashed up from the floor, the hard, sharp scales striking Kane across the shoulders with enough force to launch him and Hannah across the length of the wide control room. With a twist in midair, Kane took the brunt of their landing on the tough muscles of his back. They slid to the floor, Kane's head swimming from the impact.

"Holy shit!" Grant snapped, bringing up his Copperhead, its magazine emptying on full-auto. The shape that rose from the floor was huge, but bullets smashed into scales that appeared to be made out of steel plate rather than standard keratin.

"I haven't shit yet," Durga growled, the monstrous coil of his lower body writhing beneath him. "Maybe after I devour you and your companions, Grant, I'll turn all of you into my first shit as a god."

Kane lurched onto his knees. Between recovering from the anaphylactic shock of Durga's venom and the whiplash that would have broken his collarbone if it hadn't been for the protective nature of his shadow suit, he could barely stand up. A long, powerful arm reached out, fingers wrapping around Grant's torso.

Domi leaped on Durga's arm, firing her .45 at contact range into the crook of the monster cobra's elbow. Involuntary reflex bent the arm, surprised and numbed fingers releasing Grant. A backhand brushed the side of Domi's head as Durga attempted to knock her off his arm. It was only a grazing blow. Domi's lightning quickness prevented the massive abomination's hand from crushing her skull or breaking her neck.

Hannah dragged Kane to his feet, then pulled him into a side tunnel.

"Move it, Kane!" she bellowed.

Kane grimaced, then stomped one foot down to brace himself against Hannah's urgent tug. "I'm not abandoning my friends!"

With a twist, he pulled free from Hannah, Sin Eater snapping into his hand. Maybe Durga's hide was invulnerable to small-caliber bullets, but the machine pistol fired rounds that could penetrate the hull of an assault helicopter.

Whether it worked or not, it would buy his allies time to escape.

Kane charged at the enormous snake beast, his Sin Eater hammering out a staccato challenge to the Nagah who would be a god.

Chapter 24

Austin Fargo saw Durga twitch, then turned and ran. He had seen the interface's options, and there was nothing like that, but then, Fargo hadn't remained in contact with the interface that long. There was also the matter that Durga's blood, flooded with nanites, had permeated the uneven floor of the command chamber. Suddenly infused with the large area of stone and metal in the floor, the nanomachines could have added a couple of hundred pounds to Durga's mass.

How Durga could have survived was answered by the little knot of knowledge that weighed behind his eyes like a twenty-pound metal barbell. "The nanomachines obviated the necessity for blood. The true pool became infused with his body, providing his central nervous system with the nutrients and oxygen it required. This allowed his blood to soak into the earth beneath our feet."

"I thought you'd left me," Fargo panted as he ran. He didn't recognize this particular tunnel, and realized that he'd retreated down the wrong bolt-hole. He looked back, hearing the sound of floor-shaking fists and automatic weapons crackling.

He was not returning to the hub to find the right direction.

"Stay on this path, Fargo," the interface told him. "You said that you wanted the knowledge that would guide you to the secrets lost by humankind. As such, I was constructed between your frontal lobes. I am your adviser, and your resource."

Fargo gulped down breath. He hadn't been this exhausted by a run for his life since his first flight from an irate Durga. "How big is he now?"

"Extrapolating the amount of soil and loose stone his blood contacted, it's possible that Durga quadrupled his mass. Eight hundred pounds," the interface told him.

"What could stop him?" Fargo asked.

Fargo saw the disembodied face of Enki smiling at him. "Knowledge, Austin Fargo."

"Which is why I'm asking you!" Fargo snapped.

"You wanted knowledge to guide you," the interface told him. "I simply cannot hand you an answer. When you made your request, you wanted to still be able to have your adventure."

Fargo would have smacked his palm into his forehead, but his skull ached as it was. He hung his head. "I wish I had one of my improvised… Oh, fuck no! The bombs I planted?"

"More along the lines of their placement," Enki responded.

Fargo chewed his upper lip. "I'm not fast or strong enough to bait Durga into a trap."

The sound of scaled feet slapping the floor resounded up ahead. There was some form of cross tunnel. The archaeologist pulled his revolver, but held his fire as Hannah rushed into view. She froze, pistol locked in her fist.

"I see you took discretion as the better part of valor," Hannah said, sneering.

Fargo nodded. "We don't have time for that now. I left a bomb underneath the statue of Garuda. It's set so that when it detonates, it will send a sheet of ignited natural gas throughout the central mall."

"Saboteur," Hannah snorted.

Fargo waved his hand. "There's no time. We have to lure Durga out of here and into proximity of that bomb."

A grenade blast rumbled from the central hub, Fargo and Hannah forced to look toward the center. Smoke billowed.

"The four of them have communicators, but there's too much interference to get through to them, even if we had a radio that operated on their frequency," Hannah said.

Fargo seemed to fade out for a moment, then he looked her in the eye. "I figured out their frequency. Come on! We need to get to a radio!"

Hannah looked back toward where the Cerberus warriors engaged in conflict with the newly serpentine horror that used to be Durga. Fargo grabbed her hand and they ran into a cross tunnel, winding their way back toward the cobra baths.

DURGA WAS REELING from the detonation of a grenade that had been thrown literally in his face. His vision was blurred, and he balanced unsteadily on the thick atroxian body that had grown out of his lower torso. He lashed about with his long, powerful tail, but all he was doing was smashing consoles, flailing blindly about to destroy the interloping humans who had dared to shoot him.

"Mammals! It's time to join the dinosaurs!" Durga bellowed.

"I visit them every weekend, asshole!" Grant taunted back.

The chatter of his submachine gun heralded a new prickling sensation as the 4.85 mm bullets flattened and deformed themselves against his powerfully armored hide. Durga reached out in the direction where the discomfort originated, jamming a long arm to snatch up the black outlander. Rather than grabbing a torso, Durga winced as he jammed his fingers painfully into the wall, sticking them into thick stone up to the second knuckle of each digit.

A weight impacted Durga's shoulders, hammer blows bouncing off the top of his skull. Familiarity with the authoritative impacts of these particular bullets informed the Nagah godling that it was most likely Kane, blazing away at contact distance. With a lurch, Durga drove his head and shoulders into the domed ceiling, the muscular length of his serpentine lower quarters rocketing him up with enough force to pry his stuck fist out of the wall and to smash the stone above.

The impact stunned Durga, and he crashed back to the floor, catching himself on his hands.

"Accursed, chattering monkeys," Durga cursed. He coughed, then drew back into himself, bringing up the interface in his mind's eye. There was a quick scan of the options open to him and he chuckled internally.

Returning to reality, the nanomachines had repaired the damage done to his optic nerve by the explosion of the grenade in his face. Durga's headache was fading rapidly as the miniature builders shut down pain receptacles and shored up the damage in his body.

The control room had emptied, however.

"Aw, I have a new toy, and there's no one to share it with," Durga said.

A quick visit to his interface, and Durga activated the ability to divine the infrared portion of the spectrum. Amid the still hot brass ejected by the guns of the outlanders, there were footprints that had scattered down four separate tunnels. Durga managed to differentiate the different tracks by the size of their feet. Picking Kane as his primary target, he swung his head into a tunnel, then extended his fangs.

This time, instead of venom, fire issued on the spit of the cobra godling, a stream of blazing flame that curled through the air, illuminating Kane's retreat.

Durga sighed as the blast of fire didn't have the reach to catch the fleeing Cerberus leader. With a lurch, Durga forced himself into the confines of the corridor, slithering after Kane.

KANE LOOKED OVER his shoulder. Durga was following him, which would give his allies time to regroup. Apparently, in his attempts to smash the companions into a bloody pulp, the cobra prince had destroyed whatever machinery had been jamming their Commtacts. Lakesh's voice crackled sharply in his ear.

"Kane! Kane, can you read me?"

"Nah, you're a closed book to me, old man!" Kane snapped back. "Can we chat later? I'm being chased by a fire-breathing, twenty-foot-long snake centaur…whatever the fuck they call those creatures."

"Good Lord!" Lakesh marveled. "Was that a creation of Enki's you uncovered?"

"No. It's Durga after he infused a shitload of nanites into his bloodstream," Kane answered. He swerved as he rounded a corner into a cross tunnel. Kane dropped an implode grenade behind him and accelerated to the next crossway.

The tunnel behind the Cerberus exile lit up as Durga breathed fire once more. Kane dived for cover, somersaulting through the next intersection. A double thunderclap filled the air as ignited fuel saturated the atmosphere, creating a vacuum in its wake. The rush of air buffeted the enhanced

Durga, making him grunt. Kane glanced back and saw that the mutated Nagah slumped onto his forearms. Scales cracked and flaked off, exposing raw flesh underneath, but Durga still breathed, his enormous back heaving and falling as he struggled to regain his senses.

Kane opened fire with his Sin Eater again. "Lakesh, we've got trouble. I just hit Durga with an implode grenade, and all it did was knock the wind out of him."

The Sin Eater's heavy slugs tore into sections of bared flesh, but no blood trickled from the scale-shorn flesh. Durga lifted his head, golden eyes filled with fury and disdain for the human who simply would not die.

"Keep fighting, mammal," Durga growled. "The longer you survive, the more time you give your friends to make peace with their gods."

"What makes you think you'll survive killing me?" Kane called back.

Durga laughed, rising to rest on the coiled trunk of his serpentine lower half. He hadn't recovered fully yet, but scales began to form over the flesh that had been scoured by the implosion grenade. "You amuse me, Kane. I'll name my first extermination camp after you."

Kane whirled and continued racing through the tunnels. He checked the load on his Sin Eater. He had one and a half magazines left, having burned off the rest. For all the good that the machine pistol did, Kane might as well have been throwing rice at a charging rhinoceros. The one thing that seemed to hurt or slow Durga was his own savage strength, or a grenade set off right under his nose. *Hurt* was a relative term, however. The nanites granted Durga a regenerative ability that was maddeningly quick.

Throw in the fact that Durga had been able to bleed out completely without undue harm, probably another gift of the nanomachines, and Kane would require an antitank missile to deal with the monstrosity chasing him.

"Kane, you need to get out of there, and up into the main mall of the city." Hannah's voice cut in on their Commtact.

"Who gave you our party line?" Kane asked.

"Fargo," Hannah said. "He's acting pretty strange. Says he has a nanite construct in his brain."

"Really?" Kane asked. "Tell him to hold still, I'll remove it for him."

"Damnation!" Fargo snapped. "There's a bomb under the statue of Garuda. It was designed to inflict massive losses among the Nagah population as a distraction for the consortium's attack. However, the explosives plus the natural gas should be enough to kill Durga."

Kane charged on, keeping one turn of a corner ahead of Durga at all times. Sooner or later, his endurance would begin to flag. Fargo had a good idea. The explosion would be a more intense variant on the implode grenade. It could work. Kane tried to subvert his distaste for the original intent of the killer bomb, however. The archaeologist had designed the weapon as a mechanism for mass murder. Only circumstance had transformed it into a possible salvation from the rule of an inhuman snake god.

"Once I'm done, you and I are going to have words," Kane warned.

"Whatever! Get the hell up here now!" Fargo commanded.

Kane raced, weaving his way back toward the ladder that had brought them down into this crimson-tinted hell. He hurled his last grenade down a tube to buy himself some time against the pursuing monstrosity. The thunderclap still brought the snake monster to a halt, and Kane climbed as fast as he could.

GRANT HAULED KANE OUT of the mouth of the pit, then slammed the hatch down, engaging the locks.

Kane looked at it. "Is that a good idea?"

"Fargo, you suddenly got some magic brains," Grant said. "Would the security kill everything in the city?"

"It's a conventional explosive that would seal the pit," Fargo replied.

"Then let Durga break this door down," Grant concluded.

"If that's powerful enough to seal the catacombs," Kane said, making certain that Domi and Brigid were in one piece, "it could stop him cold."

Domi cradled her arm, wincing in pain. Grant looked as if he had trouble breathing, which indicated a broken rib. A cut ran across Brigid's forehead.

"And cut off whatever secrets Durga hadn't smashed down there," Brigid said.

Domi looked at the hatch. The floor shook beneath their feet. "It's time to run."

The outlanders raced out of the chamber of the cobra baths as the pit shook again. The vibrations of Durga's impact against the secured hatch rumbled through the soles of their boots as they ran.

"He sounds mad," Brigid commented. "Let's hope that he doesn't get stronger the madder he gets."

A wave of concussive force billowed out of the cobra baths, running the length of the hallway that the four adventurers charged through. They were unable to outdistance the shock wave and were bowled over. The floor heaved, flexed and cracked, large fissures cutting into the ground. Kane tumbled into one particularly deep crack, his shoulder gouged by jagged stone. The shadow suit protected his skin from being torn open, but the pain of the jab still stunned him. He crawled out of the furrow in the floor, then looked at Grant, Domi and Brigid.

"We're fine," Grant said with a wince. "Though that earthquake didn't do my ribs any good."

Kane helped his friend up. "Well, nothing could have survived that."

Brigid buried her face in her palm. Behind them, rocks clattered as they bounced into the hall.

"Kane!" Durga bellowed. "I'm going to tear you in two and suck out your organs!"

Kane grimaced. "Grant, get to cover. You, too, Domi."

"Arm broke, not leg," Domi replied in a guttural snarl.

Kane glared at her. "And if Brigid and I get roasted, you and Grant are our backup plan."

Domi frowned.

"Go!" Kane yelled.

Grant and Domi limped off down a side tunnel, looking back as they reluctantly abandoned their allies.

Brigid sighed. "You've seen how fast he is."

Kane nodded. "But we still have to bait him toward Fargo's bomb."

Brigid looked at him. "Which we most likely won't survive if we're bait."

"I'll draw him right to the statue," Kane told her.

Brigid was about to argue when Durga's hand wrapped around the wrecked archway leading into what used to be the cobra baths. The mighty serpent looked as if he were trying to drag himself out of a landslide. Furious golden eyes burned with hatred toward the humans in the hall.

"Kane. Baptiste," Durga called in a friendly singsong voice. His tone dropped several octaves. "I was hoping to have you two for dinner!"

Kane opened fire with his Sin Eater, emptying his half-full clip into Durga's face. Bullets sparked as they rebounded off the plates of his reptilian visage. Another shrug tugged the serpentine monster farther into the hall. That was the outlanders' cue to run for their lives. Durga's flames lashed at their heels as they raced toward the main central hall of the Nagah city.

DURGA SURGED ONE LAST TIME, freeing the end of his tail from beneath the tons of rubble. Ugly gashes had been torn in his nanite-transformed flesh, but they were slowly sealing again. He lowered his head, screwing deep down for reserves of strength.

The interface came up in his mind. "Your body is nearly at the limits of what strain it can take. You need to allow a rest—"

"Quiet, you microscopic shits!" Durga bellowed. With a sweep of his arm, he widened the shattered entrance of the cobra baths. His forearm ached where he had pulverized concrete. He glared down at the limb, some part of his mind informing him that the mechanisms coursing through his body had altered his form, but their efforts at repairing the horrendous damage inflicted by bullets, bombs and grenades had drained them.

It didn't matter. Even covered in scars, Durga still possessed more than enough strength to rip apart Kane and Baptiste. The other two had disappeared, but considering the hammering he had given them, they were most likely in hiding, licking their wounds. He slithered along, vowing that he would rest before hunting down the injured humans.

"How's that for a compromise?" Durga asked the interface.

"Altered cellular structure integrity failing," the machines in his body said. "Altered stone and metal additions to natural form are experiencing rejection. Recommend conversion to normal mass and form."

"Nattering little pussies," Durga spit as he turned the corner, spotting the central hall. Kane stood alone at the base of Garuda's statue. Durga sagged against the archway connecting the two corridors, then sent the command to the molecule-sized machines to expunge the six hundred pounds of mass he'd absorbed into his new, gigantic form. Stone and scrap metal tumbled onto the floor around him, and he took a deep breath. The shed material crumbled to dust, and Durga sucked in a breath.

The human braced himself and Durga smirked.

"I don't need a damned superbody to kill you," Durga growled.

Kane opened fire on the renegade serpent prince. The Sin Eater bullet tore through Durga's chest, and the interface whinged once more about its nanomachines working too hard to heal itself.

"What's the matter, Prince? Took too much of a beating?" Kane taunted.

Durga shook his head, the wound closing even as Kane watched. "Enki's gifts have made me a protean god. Cut me, shoot me, it doesn't matter. I don't bleed."

"But we rock you with a grenade, you feel it," Kane continued, egging the cobra prince on. Durga squinted, his eyes focusing on the human and his surroundings.

Kane opened fire again, scrambling Durga's infrared vision as the bullet glanced off the enhanced being's forehead. The Cerberus leader had been informed by Fargo that the nanomachines had offered a range of visual perception that could easily have located the bomb hidden beneath the statue.

Durga continued to walk forward, starting to laugh. "You cleave to my father's form. Why? You thought that a big snake man made of stone might provide you with a little protection from another one like him?"

Durga spewed his flaming venom again, and Kane lunged backward between the legs of the statue. The prince strode more quickly now, the microscopic robots now powerful enough to restore his health since they didn't have to deal with the extra bulk he'd absorbed. In seven strides, Durga had enough speed to leap across the main hall, striking the statue of Garuda in the chest with both feet.

Kane lunged out of the path of the falling sculpture as it tore loose from its pedestal. The flaming spear was held in place by the pipe system that fed its constantly burning natural gas lamps. Durga stood on the broken effigy of his father, laughter pouring out of him in a torrent.

"I shot this dumb bastard as he looked on me with approval," Durga said to Kane. A kick smashed the jaw off the statue, skittering it across the floor. He turned toward the human, ignoring the pinpricks of pain as Kane's bullets lashed his chest.

Kane got to his feet, pulling his combat knife.

"Oh, blades versus fangs?" Durga asked. "Of course, that

little bodkin isn't going to be any more effective than your gun, is it?"

Kane's eyes narrowed. "I never was one for going quietly."

Durga's laugh trailed off. "I just hate stubborn people."

"And I just hate megalomaniacs," Kane replied. "Come on, I'm not getting any younger."

Durga motioned for Kane to come closer. "One last free shot. I want to see what you think can stop me."

Durga spread his arms wide, leaving himself open to Kane. "Go on. Stick a knife into an indestructible immortal."

Kane leaped, slamming into Durga and driving him back into the burning spear as it wobbled on the pipe that fed it. With all the strength he could muster, the Cerberus warrior plunged the blade into Durga's forehead. A spearing sheet of steel cut through the Nagah's brain, filling his head with painful static.

"Warning! Central nervous system compromise!" the interface howled in his mind. "Emergency recovery protocols activating!"

Durga hurled Kane away with such strength that the human landed a dozen yards away, tumbling across the floor like a ragdoll. The knife was still stuck in Durga's head, and the Sin Eater had been dropped when he had pulled the knife.

The Nagah prince reached up, limbs impelled by the nano-machines to wrench the blade out so that they could begin repairs on the pinioned brain. Durga coughed, chuckling.

"Nice...effort..." Durga laughed. The knife crunched through bone as it was released from the prince's skull. "But the nanites are keeping my brain running, despite what bits you separated with this."

Durga tripped, wincing as his strength faltered. "It will take a minute, but then I'll enjoy pulling your arms and legs off...."

"Take a look at where you're standing. On radar, if you can," Kane offered.

Durga blinked, then looked down. "Interface, you heard the monkey."

He heard the sound of retreating feet as he focused on a square block of some form of substance. A pulse hummed through the air. Glancing up, he saw Hannah's unmistakable profile on his radar vision, standing at least a hundred yards away. She had something noisy in her hand, emitting a signal pulse.

"Call this a divorce, Durga!" Hannah shouted.

The object in her hand flared so bright that it blotted out the godling's enhanced vision.

The world vaporized a heartbeat later, a natural-gas-powered fuel-air explosion smashing Durga apart with a thoroughness that the nanomachines couldn't counter, their own microscopic mechanisms incinerated in the cleansing flame.

Kane had been hauled behind cover by Brigid, and he rode out the blast in her arms. As the roar faded, the two people lurched from behind the heavy barrier that had protected them.

Hannah crushed the detonator under her heel, then regarded the humans coldly.

"Too merciless?" Hannah asked.

Kane looked at the blast crater created by Fargo's device. The vaporizing fireball had a radius of thirty feet. Even so, the overpressure of the shock wave had torn up marble columns and flagstones for another eighty feet. Had the hall not been evacuated for the duration of the emergency, people within 150 feet would have been killed. Kane's mad dash had taken him out of the kill zone.

"Sometimes a little overkill doesn't hurt," Kane replied.

Hannah frowned, then nodded. Her dour mood lightened. "And a little compassion…will make things a bit better for everyone involved."

"So what now?" Kane asked.

Brigid helped the battered Kane by letting him lean on her. "It would be wonderful if the Nagah could…"

"No," Hannah said.

"But all we did…" Brigid spoke up.

"No. Not right now," Hannah explained. "Our people have suffered. Enormously. The hangar, in case you didn't notice, is more wreckage than working aircraft."

"You don't have enough to spare," Kane agreed.

"Plus the deaths caused by the insurgents, and the loss of Durga's personal guard…" Hannah sighed. "We have half a government left. Maybe in a few years."

"Years," Kane repeated. "We'll try to keep the planet together for you until then."

"If you don't mind, I'd prefer you return to Cerberus tonight," Hannah said. "We have one helicopter capable of taking you to the temple."

Kane nodded. "I wish we could have saved the interface to reprogram the cobra baths."

Hannah managed a weak smile. "Manticor is a strong man. And he told me, 'You don't need feet to be a husband.'"

"One more thing—where did Fargo go?" Kane asked.

Hannah sighed. "I let him go. Repayment for the weapon that destroyed Durga."

Kane nodded. "I'm too tired to kick his ass anyway."

Hannah managed a soft chuckle at that remark.

He held out his hand. "Good luck rebuilding, even if your people decide to never talk to us again."

She accepted the handshake. "And maybe someday we'll be able to forget the likes of Fargo and the consortium, and just concentrate on good people like you."

Kane rested his arm around Brigid's shoulder. The two explorers turned and began their long trek to the hangar. The journey around the planet wouldn't take long, thanks to the power of the interphaser, but the losses of the past few days would make it feel long. The destroyed twentieth-century technology and the burial of Enki's secrets beneath thousands of tons of collapsed stone paled in comparison to the death of a kind matron and dozens of her loyal subjects.

Their consolation, though, would come in the thousands who had been saved.

That, and the fact that they weren't leaving a nest of angry vipers.

When the Nagah would next appear to humanity, the Cerberus envoys would be there, ready to offer friendship. once again.

Kane rested his head against Brigid's. "Let's go home, Baptiste."

The Don Pendleton's Executioner®
HOSTILE ODDS

A small town is caught between warring factions...

The illicit activities of an organized crime family take Mack Bolan to California, then to Oregon, where he uncovers a deadly power struggle. Profits from prostitution and drugs tied to local businesses are being funneled to a radical ecoterrorist group willing to strike out against anything—and anyone—in their way. A war is brewing and, faced with mounting casualties, Mack Bolan will have to use his own methods to clean up the environment.

Available March 2009 wherever books are sold.

GOLD EAGLE®

GEX364